REGENERATION

REGENERATION

A THRILLER

MAX ALLAN COLLINS AND
BARBARA COLLINS WRITING AS

BARBARA ALLAN

THOMAS & MERCER

Text copyright © 1999 Barbara and Max Allan Collins
All rights reserved.
Printed in the United States of America.
No part of this book may be reproduced, or stored in a retrieval system, or transmitted in any form or by any means, electronic, mechanical, photo-copying, recording, or otherwise, without express written permission of the publisher.

Published by Thomas & Mercer
P.O. Box 400818
Las Vegas, NV 89140

ISBN-13: 9781612185262
ISBN-10: 1612185266

For the class of '66

AS IF READING HER MIND, LARUE SAID, "IT'S THAT SECOND CHANCE EVERYONE DREAMS OF, BUT SO FEW RECEIVE."

Joyce felt as if she were in a dream. "Yes … yes…."

"Let me explain how it is that you came to fit our ideal profile. In addition to your outstanding achievements in your chosen field, you have few ties, few strings. Your parents have passed on…. No close relatives, really…."

"Yes. Only my mother's sister, my Aunt Beth … she lives in De Kalb. We're not … terribly close. I see her at Christmas."

"You'll no longer be able to do that, Joyce. For your new life, you'll need a new name—and you have to leave your own life behind."

"I just … disappear?"

Larue shrugged. "We have clients who are able to use that option, yes. But you are much too well known in Chicago, Joyce—you would be missed."

"Considering the way my job interviews have been going, I find that hard to believe."

"You will need to" —he made quotation marks in the air, with his fingers— " 'die.' "

Hope I die before I get old.
—Pete Townshend, "My Generation"

Prologue:

"EVE OF DESTRUCTION"

(Barry McGuire, #1 Billboard, 1965)

The homeless man leaned against the granite wall of the Kafer Building on Wilshire Boulevard in Los Angeles, enjoying the coolness of the stone, waiting for the white-collar workers to leave the building for the day. He was nearly six feet tall, or at least had been, before slouching into anonymity, and the handsome man he'd once been could be discerned by anyone who took the time (which was no one): Indian-sharp cheekbones, skin tanned from the sun, gray-streaked hair pulled back in a ponytail with a rubber band he'd found on the sidewalk.

Wearing faded denim jeans and his best T-shirt, which bore only a few permanent stains, he prided himself on being better dressed than his fellow rabble roaming the streets of the City of Angels. And he was more polite than his piss-stained peers, too, making sure his demeanor was unthreatening whenever he asked the working class for spare change, because he made out like a bandit that way.

He hadn't always been homeless, of course, though he knew plenty who had grown up a part of this under-est of underclasses. But even the riffraff who'd raised themselves on the fringes of L.A.

1

had histories. Ben was no exception—he wasn't just another sad, tortured creature rummaging in dumpsters and sleeping in parks. He was a man, a person. He had a past.

Benjamin Franklin McRae was born and raised in a small river town in Missouri where he grew to be captain of the football team in high school, a three-point senior with a bright future looming after graduation in '66. He and his steady, Betsy Jane, had been in the homecoming king and queen's court, and they'd gone to Kirkwood Community College together. They were engaged in the summer of '68.

But that same turbulent summer, he drew an unlucky draft number, and instead of finishing college as planned, he left his life and future wife behind and soon found himself in Da Nang, knee-deep in rice paddies, no longer breathing in clean fresh Midwestern air, but the pungent aromas of napalm and Agent Orange.

He had killed people and seen people killed. While he had no atrocities on his conscience, personally, he had seen the ditches filled with Vietnamese civilians, families, fathers and mothers and sons and daughters, sleeping wide-eyed in those silly pajamalike outfits, riddled with slugs, soaked with blood. He had walked the tall grass and seen his buds fall dead beside him, a bullet through the throat, through the chest, through the groin, disappearing into the brush as if swallowed by the earth; he had shot upward at trees and, like weird falling fruit, snipers dropped to the ground near his feet, teenage boys with empty faces and full rifles.

And, too, he'd seen sweet innocent kids—four or five at most—hurling homemade hand grenades.

After two tours of duty, Uncle Sugar returned him to the States—many in his platoon were not so lucky—and, with his mom and dad dead and Betsy Jane married with two kids, he had left Missouri for the promise of sunshine and prosperity the Beach Boys had sung about. Settling in Los Angeles, he grew his hair out, fell in with the make-love-not-war crowd and never let any of the hippie chicks he was banging or longhairs he was scoring dope off of know he was one of the baby murderers they so disdained.

One day he woke up, shook the drug hangover off, and walked back into the real world. Within days, he was pouring cement for the construction business, which was just the sort of mindless labor he craved. But terrible nightly dreams began taking him back to the jungle and the rice paddies and he would wake shivering, sweating, not even wanting to try to go back to sleep. So he would drag into work half-dead, and perform his job half-assed.

A rash of illnesses followed, including fatigue and depression, causing him to lose one job after another. The doctors at the veterans hospital had some kind of term for it—delayed post-combat stress fatigue syndrome or some such shit—and put him on a variety of antidepressants.

Drugs again.

But these, whether uppers or downers, only made his constant fatigue worse. Drinking helped numb the hurt, but didn't do much for his job prospects.

Ben wanted to work, he really did, and, yeah, he drank some, but he was no rummy, he had never been one to drink on the job; but even if he felt better and his fatigue went away, who would hire him now?

Now that so many years had slipped through his fingers, and he was pushing fifty?

It was a little after six o'clock in the evening and dusk was beginning to sneak in like Cong from the east, the buildings casting long shadows over the city. Ben had been there since four that afternoon, to catch the older executives slipping away early for the day, heading out to the links for a round of golf before dinner. He generally did well with them, especially if he mentioned he was a Vietnam vet; these were his classmates, from the late '60s and early '70s—they looked at him and saw the shell of their brother who got killed over there, or the best friend they'd lost contact with a million years ago. So they would hand him a buck or two, perhaps feeling guilty that they, too, hadn't gone off to that sense-less war, as if Ben wouldn't have stayed home if he could.

But Ben had learned that the professionals who left later, between five and six o'clock—younger ones in their twenties and early thirties, Generation X, wasn't that what they were called?—were a cold, callous lot. The only thing he ever got from them was a blankly contemptuous stare, if they bothered to look at him at all.

He was ready to call it quits for the day, when a young woman he'd seen before, wearing a fetching, formfitting red suit with an oversize collar and straight skirt, stepped out of the building onto the sidewalk.

A smile tickled his stubbly face. There was always time to take a look at this one. Not that good-looking women were exactly rare in this part of the world—but there was something about her, something that reminded him of the girls he'd dated, of Betsy Jane and the backseat of his Chevy Nova.

She had shoulder-length auburn hair and pink satiny skin that seemed to glow. Her face was youthful, her features exquisite, as beautiful as any of the Hollywood wannabes he'd seen on these streets.

She paused in front of the building, looking up Wilshire Boulevard, then down. He remained where he was, leaning against the building, too intimidated to ask her for money.

No, not intimidated—embarrassed. It was goddamn hard to embarrass a homeless beggar like him, but this vision, this reminder of a life lost or anyway misspent, made him ashamed. Made it all his own fault, somehow.

Then something extraordinary happened: She walked over to him.

"I'm afraid I don't remember where I parked my car," she said with a little laugh, as if he were a casual friend or coworker. The laugh had a falling, tinkling cadence, like a wind chime.

Ben looked into eyes as green and glimmering as an emerald. Cleared his throat. "White GM, right?"

She had an odd look on her face, like she couldn't even remember the make of her car. Was she on something?

"White GM," he repeated.

Then she nodded. "Thanks for remembering. Funny—I've seen you standing over here. You look at me, sometimes."

Ben did something he hadn't done since high school: He blushed. "Yes, I ... I didn't mean anything by it...."

"No, it's okay. But isn't that funny? I remember that you stand here every day, but I don't remember where I put my own car?"

Another tinkling laugh.

"Yeah, uh, funny," he said.

"Hysterical.... Can you help?"

"Sure," he said, and pointed across the boulevard. "I've seen you park up that side street sometimes. I wasn't here this morning, but it's worth a try."

"Thank you," she responded with a little smile. "You're very kind. You have nice eyes."

Was she flirting with him? That was insane. He remembered his place.

And he took his best shot. "Uh ... you wouldn't happen to have any spare change, would ya? I could use a hot meal."

Her confused emerald eyes turned compassionate. "I'll look," she said, and dug into her black purse. She withdrew a twenty and handed it to him. "Will this do?"

"Ah ... yeah," he said, stunned by her generosity. And touched. But before he could thank her, she turned away.

He watched her walk down to the corner and wait for the light to turn green. When it did, she began to cross the busy intersection, the hem of her silk-linen red dress rising up her luscious Betsy Jane legs with every step.... And he wished he was eighteen again and captain of the football team and the prom, the goddamn fucking prom, was tonight.

Suddenly a tan sedan with tinted windows squealed around the corner, the driver apparently not seeing her crossing the street.

Ben shouted a warning, but it came too late, the impact of the car sending her up over the hood, with a terrible splash of blood, hurling her like a rag doll up and over the car, then down again, bone-crunchingly hard on the cruel pavement, behind the vehicle with another ghastly splash of blood, tossing her crumpled form, limbs askew, head at an unnatural angle, to the cement.

The driver did not stop. And Ben saw something more grotesque than he'd ever seen in a life filled with grotesqueries: As the sedan sped away, the driver—through the tinted windshield Ben barely made him out, sunglasses, dark hair, male, twenties—turned on his windshield wipers and wiper solvent shot up and helped the blades wash away the blood.

Ben was already breaking into a run, dodging in and out of traffic that was shrieking to a halt, and within seconds he reached her and, dropping down on his knees, gathered her broken body in his arms, her blood as red as the dress.

And then he was back in the rice paddies, screaming, "Medic! Medic!" telling her to hold on, to hold on, a chopper was coming….

But she just stared back at him with lifeless green eyes, and the EMT boys—when they finally came—were confused that Ben kept calling the dead woman Betsy Jane when her ID said something else.

Part One:

BEFORE

Chapter One

"BIG GIRLS DON'T CRY"
(Four Seasons, #1 Billboard, 1962)

Joyce Lackey stood at the wide window in her well-appointed office of polished granite and brushed steel on the sixty-third floor of the John Hancock Building in downtown Chicago. Looking out over the tops of the other buildings toward the soothing shoreline of Lake Michigan, she took in the carefree joggers and bikers and in-line skaters moving in miniature along a cement path under a continuous canopy of trees vivid with fall colors. The late afternoon sun spilled its rays downward like an endlessly unspooling bolt of gold lamé, while here and there, sailboats drifted lazily in the breeze across the turquoise lake.

The view from this window was one Joyce—fifty-five, senior account executive at Ballard, Henke and Hurst Advertising—had worked long and hard to attain. It was a view she relished. It was a view Joyce knew she would never likely see again.

With a sigh, the shapely brown-eyed blonde turned back to her massive mahogany desk where a tan leather Vuitton suitcase (no cardboard box for her) lay open, filled with the few office belongings she was allowed to take with her, a sadly austere culmination of thirty years of faithful service.

The executive desk set—blotter, appointment book, pen and pencil holder with Seiko clock, along with the expensive MontBlanc pens—was her own, purchased some years ago in the basement of Neiman Marcus with her first bonus check, long before the company became prosperous enough to hand out MontBlanc pens to the executives like they were Bics. The crystal heart-shaped Swarovski paperweight was a gift from Henry Ballard, one of the founders of the company, a Robert Young-esque father figure she had adored (in both boardroom and bedroom).

Henry had been the kindest, most handsome man she had ever met. Unfortunately, he was also a married man, with an atrophying trophy wife, four children and (at least during the years Joyce knew him) five grandchildren. It had been clear to Joyce from the beginning of their long affair that Henry would never leave his wife, whose Evanston family remained prominent social fixtures in Chicago, and investors in the firm. Oddly, Joyce never particularly wanted Henry to leave Doris, rather was content to see him at work—and after, when they would sometimes go to her condominium up the Gold Coast—instinctively realizing that her job was really her first love.

And even if she did, from time to time, in the afterglow of fantastic sex, fantasize that one day Henry might show up at her door, suitcase in hand ... that fantasy ended two years ago with his coronary over a plate of rare prime rib at the Cliff Dweller's Club.

She gazed across the room at some of the numerous awards arranged on small marble pillars that she had won for the advertising firm during her tenure; they would have to stay behind, along with others on the agency's walls and in the reception-area display case. Which was all right with her. The way she felt now—that is, betrayed—the awards would only have wound up in a dumpster.

Being forced into early retirement was an eventuality that had never crossed her mind. In fact, retiring at all had never crossed her mind. For Christ's sake, she had *years* of quality work left in her. She was at the top of her goddamn game!

So why was the company doing this to her?

Idly she toyed with the Petek Philippe watch on her wrist, a gift the board had given her last week in place of her job. Now she wondered if she had priced herself out of the market by asking for all those raises over the years … though God knows she certainly deserved them.

When she was hired straight out of Northwestern as a copy writer in the 1970s, Ballard and Henke had been a struggling advertising outfit at the bottom of the local heap, until she catapulted them to the top of the business in the early 1980s with her "I'm worth it" campaign.

With billboards and radio and TV spots trumpeting her slogan in every state of the union, Joyce had found herself profiled in *Chicago* magazine, the *Tribune* and *Sun-Times*, and even the giveaway *Reader*, which had singled her out for a tongue-in-cheek piece that put her on a pedestal of irony, picturing Joyce as the poster child for the Me Decade. This leftist, left-handed compliment had only boosted her standing in the industry.

Then in the '90s, sensing people were feeling guilty with their excessive spending—even though she herself never felt that way, particularly—Joyce had coined the phrase "provisional hedonism," understanding the need for people to rationalize away their expensive purchases. This phrase remained within the industry itself, but her slogan for the public—"Buy it as an investment!"— became a new creed for the Baby Boomer generation, and one she personally had followed.

But apparently, as all of this success had built her into the highest paid account executive in the city, she had unwittingly become too expensive a commodity to jibe with the job she loved—and there was nowhere upstairs for her to get kicked to, in Ballard, Henke and Hurst: Males held down those choice slots.

And as if this glass-ceiling indignity weren't enough, now she would be replaced by a cheaper, younger—and, she had to admit, prettier—this-year's-model named Heather.

Joyce sighed and shook her head. Jesus! Were the Heathers of the world *really* old enough already to hold executive positions? What next—Brittany?

Oh, the company didn't think she knew about her replacement, but Joyce did. She had run into Heather in the hallway yesterday as the young woman came out of the Human Resources office.

"You're Joyce Lackey!" the woman had said breathlessly. She wore a pale gray suit and white blouse—very dull, to Joyce's way of thinking, though her slender, suspiciously busty figure was well served by it—the little bitch looked like Ally McBeal with breasts.

"Yes, I've been Joyce Lackey for some time."

"This really is an honor. You're a legend in our business."

"I like to think of myself more as a reality. And you are...?"

"Sorry!" The young woman smiled, her skin so fresh and young it barely creased. She extended a well-manicured hand. "Heather Blake."

They shook hands; Heather's grip was cool and firm.

Heather was shaking her head admiringly, short platinum tresses shimmering. "I've heard so much about you, read about you, since I was ... do you know that your ad campaigns were discussed in my advanced advertising class at Northwestern?"

"Well, I have spoken there a few times...."

"I must tell you, personally, I'm very surprised that you're retiring. I would think someone of your skills and accomplishments would just"—Heather's voice turned cute, and she swung a Mary Tyler Moore fist in the air—"hang in there and keep pitchin'! But nobody deserves a rest more. I mean, who better to lay back on her laurels than Joyce Lackey?"

"What position are you applying for, Heather?"

"Oh, I'm not applying. I've been hired. Didn't you know? I have the unenviable challenge of taking over for you."

"Really."

"But I don't how I'm *ever* going to manage to fill *your* shoes."

That was true enough, since Joyce wore a size eight, and Heather's tiny feet looked bound at birth, which was yet another reason for Joyce to hate her.

"I hope you won't mind the occasional phone call, Joyce … may I call you Joyce? You know, just to help me understand the lay of the land."

From the look of her, she already was the lay of the land; probably had something to do with getting the job.

"Well, I'll make sure to leave my phone number for you," Joyce said to her and walked on, casting her replacement back a smile so believable, Joyce practically bought it herself. But, then, that was her speciality, wasn't it? Selling things to imbeciles?

But the woman had watched Joyce go with such a funny expression on her flawless young face. Could that possibly have been guilt? Joyce could only laugh—Heather wouldn't make it very far in advertising if she felt sorry for the other guy.

Joyce slammed the suitcase shut. Then again, she thought, money may not have been the be-all-and-end-all of her forced retirement. After all, she had never really seen eye to eye with the company's new partner, Tyler Hurst, a thirty-something male whose Armani suits looked sewn directly onto his body. Hurst bought into the partnership after Henry died. Joyce had had the option, but not that kind of capital.

And she had tried to get along with Tyler, she really had. But from their very first meeting they had rubbed each other the wrong way—a clash of styles, a clash of generations.…

The client had been an R.V. manufacturer who, in the positive economic climate of the late '90s, was ready to give Winnebago a run for the market share, and Joyce had worked up the preliminary concept for Tyler's approval, before turning it over to the creative team. But when she presented it to Tyler in his office that rainy overcast morning, he shook his head.

"The target should be Generation-X," he'd said flatly.

The wind rattled the windows on the sixty-third floor, trying to get in; beyond, Lake Michigan was choppy and murky.

"Generation-X?" she'd blurted. "*They* don't have any money!"

"Many of them are starting to. And that's our market."

"But that's crazy—retirees have always dominated the R.V. market."

"Many markets suffer generational shift, and this is one of them." He sighed, tossing the art she'd brought in across his desk carelessly, as if discarding it. "And, considering your reputation as an innovator, Joyce—I would expect bolder, less traditional thinking."

Hurst's thinking was so bizarrely wrong it made Joyce's head whirl. "Some markets *are* traditional in nature, Tyler—you sell tractors to farmers, you sell airplanes to pilots, and you sell fucking R.V.s to fucking retirees!"

"I don't think we need that kind of language here, Joyce." He checked the knot of his tie, as if her profanity might have loosened it. "That may have been ... chic, or ... hip ... in *your* day, but we'll show more respect for each other, here. From now on. Understood?"

Her day?

"I apologize," Joyce said numbly. "But my point is, retirees are the natural market for this product."

Hurst looked at her with cool, gray eyes that matched the dismal sky. "Yes. Retirees who lived through the Depression and understood the necessity to save in order *to* retire. But they're dying off, replaced by a generation of spoiled brats who've had everything handed to them on a silver platter and who won't have any money to face their well-deserved bleak futures."

Joyce smiled in astonishment, put one hand on her hip. "Of course they'll have money. Lots of money ... just like they have now."

Hurst laughed soundlessly. "No. They've spent it, mortgaged it, leased it, plastic-carded it, and haven't saved."

She had no rejoinder for this—because, in her case at least, all of that was true.

"The Baby Boomers are soon to lose their position as a vital demographic," Hurst said, then added with a smirk, his voice taking on a more personal tone, "They won't be able to afford a pot to piss in, let alone an expensive R.V. to vacation in."

So he could say "piss," but she couldn't say "fucking." Interesting ground rules.

"Then they'll buy the damn thing to *live* in!" she snapped, fed up with his smug attitude. "Boomers are still the only market that counts, because there are seventy-six million of them!" *Of us!* she thought. "*They* set the trends. And if they have no money, and have to live in an R.V., then *that* will become the trend."

"You're reaching, Joyce."

She laughed humorlessly. "They'll be Easy Riders, only with R.V.s instead of motorcycles, cruisin' down the highway. And it'll be cool, because whatever the Boomers do defines cool."

He looked at her with barely veiled contempt, arched an eyebrow, and said, "You really think going down the tubes will be 'cool'? Well, you're right on one account, Joyce—it will be a trend—only that will be one trend we'll have a great deal of difficulty finding a way to make any money out of."

After that, the two barely spoke to each other, and within the year Hurst gave her an ultimatum of taking early retirement or being "let go," a decorous way of saying "fired."

"We need fresh blood," he had said, which made a lot of sense to her, coming from him: He was a vampire, after all, sucking the joy and creativity out of her work. So it was just as well she left.

She had considered, briefly, an age discrimination suit. And that might have won her a handsome settlement, but would have ended her career, forever branding her a trouble-maker—and old.

Joyce moved her Vuitton suitcase off the desk and set it on the floor. She looked around the office, feeling a sense of loss unlike any since her parents died. It brought tears to her eyes and made her stomach churn.

"Hi!" In the doorway stood Julie, her secretary; she was twenty-something, with curly brown hair and big round glasses, apparently borrowed from Velma of *Scooby-Doo.*

Today Julie was wearing a baggy blue sweatshirt and jeans, this being "casual Friday," an idea Joyce had opposed, believing sloppy attire promoted sloppy work. That was why she, Joyce, always wore a suit, like this navy and gold St. John knit she would be wearing when she left this job.

"Just wanted to say 'good-bye' and 'good luck' before you went," the woman said chirpily.

Joyce, from behind the desk, said, "Thanks."

She had always just tolerated the peppy Julie, who seemed to have drifted into the ad game from a road company of *Up With People.*

"You still have some things in the lunchroom," she reminded Joyce. "That Milano expresso maker, I believe, is yours...."

"You girls can have it."

"Oh really?" Julie said, then smirked. "Martha was eyeing it today.... She said if you didn't take it home, she would." Martha was Tyler's secretary, the company gossip and her boss's spy—universally disliked, and yet *she* had a job.

"All right, all right," Joyce said dismissively. "I'll take it home." Julie smiled. "Good." And then she was gone.

Joyce picked up her suitcase and took one final look out the window; dusk was moving in from the lake, creeping over the city, smothering it with a misty blanket—or was that just her eyes? She walked across the room on the thick mauve carpet for the last time, and out the door, not bothering to turn off the light, a petty decision to cost the company a few cents. Boy, that would sure hurt them.

With that, she left her world behind.

Suitcase in hand, Willy Loman-like, she trudged down the corridor, and then down another, to the lunchroom, which was dark and silent.

She flicked on the light.

"Surprise!"

Joyce almost dropped her suitcase; she leaned against the doorjamb, one hand to her chest.

"Jesus Christ," she gasped, wide-eyed, at the little group that stood around the kitchen table, on whose top a cake and several presents rested. "You really scared me!"

Julie laughed. "Sorry … it's traditionally done this way. I mean, it is a surprise party!"

Brian, manager of the mail room, wagged a scolding finger at Julie, and said, "Want to give the 'old girl' a heart attack before she can even start enjoying her retirement?" His receding hairline seemed at odds with a round boyish face.

The others in the small group were Mary Irene, from accounting, a tall, thin woman in her mid-forties, whose hatchet-faced efficiency reminded Joyce of *The Beverly Hillbillies'* Miss Hathaway, and Linda, the receptionist, an overweight thirty-something with cow-eyes, who didn't remind Joyce of anybody.

Missing from the little celebration, and obviously distancing themselves, were the copy writers and art directors she'd bought so many lunches for, and her fellow account executives, all of whom she thought were her friends, none of whom seemed to be able to attend one lousy little going-away party....

"You shouldn't have gone to any trouble for me," Joyce said lamely, and truly wished they hadn't; she hated surprises, and had hardened into hating sentimentality—and now she had to be pleasant and upbeat, when all she wanted to do was go home and crawl under the sheets and bawl.

"It was no trouble," Linda told her with a smile so sweet Mary Poppins would have considered slapping her. "We couldn't let you get away without having a little party of our own, now could we?"

"Damn straight," Brian added. "Now get over here and open your presents."

Suddenly she felt strangely moved. Brian was just such a sweet kid, untouched by office politics, it got to her.

Joyce put her suitcase down and walked over to the table. "Which should I open first?" she asked; even such a simple decision was more than she could handle right now.

"Take your pick," Julie said, bubbling with vicarious pleasure, brown eyes behind the round glasses shining like bright copper pennies.

Joyce picked up a small floral bag with lavender tissue paper sticking out of it.

"That one's from me," Mary Irene said, her hands clasped primly in front of herself.

Joyce stuck her hand in the sack and withdrew the contents: a Funjet Vacation to Cancun.

"Oh, Mary Irene," Joyce said, sincerely affected. Now she felt bad about every unkind thought she ever had about the accountant.... Like thinking she'd never had sex—with a man, anyway.

"You can use the tickets anytime you want," Mary Irene explained. "And I'll expect you to send me a postcard when you get there."

"I will." She clasped the tickets to her bosom. "I promise."

"Now this one," Julie said, pushing a familiar pink and gold striped box with hearts toward Joyce. "It's from Linda and me."

Joyce lifted the lid of the Victoria's Secret box and pushed the tissue paper aside and pulled out a sheer black negligee; it had a black feather boa around a plunging neckline that went down to the navel.

"My," Joyce said with a forced smile. "Isn't this nice." But it was more a question than statement.

"You can take it on your trip to Cancun," Linda said brightly. "You never know who you might meet!"

"Uh-huh," Joyce said holding the negligee out, noticing the XL size label. She wasn't fat, was she? She knew she could stand to drop a few....

"I hope it fits," Julie lamented, then added, "But it should.... Linda tried it on."

I am fat, Joyce thought.

"You should have seen her prancing around," Julie laughed.

Linda giggled. "Yeah, after a while we felt we had to buy it."

"Okay, guys, that's way more information than I need," Joyce said, kidding on the square, trying to banish the image her coworkers had just summoned, and tucked the nightgown back into the box.

"This is from me," Brian said, and handed her a business-size envelope.

She thought it was only a card, but inside found season tickets to the Chicago Bulls; she wasn't sure what his salary was, but the gift must have been a big sacrifice, down the food chain as he was, with a wife, four kids and a house in Elmhurst.

Joyce touched his arm. "Oh, Brian," she said, choked up, "this is so sweet of you.... I've never had season tickets." The company bought any number of tickets, to all kinds of events, but they were strictly to be given to clients.

"I always buy presents *I'd* like to have," he explained, grinning shyly. "So, if you ever can't make a game, I guess you know who to call!"

She looked at the others. "Thank you all so much for the gifts," she said, and wondered if she would have been so thoughtful and generous if it had been any of them who were leaving.

Possibly.

Maybe.

Probably not.

Over pink champagne and slices of the two-layer cake lettered in darker pink *Happy Retirement, Joyce* on white frosting, they talked about getting together for lunch in the future, but she knew that would never happen.

It would only be awkward and painful. Friends made at work were like friends made in childhood: They happened to be whoever lived on your block, or in your apartment building. It wasn't that company friendships weren't real ... it was just that without the context of the workplace, future conversations became stuck in the past, as painful and ungainly as standing around trying to chat at a high school class reunion.

And the last thing Joyce wanted to hear from her former coworkers was how well her replacement was doing, or for that matter, how terrible, which would make Joyce wish she was still on the job—not that the latter wouldn't at least give her some smug satisfaction. Truth be told, however, she secretly hoped the whole company would go down in flames ... taking everybody with it. Including these nice, sweet people who'd taken time to say good-bye to her.

After the party, her arms laden with her suitcase, coffeemaker and gifts—like consolation prizes from a game show—Joyce took the elevator down to the parking garage, which occupied the center of the Hancock building, and made her way through its cavernous, cement tomb to her reserved parking space, where a silver BMW awaited her ...

... a company car they would let her keep until the end of the week.

She threw everything unceremoniously in the backseat and slid into the front. When she turned the key in the ignition, the radio also came on, tuned to her favorite oldies station, and the Grass Roots doing "Live for Today" blared like a car alarm.

Twitching a grimace, she twisted it off with a *click*. As she wheeled the BMW down the narrow spiral exit ramp to the street, Joyce wondered how much a car like this cost these days—then she wondered what *any* car would cost, since she'd never had to shop for one, and never had an auto-manufacturer account, either.

From this she had the sudden realization that, in some respects, she was like a sheltered, spoiled child, being cast out into the world by parents who had finally got fed up.

The autumn evening was darkening, as was her mood, the traffic heavy, as she headed north on Lake Shore Drive. Maybe it wouldn't be so bad driving a smaller car, she thought. She wouldn't have to worry so much about car theft, and she could practically invent her own parking spaces on the street, which was a plus in Chicago. Also, the insurance would be a lot lower—she assumed.

She'd never had to buy car insurance, either—that had been a perk attached to the company car.

Still, by the time she arrived at her rented lake-view condo up the Gold Coast, she was feeling a little better. She threw her keys on the ornate wrought-iron-and-glass entry table, kicked her Stuart Weitzman heels off and padded in nyloned feet back to the art-deco black-and-white kitchen, where she poured herself a glass of Chateau Latour from a crystal decanter and downed it in a few gulps.

Her mind beginning to numb from the wine, which was precisely the desired effect, she wandered the spacious apartment that had been her home for the past ten years, like a thief casing the joint.

After a while, she entered the master bedroom, which had recently been redecorated with the expensive King Louis XV furniture she had convinced herself would be a good investment, buying into her own campaign. *Fool for a client*, she thought. There she sat at a small writing desk, opened a drawer and pulled out her financial statements.

Her money market account had the equivalent of two, maybe three (if she behaved herself) months salary. Her investment portfolio, once healthy, was now non-existent: The mutual funds had gone for the furniture; the annuities, for a younger man she'd met in a bar on Rush Street after Henry died, and thought she might want to marry, as her biological clock was still ticking, then. They had taken a romantic world cruise and spoken of love and the future and then her money had run out, and so had he.

Yet another bad investment.

Now she wished she had taken company shares instead of cash over the years, but then, she'd thought there would be plenty of time for that kind of thing.

Joyce got up from the desk and went over to the four-poster bed and sat down on the peach satin bedspread and stared, trying to imagine what it would be like to live in an R.V.

She shook her head. She'd made a lot of money over the years.... Where the hell had it all gone? She sighed. It cost a great deal to live the good life in an expensive city. And, at her age, it took more and more cash to get her ready to face the world each day ... the facials, the hair styling, the manicures, the workouts, the clothes.... After all, she had an executive image to uphold, and clients to impress.

Her eyes traveled to a walk-in closet the size of the Batcave, where enough designer clothes hung for her to open her own Michigan Avenue boutique.

Something caught her attention and she got up from the bed and went over. An Ellen Tracy dress she'd bought on a whim a while ago, still had the store tags on it! She could return it for cash, if she could only find the receipt.

She returned to the desk and rummaged frantically around in the drawers, making a mess, and the pathetic need to find the receipt in order to get a few hundred dollars—which really wouldn't do her much good, anyway—caused her eyes to well up.

First thing tomorrow, she'd cash in the Cancun flight and sell a scalper the Bulls tickets. The negligee she'd hang onto—it might help her the next time she got screwed.

A tear slid down one cheek and splashed on the Petek Phillipe watch on her wrist. She wondered what a pawnshop would give her for it—assuming the goddamn fucking thing was waterproof.

Chapter Two

"IT'S OVER"

(Roy Orbison, #9 Billboard, 1964)

The receptionist—an icily attractive woman of perhaps twenty-five with porcelain skin and blond hair pulled back from her face in a simple chignon—looked at Joyce with glazed politeness.

"Mr. Thomas will see you now," she said in a monotone worthy of a waitress in a low-end fast-food joint.

Like her makeup, the receptionist's outfit was stark—beige cardigan and straight skirt—which provided quite a contrast to Joyce's elegant pink Chanel suit with its gold buttons and splashy jewelry (she hadn't been able to make up her mind between a heavy chain necklace or the long pearl one, so she'd worn them both).

Joyce rose from the comfortable if somewhat stained and threadbare burgundy upholstered chair where she'd been sitting in the reception area next to a plant badly in need of re-potting. She gave the young blonde her friendliest smile.

"Thank you, Diane," she said, picking up on the woman's desk nameplate. After all, Diane here might one day be *her* secretary. And if so, one of Diane's first new jobs would be to keep the reception area spruced up, for Christ's sake, and to work on her lackluster people skills. There were clients to impress!

The inner office was masculine in decor, and also rather untidy. On the wood-paneled walls hung pictures of ducks and geese mixing oddly with autographed photos of sports figures, and here and there a plaque or two, awards won by Thomas Advertising, an outfit that was not just lower on the totem pole than her former employer, but barely in the same tribe.

This should be a slam dunk, she thought, staying positive, despite the dozens of disappointments in recent days.

Behind a desk so littered with papers and files the glass top could barely be seen sat Frank Thomas, owner of the firm. Approaching sixty, his thick hair a steel gray, he wore rather old-fashioned heavy-black-framed squarish glasses that suited his chiseled, character-lined face, which—unlike hers—had only gotten better with age.

Frank was wearing a navy polo shirt and tan pleated slacks, rather casual attire for the top man, Joyce thought, unless Thomas Advertising had a "casual day" other than Friday. As she entered the room, he stood up, smiling broadly.

"Joyce," he said, beaming, extending a hand across the desk. "I've been looking forward to this! What a pleasure to see you somewhere besides the Addies!"

"Frank," she said, genuinely happy to be in his presence. "It's good to see you again, too." And she took his hand, which was warm and firm.

"Please, please, have a seat." He gestured to another burgundy chair—not stained, though equally threadbare—in front of the desk.

She sat.

Frank leaned back, his chair creaking. "I read in the *Trib* you'd retired. I couldn't believe it! I was sure I'd beat you out to pasture by a long shot. Leave it to Joyce Lackey to figure a way to retire early. You always were smarter than me."

Joyce smiled, putting just a hint of something unbusinesslike in it. "And *you* still know how to make a woman feel good," she said.

Years ago, they had met at a business function, became close friends, then lovers; he had even proposed, being one of the rare men she'd been attracted to who wasn't already married. But she hadn't wanted to make that kind of commitment, yet—she was too devoted to work, and having too much fun after work. And a man couldn't be expected to wait around forever.

"And how's Maureen?" she asked.

"Fine. Just fine."

"Did she ever get a handle on those migraines?"

"Oh, yes, they've got some wonderful new medication. If I'd bought the right pharmaceutical stocks, we'd both be retired right now, kiddo!"

"And your boy—Ted?"

"We're up to three grandkids, now, thanks to Teddy." He gestured to a small three-framed photo, lost in the sea of papers on his desk. "Janet's married, too, but no little deductions yet."

She smiled and nodded. Suddenly she felt stiff, even awkward, around this man she'd known so well: She was fresh out of small talk.

"So, Joyce—what brings you out to the suburbs?"

Bless him, he knew her so well; everything she did had a purpose.

She took a deep breath, shifting in the chair, her gaze dropping from his eyes to the files on the desk. "Well ..." Suddenly, despite the industrial-strength deodorant, her underarms felt damp, adding to her discomfort. "I heard through the grapevine that you're looking for a copy writer."

"Well that's right. Why, do you have a candidate in mind?"

"Yes."

He shook his head, smiling a wry half-smile. "I guess we all have a nephew who wants to get into the advertising business, right? Or a niece! Got to watch the sexist stuff, you know—close me down overnight."

"You were never sexist, Frank. You were always as fair a man as this unfair business ever knew." This was a line she had prepared and rehearsed and she prayed it had sounded spontaneous.

"Well, gee whiz, like we used to say back in Muncie ... that's sweet of you, Joyce."

"Frank ..." She paused. "The person I had in mind was ... me."

He laughed. "Yeah, right."

She said nothing. Swallowed.

Frank's smiled faded a little. "You are kidding, of course."

"I wish I were."

He leaned forward, the chair making the same creak. "Surely you must know that all I have is an entry-level job, Joyce—not even head copy writer. You'd be reporting to a damn kid who has half your qualifications and a tenth of your experience."

"I don't care. I just want a chance."

"But, Joyce ... you're *beyond* overqualified."

"That doesn't matter."

"And the pay is pitiful ... not even in your ballpark."

My ballpark, she thought bitterly. *Can't you see I've been sent down to the minors?*

"Frank ..." she began.

"Joyce, you know I'd do just about anything for you...."

Please, she thought, trying to send him a mental message, *don't make this any harder for me. Don't make me beg....*

Maybe he had read her mind, because his face took on a tortured look and he said haltingly, "Joyce, I ... I just don't think you'd be happy starting over. With your reputation, you should open your *own* agency." Then he added with a little laugh, "Though I wouldn't welcome the competition."

She looked down at her hands in her lap. "Yes, well, that takes capital, doesn't it."

"Oh. But with all the loot you made over the years ..."

"Bad investments. No retirement package. Nothing."

Now he swallowed. "I see."

She sat forward in her chair. "Frank, I'll level with you. Despite that bullshit in the papers, I was forced to retire … and you *know* me, Frank, you know I don't have anything but my work. Even if I didn't need money to exist, I'd still want to work—*that's who I am* … that's … all I am."

"Joyce … I really didn't know. The papers made it sound so convincing.…"

"Who do you think wrote the news release? And, Frank—I do need the money … no matter how 'pitiful.' " She sat back in the chair, and added slowly, "I just thought that *you* might be able to help. For … for old times sake."

She hated herself for leaning on their past, for calling that marker in. But it was the only card she had left to play.

Frank stood from his chair and turned his back to her and looked at the wall where an autographed photo of Ernie Banks stared back; perhaps he was hoping the legendary Cubs ballplayer would give him some guidance, help him find the words.

When Frank turned around his voice was soft. "Joyce, my company needs young blood."

God! Couldn't a veteran adman come up with a newer phrase?

"Oh but I *have* young blood," she said, not letting him off the hook. "I just had a complete physical. The clinic says I'm as fit as a thirty-year-old woman. I never smoked, never drank to excess, and I still work out—"

"You know what I mean … young ideas."

Joyce studied his face. "I see," she said icily. "Of which I have none?"

"I didn't mean that," he said, and came around the desk, pushing some files back, sitting on the edge. "*I* know your past accomplishments, everybody in Chicago knows. Hell, everybody in the goddamn country does."

That melted her a little.

"But this new millennium needs the kind of fresh perspective that only youth can provide."

Horseshit! she thought, and was about to flail into him verbally, when he lowered his voice and went on.

"And there's something else I should tell you."

She looked up intently at him.

"I'm thinking of merging with a bigger company."

She blinked. "You *want* to be taken over?"

He nodded. "The Davis Group. It's either that or go under."

She stared at the wall behind him. She didn't know business was that bad. That ... threadbare.

"And if that happens," he said with a sigh, "you know what it's going to be like around here?"

She did. She'd gone through it with her old agency: utter turmoil. Turmoil from without, by irate clients who don't like the change and take their business elsewhere, and turmoil from within, by merging two different sets of employees, and fighting over which ones got to stay.

"As our newest copy writer," he said, "you'd likely be one of the first to go—no seniority, no history."

"Maybe. But, Frank—if I do hold on, and help the merged company keep from losing too many clients from both their lists, I could rise to the top. Cream always does."

"I don't know, Joyce...."

"And, Frank, when the company goes public—and that's where you want to head, don't you?—there'd be plenty of money to go around."

"You do have a point."

"Merger or not, I still want to be considered for the job," she said firmly, eager to take the chance. Besides, she had no other prospects on the horizon.

Frank put one hand on her shoulder. "All right, Joyce. Okay. I'll see what I can do."

Hoped blossomed within her, and she rose from the chair and grasped his hand. "Thanks, Frank, I knew I could count on you."

He smiled weakly. "Sure, Joyce. I'll call you by the end of the week."

She exited the office into the hall with the old bounce back in her step. Frank would come through for her, she knew it! After all, he was still president of the company—for now, anyway. Pausing at a drinking fountain, she sipped cool water, feeling reinvigorated, thinking how this lowly agency was no different from Ballard, Henke and Hurst when she'd first come aboard. She wasn't starting back at the bottom, no—she was back on the launching pad!

Dreading the commute into the city in slow, rush-hour traffic, she wandered down the corridor to find a rest room.

She was in the last stall, straightening her skirt, and about to flush the toilet, when female voices trailed in.

"So," a sarcastically tinged female voice said, "who was the rhinestone cowgirl, anyway?"

Joyce could see her through the crack of the stall door, at the mirror, applying lipstick, a slender girl, with shoulder-length brown hair.

A voice from a stall down the line answered, just as acidly: "Somebody who used to be somebody, I think. If you can believe it."

"Couldn't she find *one* more necklace to wear?"

Joyce, standing in the stall, touched a hand to her throat; maybe two *was* too much….

From that stall down the line the other woman laughed. "Maybe she forgot she already had one on. I think she was an 'old friend' of Frank's. Anyway, that's how I read her body language."

Joyce froze in the stall, finally recognizing the secretary's voice. It wasn't so monotone, now.

"*Old* friend is right," said the woman at the mirror. "Hasn't she heard, less is more? Move over, Tammy Faye! So what did she want?"

Joyce frowned. She didn't wear *that* much makeup! Did she?

A toilet flushed. The secretary joined her friend at the mirror. Washing her hands, checking her makeup, the blonde asked, "What makes you think I listened?"

"Ha! Spill."

The secretary was touching up her lipstick. "She was asking about the copywriting position."

"Really? Did she come out with runs in the knees of her nylons?"

"Don't knock it. It worked for Monica—maybe it'll fly for the Geritol set, too."

"You think she takes out her false teeth?"

Both women laughed and it echoed like mocking thunder.

Joyce was shivering—it was cold in there.

Then the first woman said, "Hey, I thought that position was already decided on. You know, that cute black guy from Northwestern. Nice buns!"

"Yeah, but gay."

"All the good-looking ones are gay!"

The secretary shrugged. "I guess poor Frank just didn't know how to tell her the job was filled."

The other woman's laugh echoed in the room. "He's such a soft touch. He should have let *us* do it."

The voices trailed out, as the bathroom door wooshed open and shut.

After a few moments, Joyce came out of the stall and stared at the mirror, where a tired-looking, middle-aged woman wearing overdone makeup, an outdated suit, and too much jewelry, stared back at her. Tears spilled down her cheeks, washing some of the makeup away—was that really better?—and she got a paper towel and ran cold water on it, and dabbed her face with it.

She didn't remember leaving the building, nor did she remember driving back into the city and up the Gold Coast, parking in the underground garage of her condo and letting herself in the front door.

But she did remember standing in the dining room with its beautiful parquet floor where she had, over the years, entertained VIPs, from publicists to politicians, royalty to rock stars, at her elegant dinning room table, which she'd had to sell at an auction house. The Louis XV furniture had been the first to go, at a considerable loss—so much for "provisional hedonism."

And she remembered going into the kitchen and pouring herself a large glass of Chablis, and entering the bathroom, getting a bottle of sleeping pills, and taking them all with the wine. Then she combed her hair, and fixed her makeup—with a new, lighter touch—and, returning to the bedroom, she put on her finest silk nightgown—not the black-boa thing; she wouldn't be caught dead in that—and reclined on the bed, arms folded upon her chest, as if giving the mortician guidance to how she should be laid out in her casket.

Never before in her life had she ever given the faintest, slightest consideration to suicide. She was much too selfish for that. And, anyway, advertising people were tough! They were used to criticism and rejection.... It happened every day. So what was the matter with her? Had her tough skin gotten thin over the years?

All she knew was that she was tired, so very, very tired—or was that the drugs kicking in?—and there was a limit to the rejection one person could take. When they took her job away from her, they took her life—suicide was just a formality.

Idly, hazily, she wondered if the toilet bowl was clean and what kind of junk was fermenting in the fridge. And finally, what Aunt Beth in De Kalb—her only living close relative—might think about the crotchless panties she would inherit.

A phone rang on the floor by the bed—very far in the distance, it seemed, hundreds and hundred of miles away—and the answering machine picked up.

A once-cheerful, vibrant Joyce told the caller to leave a message. So he did.

"This is Jason Larue with the X-Gen Agency. We understand you are available for a new employment position. I'd like to meet with you as soon as possible about a job I think you may be interested in. We're excited about the prospect of working with you, and hope you'll feel the same about our company."

Joyce's eyes flew open, and she jumped out of bed, ran into the bathroom, stuck her finger down her throat and happily threw up.

Chapter Three

"SIGNED, SEALED, DELIVERED"

(Stevie Wonder, #3 Billboard, 1970)

The man who appeared at Joyce's apartment door the following afternoon was about five foot ten—just a few inches taller than Joyce—and young (twenty-five?) and slender and rather blandly, boyishly handsome in that Brad Pitt manner that had always eluded her.

His dark curly hair had a frosting of blond, as if the tip of his head had been dipped in bronze; his tanned cherubic face wore two-day stubble—an affectation she didn't understand (would she go out without shaving her legs?)—and he wore a single, small golden earring. He would have been an excellent male model in *GQ Magazine*, if it weren't for his pale blue, rather bloodshot eyes.

Did a workaholic or alcoholic lurk behind this slick facade? she wondered. Or maybe both?

Still, the overall impression was of a well-brewed blend of professionalism and sex appeal. Conservatively though expensively dressed in a sleek black suit, dark gray tie and pale gray shirt with white collar, and carrying a black briefcase, he would have seemed more likely a religious zealot, going door to door handing out tracts, than a corporate headhunter—if it hadn't been for his smooth manner and casual charm, and the Continental cut of that suit.

With her many years in the ad game, Joyce was skilled in the art of quickly sizing people up, ascertaining the phonies, discerning the sharks, pinpointing the occasional decent human being. But she felt uncertain about this visitor—sending herself mixed signals.

Immediately, instinctively, she had felt a wave of dislike; then he flashed a charming, disarming smile—those *had* to be caps!— and all her inner shit-detectors shut down, and she found herself drawn to him.

She tried not to betray any of these conflicting feelings as she invited him inside. "The living room is this way. You'll have to excuse the … transitional phase."

"Thank you, Ms. Lackey—or may I call you Joyce?"

"Please."

Earlier, when she had returned his phone call, he had insisted on coming to her apartment rather than receiving her at his place of business. She had found this strange, even inappropriate; but perhaps he just wanted her to feel comfortable, and, not wanting to seem difficult, eagerness and desperation clouding her better judgment, she had consented.

She ushered the boyishly hunky headhunter through the empty entryway into the sparse living room, the only furniture left being a mauve chintz couch, mahogany coffee table and brass floor lamp, huddled in front of the ornate fireplace like three very unhappy campers.

"Won't you have a seat, Mr. Larue," she said, gesturing to the couch.

"Make it 'Jason,' please."

"Jason. And, again, please excuse the state this condo's in…. I'm redecorating, and my new furniture hasn't arrived yet." She hoped the lie wasn't too transparent. She then asked, "Can I get you something? Coffee? Tea?"

Me?

"No, thank you," he said, sitting down.

Joyce, dressed modestly in a beige silk blouse, brown skirt and flats, and no jewelry, joined him on the couch. Nervously, she clasped her hands in her lap to keep from fidgeting; she never wanted anything in her life as much as she wanted this job. She wondered what it was.

Several things did bother her, however, despite her eagerness. Like anyone in advertising worth his/her salt, Joyce had spent the morning doing her homework on the X-Gen Agency. But because her pitiful financial condition had caused her to drop her Internet provider, she had to trek down to the Chicago Public Library to do so.

There, she could find very little regarding the company other than ascertaining its existence, and that its HQ was located in the western suburb of Schaumburg. A call to the Better Business Bureau, using the library's pay phone, confirmed X-Gen was indeed a job placement service.

Checking the reference book *Who's Who in American Colleges*, she found a listing for a Jason Larue, graduating from Drake University (MBA) with honors in 1997. All of this was helpful, but she wanted more. Joyce Lackey was never one to go into a meeting unprepared. Still, maybe the X-Gen company was just too young to have much of a track record.

What disturbed her more, though, was that *she* had never contacted *them* ... so why were they contacting her? Was Frank behind this? Feeling guilty for not giving her the copy writer's job? Or had X-Gen simply read about her retirement in the papers, and Larue was ambulance-chasing?

Larue cleared his throat. "We at X-Gen are very impressed with your long history of achievement, Joyce. We know you've dedicated your life to your work, and we find that sort of work ethic, so often lost these days, highly admirable. Therefore, out of respect to you, if you don't mind, we'll get right down to business."

"Please do, Mr. Larue."

"Jason," he corrected her, then went on. "Before we discuss your future, however, I'm afraid you'll have to sign this confidentiality agreement."

He removed a single folded sheet from his briefcase, handed the paper to her, and a pen—MontBlanc.

Joyce took the sheet and looked at it; it was a simple form—merely a pledge to keep the terms of X-Gen's offer to herself, whether she took it or not.

But not wanting to seem overeager, trying to project a cool, cautious air, she said, "Mr. Larue ... Jason. If you know as much about me as you say you do, I'm sure you don't expect me to sign something without running it past my attorney, first."

With a frosty smile, Jason rose, snapping shut his briefcase. "Then I'm afraid we've misjudged you," he said, looking down at her, making her feel small on the couch. "If you'll just return the form, and pen, I won't be any further nuisance to you."

"I merely meant ... Jason, Mr. Larue, it's just not professional...."

"It's a simple form, a few sentences. It requires no legal interpretation."

"Well, just a moment, let me review this.... Ah, well, yes I see that you're right, of course—no, uh, legal counsel is necessary for something this rudimentary."

And she signed the paper.

"Good," Larue said, sitting back down, the charm back in his smile. He smelled good—was that a Calvin Klein scent? "I'm here to offer you a job on the West Coast. Los Angeles to be exact."

Joyce nodded. "I see." She was trying to keep the excitement out of her voice and her expression. She adored L.A.! She had frequently done business there and loved the sun, the glitz, the sophistication. And there was certainly nothing to keep her in Chicago.

"You'll be working for C.W. Kafer Advertising, in the capacity of vice president in charge of new corporate accounts."

Now Joyce simply couldn't contain herself: her jaw dropped open and her eyes popped wide. C.W. Kafer was one of the largest, most prestigious agencies in the country, primarily handling the motion picture industry. Finally, finally, finally, her luck had changed for the better!

Recovering, she said, "Well, obviously that's a highly prominent firm—similar to the level of my previous company. But I have to say, the notion of corporate accounts is somewhat, uh … less than thrilling."

"Corporate accounts can be difficult."

"Difficult, and dull, and boring … not to mention a royal pain in the ass. The only thing worse is industrial accounts."

"I realize your specialty has been consumer-related accounts."

He put a hand on her shoulder—it was a fatherly gesture, odd coming from someone so much younger; she didn't sense any sex in it, exactly—and she was trying.

"But, Joyce, it takes a special kind of person to handle the bigwigs of corporations … someone with the kind of maturity, talent, and insight required to understand a corporation's dry mission statement and transform it into a great ad campaign. Someone like you, Joyce."

He was manipulating her, of course; but she didn't mind. This was better than sex.

"And," he went on, removing his hand from her shoulder, his voice as casual as if they were discussing the weather, "I understand part of your job will be finding celebrity spokespersons for these corporations."

"Really?" Suddenly she had a change of mind about the stuffiness of corporate advertising.

In the 1970s new ground was broken when high-profile celebs like Bob Hope, E. G. Marshall, and Bill Cosby were featured in advertisements and commercials. It was a concept that proved highly successful with Baby Boomers who identified with these beloved public figures.

Joyce sighed. "Matching a compatible star personality with the image a corporation wishes to portray ... that can be a very time-consuming undertaking."

"Yes. You may have to take meetings and lunches with some very difficult, egotistical people. Celebrities can be such children."

Yes, she thought, *she would just have to suffer through those lunches with the likes of Tom Hanks, Mel Gibson, and Leonardo DeCaprio. Well, maybe Leo was too young for the corporate image, but she'd be willing to find out....*

"But there are compensating factors," Jason continued. "Your starting salary, for example, which will be thirty thousand above what you were being paid at your former job."

Joyce damn near fell off the couch. Would the good news never cease? She stared at him speechless, not knowing whether to laugh or cry, or both.

"Jason," she said, "you're going to have to be careful, or you'll give corporate headhunters a good name."

A half-smile dimpled a boyish cheek. "Well, every silver lining does belong to a little cloud or two—I have no intention of misleading you. If you decide to accept this position, you and X-Gen will enter into a long-term arrangement. In perpetuity. It's vital that we be honest with each other, and that we share a mutual trust."

"Oh-kay," she said, ready for the other shoe to drop.

"X-Gen will be taking its fee from your earnings, which amounts to half of your annual salary."

So much for the good news. "*Half* my salary?" she said. "You must be joking."

"A sense of humor is not my long suit, Joyce. I am quite serious."

"For how long? The first year, I assume."

"No. For as long as you hold the position."

She blinked, looked at him as if his face was smeared with jam. "I mean no offense, Mr. Larue, Jason ... but that seems excessive by *any* reasonable standard. Excuse me, but how do you get away with charging such a high finder's fee? And an unending one, at that?"

The charming smile was back; but the bloodshot eyes were unblinking and serious. "Because, Joyce ... Ms. Lackey ... we can."

Her laugh was harsh. "No one would agree to those terms."

"Any number of people already have—and more and more are continuing to do so, every day. And I believe you will, too, Joyce."

She felt her joy slipping away. She rose from the couch and stood before the cold fireplace, one hand on the mantle, staring into the hearth, at a fire that wasn't there.

"It's thirty thousand more than you were getting," Larue said. "And our commission is tax deductible.... Do the math, Joyce."

She already was. Even with a fifty percent cut, she would be making a nice salary. Still, L.A. was expensive; her lifestyle couldn't be what it had been.

But, then, what was it now?

And then there was that *other* math-related factor to consider: her age.

"All right," she sighed. Then, in a last-ditch grasp at self-respect, she added, "But only if you can guarantee the salary you indicated as a minimum."

"I can. Fall below it, we'll take no commission whatsoever."

What the hell, she thought. *What the fucking hell ... it beats going the Kervorkian route....*

"Done," she said.

"Done," he said lightly, his small, satisfied smile making her feel a little queasy.

She returned to the couch. "When do I start?"

"You begin in six months."

"Six months!" The words struck her like a blow. "But ... I was hoping...." She looked helplessly around.

"Don't worry," he interjected. "My company will advance you some cash, to get you by." He patted her hand with his; his touch felt warm, reassuring. "The time will fly…. You're going to be a very busy young woman."

She recoiled from his touch, however soothing it might be, her eyes narrowing, thinking his word choice peculiar; she was hardly "young."

"Doing what?" she asked.

"Going back to school, for starters."

"School?" she said in astonishment. "I'm sure you're aware I have an MBA."

"Yes, circa 1972. But a lot has occurred in almost thirty years." He paused, then said, "Our company requires an extensive, intensive four-week curriculum to bring you up to speed—and up to date."

"Just where do you think I've been since 1972?" she asked, adding to herself, *Mars?*

"It's not where you've been, Joyce—it's the context."

What the hell did that mean?

"This is a retraining of sorts—not in your field, no one doubts your mastery, there. California is not Chicago, for example. Orientation implementation is simply necessary."

"Well, that's absurd."

"It's also required."

"A deal-breaker, you mean?"

"Oh, yes."

Joyce frowned. "And just who pays for this 'retraining'?"

"X-Gen, of course. It's part of our belief, our investment, in you."

Well, as long as it didn't come out of her pocket, she'd play along.

"Where will these classes be held?" she asked.

"We want you to be comfortable, Joyce. You'll be attending Relocation Orientation at your old alma mater."

"Northwestern?"

"No—I was referring to your undergraduate years."

"Simmons College?" She found herself smiling again—she hadn't been back there since she graduated!

It might be kind of fun at that, to return and see how things had changed for the cozy little college in that quaint small-town setting. She still received the campus newsletter, though she never seemed to have time to read it.

And, once, several years ago, she had received a solicitous phone call asking for a hefty contribution because the private college was in trouble; she had politely declined—wasn't it up to the generation attending there (and their parents) to take care of that? Evidently, the college must have gotten back up on its feet.

"I'll be happy to attend some classes," Joyce said, "but four weeks is hardly six months…. What else will I be doing?"

Larue twitched a smile. "What I am about to tell you, Joyce, will change your life."

"Really?"

"Literally. What I'm about to share with you is the reason for our secrecy, the explanation for the confidentiality release I had to insist you sign."

She had felt many emotions this afternoon—despair, elation, happiness, suspicion. Now she was afraid.

"What else is in store me, Jason, if I sign with X-Gen?"

Jason responded, matter-of-factly, "You'll be receiving a new identity, Joyce."

"A new identity."

"Yes … face lift, nose job, breast implants, various nips and tucks and suctions…. Whatever it takes to turn you into the thirty-five-year-old woman that Kafer thinks they're getting."

"*What?*" Joyce recoiled again, mind reeling. "Are you insane?"

He smiled broadly for the first time, showing those perfect white teeth; the bronze-tipped hair was somehow godlike. "Some people might think so. But most of our clients have come to see

X-Gen as their savior. A savior who rescued them from a society that deemed them worthless and threw them on the trash heap long before their usefulness was fulfilled."

Joyce swallowed, trying to assimilate all of this; maybe this guy *was* a religious zealot going door to door....

In a richly modulated voice, Jason continued, shifting into higher gear. "I'm talking, Joyce, about a society that punishes *women* for growing older and, by its shallow standards, less attractive. A youth-obsessed society that denies itself the benefit of so much talent, experience and, yes, wisdom!"

He again opened his black briefcase and drew out a black binder and plopped it in her lap.

"Open it," he ordered.

She eyed him cautiously, then lifted the notebook's cover.

It contained photos of women, both before their new makeover, looking worn and haggard, and after, looking fresh and sexy—and happy.

And so very much *younger* ...

"These women, age fifty to fifty-eight, have all been successfully transplanted into new jobs across the country. Once destitute, they are now living successful, productive, *younger* lives. It's a win-win-win situation. You win, we win, society wins."

Joyce turned another page in the binder; a familiar face stared back at her. "Oh, my God ... it's ... it's Heather. Heather Blake! The woman who took *my* job."

"She was a fifty-seven-year-old ad exec from Detroit," he explained, "who got squeezed out and couldn't land another job. We gave her a new name, new body, new credentials ... a new life."

"You mean *my* life, you bastard!" Joyce said, jumping up from the couch.

Jason put both hands up in a "hold on" manner. "Hey," he said, "we had nothing to do with you losing your job—Heather didn't 'take' your position, she filled it after your company made you vacate it. All we did was restock the empty shelf you left behind."

Trembling, Joyce put both hands on her hips and glared down at him. "And I suppose I'll be replacing some other poor woman down on her luck and out of a job...."

He shook his head. "Not in this instance, no. The woman you're replacing was in the prime of life, I believe forty. She was a victim of a traffic accident."

"Oh ... I ... I see." Joyce flopped back down on the couch. She felt woozy, mentally pummeled; and yet a small, clear voice was saying, *Well, then, that's all right, isn't it? You'd just be filling the space the poor woman left behind....*

"Joyce ... shall we go on?"

"There's more?"

"I'm afraid so. If you have any further doubts, express them now."

"No ... no. Do go on." After all, she'd been ready to leave this life behind; why shouldn't she try another?

As if reading her mind, he said, "It's that second chance everyone dreams of, but so few receive."

She felt as if she were in a dream. "Yes ... yes ..."

"Let me explain how it is that you came to fit our ideal profile. In addition to your outstanding achievements in your chosen field, you have few ties, few strings. Your parents have passed on.... No close relatives, really...."

"Yes. Only my mother's sister, my Aunt Beth ... she lives in De Kalb. We're not ... terribly close. I see her at Christmas."

"You'll no longer be able to do that, Joyce. For your new life, you'll need a new name—and you have to leave your own life behind."

"I just ... disappear?"

Larue shrugged. "We have clients who are able to use that option, yes. But you are much too well-known in Chicago, Joyce— you would be missed."

"Considering the way my job interviews have been going, I find that hard to believe."

43

"You will need to ..." And he made quotation marks in the air, with his fingers. "... 'die.' "

"Die? Jesus, what are—"

"You were at a point in your life, Joyce, when many people contemplate ... forgive me ... suicide."

How did he *know* this?

"And so, Joyce, that's what you will do. A body will be found with your identification, in apparel you own, of your general build and description...."

"Stop. No—I won't be party to ... to ..."

"Let me continue. This will be a cadaver, purchased through confidential medical sources, an unknown, unnamed, unclaimed soul. By the time the body is found, it will have ... excuse me for being indelicate ... decayed past anything possible but a general identification."

Suddenly she was breathing hard. "But ... but what about dental charts, medical records...."

"You were referred to us by the clinic you frequent. All of your records are there—and they will be ... adjusted."

Her mind was reeling again. "This must be terribly illegal...."

"Oh, yes, it's fraud. Fraud designed to 'fool' a corrupt, immoral system that has driven you from your life's work. Who is hurt, here? No one. Who is helped? *You* are ... and the employers lucky enough to receive your skills and services and talent and brains."

"And X-Gen?"

"X-Gen benefits, too—financially, yes. But also in knowing that we are doing something positive for members of the most gifted generation this world has ever seen. That's *our* mission statement."

He folded his arms, sat back. As if in shock, she sat paging through the binder, as if it were a Sears catalogue—a wish book. Haggard middle-aged women transformed into fresh, pretty young girls ... oh, how she would like to be thought of as a girl again, sexism be damned....

"Can I keep the same initials?" she asked, almost timidly. "My Vuitton luggage is monogrammed." This absurdity was all she could think to say.

He patted her hand. "You would be surprised at how often we receive this simple request. Yes. Of course."

"Thank you."

"How about Joy Lerner?"

She thought about that for a few moments, spoke the name silently, then out loud, several times—actually liking the sound of it, the way it tripped off her tongue.

Then she thumped the binder cover and asked, "Who pays for all this reconstruction, this … overhaul? I suppose you 'advance' me the expense of the surgery, too…."

"Absolutely not. The expense is entirely ours. Another part of our investment in you."

"I've already had a complete physical," she told him. "Even without cosmetic surgery, I have a much younger woman's body."

"We know," he said, a tiny smile tickling the corners of his mouth.

"I forgot," she said, with a smile of her own—a weary one. "X-Gen owns that health clinic. That's where you got the referral…."

She stared at him, dazed; it was all so much to absorb. "What happens when I can't work anymore?"

"Ten percent of our commission goes into an accelerated retirement plan. Should your health fail, and Kafer's own bennies fail to cover you, we pledge to take care of you. It's all in writing…."

Larue reached into his briefcase again, and withdrew another, much fatter contract, and handed it to her—it felt heavy.

He touched her hand again, the contract in her lap. "You can keep that overnight and give it a good thorough read. But no attorney, Joy."

Joy—not Joyce.

She looked toward the fireplace for a moment, and in a strange instant thought she saw flames leaping there; then she gazed back at bronze-haired, bronze-skinned Jason Larue.

"Where do I sign?" she asked.

Interim

"GOODBYE CRUEL WORLD"

(James Darren, #3 Billboard, 1961)

Beth Peters had lived alone for many years. A handsome woman of seventy, with the same blond hair and apple-cheeked wholesome features that had served her late sister (and her niece Joyce) so well, Beth suffered few of the ailments that tended to beleaguer women her age. A little arthritis in her hands, and brittle bones (never a break, knock on wood), but otherwise Beth was fit as a fiddle, even if, truth be told, the blond hair was out of a bottle, now.

Since her husband Carl had died of cancer in '78, she had lived a solitary but not really lonely life in the rather precious Tudor-style bungalow on a shade-tree-lined side street of De Kalb, Illinois. Active in a church Bible study group (Baptist), she played bridge twice a week—with the Lady Elks at the lodge (Carl had been an Exalted Ruler) and with a group that was the remnants of a club of couples, all of the husbands having passed away (once called the Sixteen Club, they now referred to themselves as the Crazy Eight).

For several years, up till last March, she had dated a man who had been married to her late best friend, and he was sweet, and took her to the movies and dancing at the Moose; but after his death—that damn cancer, again—she decided she really just preferred to see her girlfriends at bridge and watch her stories on TV and read her Danielle Steele.

It was a small life, but it was enough; her life with Carl—their beloved son Davy had died in an automobile crash, in high school—had been plenty big. Carl had been an electrical engineer, and made good money. They'd been to Europe and on cruises and had really had a wonderful life.

If she had any regret, it was that her sister's girl, Joyce, had never let Beth in ... *emotionally* in. Helen—Beth's sister, Joyce's mother—had died when the girl was in college, and Helen's husband Dan died a few years later, of a heart attack (broken heart, more like it). Dan was a good man, a salesman who traveled, and something of a ladies' man, but he never rubbed Helen's nose in it, and he had really, really loved her.

Joyce was so pretty, and such a bright girl, and *so* successful. And Beth—who had never, in her heart of hearts, gotten over the loss of her boy—wanted so to be a replacement mom for Joyce. After all, Joyce was close to home—Chicago was just a hop, skip and jump from De Kalb—and the girl did come home at Christmas, and they were pleasant Christmases, too. Joyce had always given her aunt expensive gifts—half Beth's Hummell collection was Joyce's doing.

And Joyce was always friendly. Very friendly. Just not ... warm. Rarely did the girl call her aunt, and if Beth called Joyce, it was that darn machine and Joyce never called back, not till it got nigh on to Christmas.

And Beth would have loved to have just a little of that kind of warmth, *family* warmth, back in her life. Oh, she was happy with her life, her small life ... but there was that tiny but very empty place inside her that she wasn't happy with. The family place. And Joyce could have filled it, but for some unknown reason chose not to.

Beth wondered if Joyce—so successful in business, and in such a tough town!—wasn't secretly lonely. There was never talk of a man in her life, and once at Christmas—after girding herself for what might be an embarrassing confrontation, with a few extra glasses of rum-spiked egg nog—Beth had boldly asked Joyce if she (Joyce, that is) was ... and she didn't mean to judge ... a lesbian.

Joyce had found that very amusing, and in fact it was one of the few times Joyce had hugged her aunt, really hugged her.

This Christmas—last week—there had been no call from Joyce, and Beth had worried; for the first time Beth could remember, her niece did not spend the holiday with her. Beth had put the tree up, and a gift for Joyce had been tucked beneath.

But Joyce had never come, and the tree was down, and the gift snugged away on the high shelf in the front closet.

So when Joyce had showed up this afternoon—unbidden, no phone call—on an unseasonably sunny late December afternoon—Beth was both shocked and pleased.

"Dear, what a wonderful surprise!" she had said, and ushered the girl in (it never occurred to Beth that her sister's "girl" was in her mid-fifties).

Joyce had seemed ... strange. She was underdressed for a change—a Bulls sweatshirt, jeans, tennies—and wore no makeup at all; she looked very, very young.

And Joyce seemed ... conflicted. One moment happy, one sad, the next apprehensive, followed by hopeful. Fidgety. Relaxed. Every which way.

It took a long time for the girl to get around to dropping what she kept referring to as a "bombshell." They sat at the kitchen table, the walls brimming with Hummell plates, and drank coffee with cream and spoke of family memories. Silly little anecdotes. The time her cousin Davy had fallen out of the backyard maple onto the refrigerator-box cardboard house Joyce had made, when he wouldn't let her into his tree house, breaking his fall, and her house. The Christmas the dog ate Davy Crockett out of the Alamo playset Davy got, and Joyce had found that terribly amusing, until Davy hid her Barbie. How Joyce's parents had paid her twenty-five cents per eaten brussels sprout, and the time the two cousins had worried everybody to death by not telling anybody they were going to *Son of Flubber* and sitting through it three times.

Beth and Joyce sat and laughed and talked and Joyce even touched her aunt's hand a few times.

"Aunt Beth," Joyce said finally, "I came here today to tell you something very important."

The afternoon had long since turned to night, and Beth was cooking them up some V-8 spaghetti, a favorite family recipe.

"What is it, dear?"

"This is the last time you'll ever see me."

And then Joyce had done the darnedest thing: She began to cry.

Beth sat beside her niece and put an arm around her, cradled the girl's face in her shoulder, and the girl cried and cried.

Then she told her aunt the details of the long, strange story— how her career was at an end, how she'd almost ended her life, and how this company was offering her another chance, a new life.

In the living room, they held hands as Joyce explained the darker aspects of the deal she'd made: that her death would be faked, that she would assume a new identity, and undergo plastic surgery and retraining, to become a convincing "young person" again.

Beth tried. She really did. She tried to talk her out of it, but there was no stopping the girl.

So finally Beth accepted it, and held the girl, and hugged her, and for the first time, there was real warmth between them.

"If it's what you want, dear," Beth said.

"Oh, Aunt Beth—I want it so badly."

"Then you should have it…. Let me look at you. I want to see your mother in your eyes."

Then Beth had gone to the closet and given Joyce her Christmas gift—a lovely silver art-deco frame—and Joyce had thanked her and hugged her aunt again, apologizing for not bringing a gift, herself.

"Oh but you've given me so much with this visit, darling," Beth said. "So very much."

When Joyce had gone—promising to secretly, anonymously call each Christmas, no matter *what* the X-Gen company said—Beth sat in the kitchen again, drinking more coffee, staring at the many plates Joyce had given her over the years.

You can never tell anyone what I told you, Aunt Beth, Joyce had said, again and again. *It would ruin everything.*

But with Joyce gone, out of the house, the warm family memories and feelings exiting with her, Beth began to think. She didn't like the sound of it. Not at all. The more she thought, the less she liked it. Joyce was getting involved in a criminal enterprise … there was no other way to look at it.

Beth tried to watch the *Lawrence Welk* rerun on PBS, but couldn't concentrate. She tried to watch a *Matlock* rerun, but even that wouldn't take. When she finally went to bed, she lay on the soft mattress and thought about the hard decision she knew she must make. Staring at the ceiling in the darkness—wishing she could sleep, wishing she hadn't had all that coffee—Joyce's aunt knew she must go to Joyce, tomorrow, and stop this.

And, if Joyce wouldn't listen to reason, perhaps the police would.

That was when she sensed the figure in her room.

"Joyce, honey?" the woman said, sitting up. "Is that you?"

Some moonlight was filtering in through the sheer lacy curtains. She could make the figure out better, now: a man. A man in black. All in black. Even his face—in a ski mask.

He had something in one hand … what?

Was that … a wrench?

Heart in her throat, she threw the covers off and scrambled off the bed as the man came after her, the wrench swishing through the air, just missing her, thumping into the mattress. She had a Hummell music box, on the bedstand next to her, and she snatched it up and hurled it at the black shape, and must have caught him on the head, or face, or something, because he yelped and swore.

She whisked nimbly around him and out the door and was heading down the stairs. Frightened but exhilarated, she knew she could get out the front door before he caught up with her, she just knew it, and Mr. Benson next door was a *deputy* and she knew where the key was….

Almost giddy with fright and flight and fight, the spunky seventy-year-old woman lost her grip on the banister, her arthritis betraying her, and her ankle gave way and halfway down the steps she took a tumble, and bounced off the wall and into the banister, toppling hard on the wooden steps, brittle bones breaking with each new collision, snapping like twigs.

And when she landed, hard, just a helpless sack of human flesh stuffed with broken bones and bruised organs, she wondered if she was going to die from the fall.

But she was wrong.

The man in the black ski mask was looking down at her, and then that wrench, that metal wrench (was that Carl's wrench that he fixed the faucet with?), came sweeping down, caving in her face, ending her small life and her big life and the subsequent batterings of the blunt instrument, splashing blood and brains and bone fragments everywhere, were simply not needed, just completely gratuitous, though of course she didn't feel a thing, not after the terrible blow that had killed her.

Nor was she aware of the final indignity—that every Hummell in her house was flung carelessly into a big garbage bag, plates, music boxes, figurines, chipping, shattering, tiny precious figures colliding with each other much as Beth had coming down those stairs. They would be tossed in a garbage dump, far away, merely to provide a reason for this death, a motive, the old lady who was murdered for her collectibles.

As if death required a reason.

And when the De Kalb police discovered the name of the old lady's only living relative, a Joyce Lackey of Chicago, they received only a prerecorded message from the telephone company that the number was no longer in service.

Part Two:

IN BETWEEN

Chapter Four

"BE TRUE TO YOUR SCHOOL"
(Beach Boys, #6 Billboard, 1963)

Seventeen miles south of Des Moines, Indianola (pop. 10,000) sat on the crest of a hill, a quaint hamlet in its typically Midwestern, Norman-Rockwell-comes-to-Iowa way: clean and tidy and friendly.

Predictably arranged around a small-town square, many of the shops, whose turn-of-the-century storefronts had been carefully preserved, were owned and operated by families whose roots in the little community went back generations. And while time had not exactly stood still for the town—fast-food restaurants and a super-discount store had sprouted like plastic toadstools on its periphery—to Joyce returning to Indianola was like riding a time machine to a past she was more than happy to return to. No rose-colored glasses required.

Being back in Indianola was like slipping into a comfortable pair of shoes, just like the Bass Weejuns she bought at Wilson's when she arrived in town. She couldn't believe the store still carried the brand, which had been a staple of every college girl's wardrobe back in the late '60s (only today the shoes cost three times as much); spotting them on the shelf was like bumping into an old friend she hadn't seen for thirty years.

Now all she needed was a madras blouse to wear with the tan Chino slacks she'd purchased next door at K & D Clothiers, to make it really seem like old college times.

She'd made the trip from Chicago, driving in her tiny Honda across Illinois and Iowa farm country dusted with snow that shimmered under a brilliant winter sun shining in a nearly cloudless sky. The classes she was supposed to take at Simmons College in Indianola weren't scheduled to begin for another day, but she wanted time to get settled in at the dorm and check out the town.

Also, all she'd brought to wear were her professional clothes, which didn't seem appropriate for class, and she wanted to buy some more casual things. Not the sloppy T-shirts and baggy jeans that the girls were wearing these days, the *worst* fashion statement ever, Joyce felt.

Didn't these young women realize that this was the best their bodies were ever going to be? That cellulite and stretch marks and drooping boobs lay inevitably ahead? To hide their figures under a tent of clothing was such a waste. Not to mention another kind of waist, which went unchecked in oversized jeans and stretchy sweatpants.

When Joyce had been their age, her tight, white Lee jeans used to tell her when to lay off the Ding Dongs and reach for the Metrical. How ironic that the exercise industry, by incorporating spandex in their clothes, had been responsible for spawning so many fat young women.

Yesterday, when Joyce first entered town, she drove directly to the college, which was only a few blocks from the square on North C Street. She pulled her car into the main parking lot and got out, her high heels crunching on the snow. The school was deserted, except for a few cars by the Administration Building; it was a week after Christmas—a new year, a new beginning—and the students had gone home for semester break. Obviously, the

X-Gen corporation was making use of the facilities during the college's down time.

She stood by her Honda for a few more minutes, taking in the small campus. The original buildings, Larson Hall and Lockridge Hall, both three-story, red-brick Victorian structures built in the late 1800s, were still there, surprisingly well preserved. Also still standing was the Old Chapel, a building both loved and feared by students and teachers alike when she'd gone there, because it was believed to be haunted.

Like all incoming freshman, Joyce had heard the tall tales when she arrived, spun around sorority fireplaces and in dorm lounges late at night; apparent urban legends about a young man who hanged himself in the Old Chapel belfry after a failed loved affair. And two female students who pitched over the top railing of the staircase and plunged three stories to their deaths. Then there was the one about a teacher who lost his footing on the stairs, rolled down them and broke his neck.

And there were reports of other strange occurrences in the building: mysterious lights, disembodied footsteps, sinister apparitions. Even Joyce, late one night, hurrying across campus after a clandestine date with a married professor, trying to get to her sorority before they locked her out, could have sworn she saw a ghostly face in one of the belfry's windows....

But which, if any, of these stories were fact and which were fiction was anybody's guess.

Behind the Old Chapel, Joyce could see several more modern buildings, constructed with red brick to blend in with the older ones, betrayed by their unfunky modern lines. Curving cement walkways—bordered by great old oaks and maple trees, their giant limbs bare for the winter—led like paths out of *Alice in Wonderland*, from one building to another.

Suddenly, Joyce became so emotional that her throat began to ache, and her eyes welled with tears. There was something so poignant about being here, about recalling the excitement, apprehension and sheer terror she had back then, of deciding which path to go down … of endless possibilities and pitfalls … but remembering, too, the feeling of power and indestructibility only the young have, knowing their whole life lay ahead.

In the Administration Building, a plump, friendly young woman—perhaps a student working there—was roaming the lobby with clipboard in hand, waiting to snag students like Joyce, enrolled in the special session.

"Smith, Joyce," the young woman said, checking her clipboard and marking Joyce off a sheet littered with the likes of Jones, Smith, Harris and Johnson. "Welcome to Simmons campus—follow me."

The plump woman had long brown hair pulled back with a tortoise-shell clip, and wore a Simmons College sweatshirt, jeans and dark socks with Birkenstock sandals—clearly the ugliest thing ever invented; since when were shoes supposed to be comfortable? They stopped at a banquet-style table where various campus brochures were stacked, and the woman thumbed through a box of alphabetized manila envelopes.

"Here's your informational packet," the woman said, handing the envelope to Joyce. "Class schedule, map of the campus, dorm room key, dorm rules and regs, yada yada yada."

"Thanks. It's still a lovely campus."

"Oh! You've been here before?"

"Undergrad days—you don't wanna *know* what class."

The woman laughed. "I worked the special session last year—it's always a hoot."

"A hoot?"

"It's funny … I mean, you know, fun to see older people get into the campus swing. Remember that old TV show, *Twilight Zone*?"

"Sure."

"Remember that episode, where the old folks in the rest home became children again?"

"I missed that one."

"Well, that's what special session reminds me of. I think it's very cool. Like parents' day got way outa hand."

"Well ... I'm not anybody's parent."

"Oh, I didn't mean any offense! I think it's great. Never too old to learn, y'know?"

Never too young to lose some weight, either, Joyce thought bitterly, walking back to her car.

Mildly bummed now, Joyce drove around the back of the college to a four-story tan building with a futuristic front awning. Taking the elevator inside the lobby up to the top floor, she lugged her heavy Vuitton suitcases—stuffed with every creature comfort she had left to her name (whichever name)—down the narrow tile hallway, past a big communal bathroom, to the room number on the front of her informational packet.

When she opened the door, a medicinal smell greeted her, telling her that at least the room was clean. She dragged her suitcases in, stacked them in the center of the floor and looked around. Everything in the tiny room was tan: tan twin beds, tan curtains, tan work desks, tan tile floor and tan walls, making her glad she had pledged a sorority here and missed the whole dorm experience.

Then, again, she thought, dorm life might not be so bad. Add a couple thousand dollars worth of electronic equipment, a computer and picture of Matt Damon, and a girl could feel quite at home ... though a voice in the back of her head was substituting a lava lamp, a Smith Corona, and a poster of Mr. Spock....

She spent the rest of the evening unpacking and cursing the fact that there weren't nearly enough hangers.

Some things, at least, never changed.

On the following morning, a small group of middle-aged would-be college students gathered in a classroom on the first floor of the Social and Behavioral Building. With nervous nods and quick hellos and quicker smiles to one another, they sat at ancient wooden desk-chairs, and quietly waited for the instructor to arrive.

Besides Joyce, who had taken a front row seat, there were six other women. She had met most of them in the dorm bathroom the night before, and again in the morning, and they were guardedly polite to each other, not knowing quite what to say. First names only, as they'd been instructed.

And—except for a woman named Sally, whose outdated black coif was obviously dyed—the rest had apparently embraced old age, donning sweatshirts with kittens or apples on them, and letting themselves go gray.

Joyce wondered if they wondered if *she* was in the wrong room.

Scattered amongst the women were three men, which surprised her; she was under the impression that the X-Gen corporation only involved itself in rejuvenating women. After all, when men aged, they got character in their faces; when women aged, they got fucking wrinkles.

But then, she supposed, men were also being unfairly displaced, so why wouldn't the company help them, too? A man could just as easily encounter the "young blood, young ideas" bullshit as a woman.

Anyway, having males around could make the next four weeks a lot more interesting—even if they were overweight and balding—because she had trouble spending time with only women. She just didn't trust her own sex—not since her best friend stole her boyfriend back in high school.

The door to the classroom swung open, and a tall, ruggedly handsome man with an armful of books and papers swept in. He had an easygoing smile, which he flashed to the group, and Joyce could feel the whole room relax. With his thick salt and pepper hair and a neatly trimmed beard, he reminded her of recent-vintage Sean Connery, particularly if she squinted a little.

He wore a navy V-neck sweater over a pale yellow polo shirt, faded jeans and brown Hush-Puppies shoes, and he plopped the load in his arms down on the desk in front of the blackboard, at the same time saying, "Hello," in a low baritone, to which everyone murmured, "Hello," back.

Something stirred in Joyce's memory. Could he be a teacher she'd once had here?

"I'm Mr. Hanson," the instructor said.

Hanson? There was a Don Hanson that taught microeconomics her junior year. Old Doom and Gloom she'd called him, even though he wasn't much older than her, because of his pessimistic outlook on the American economy. On the other hand, he *had* correctly predicted the oil crisis of the late '70s, and the breakdown of family values in the '80s—neither of which she'd given a rat's ass about in his class at the time.

Now another of his predictions came to mind…. Something about the adverse effect on the economy the Boomers would have in the late twentieth century, and early twenty-first….

Joyce squinted again, this time trying to make the middle-aged bearded man standing in front of the class into the young clean-shaven teacher she remembered, and couldn't; but then, almost thirty years had passed.

And if he was that same teacher, he probably wouldn't remember her, because it had been so long—though he might know her, because after all, *she* hadn't changed that much. Not like these graying relics around her….

"If you'll open the packet you were given," Mr. Hanson instructed, "I'd like to go over a few items before we get started…."

Joyce got out the contents of her manila envelope but didn't look at them; she'd already read everything several times the night before in her room.

"First of all," he continued, "we'll be meeting Monday through Saturday, four hours in the morning … then break for lunch … and four hours in the afternoon—I'm the only instructor, by the way, so we'll all get to know each other quite well."

That was all right with Joyce.

He was saying, "In the evenings you'll be expected to attend the movie that will be showing in the student lounge.... The film will be a point of discussion the following day, so don't skip it, even in the unlikely event you've seen it before. Sundays are yours to do with as you please. Any questions about class procedure?"

"Can we go into Des Moines?" a male voice asked from the back.

"On Sundays, yes," Mr. Hanson said, then added, like talking to a kid, "Just stay out of trouble." And everyone laughed.

Hanson came around from behind the desk, and leaned against it, half-sitting, hands folded in front of himself.

"I also want to touch on the purpose of these classes, because I detect a few smirks on some of your faces...."

Not her; she may have been "thinking" a smirk, but was positive it hadn't shown on her face. But some of the classes did sound a little ridiculous—*Slang in the '80s* and *Pop Culture in the '90s*—like they were game show categories.

"After all," Hanson said, "every one of you is a college graduate, most of you with graduate degrees, and all of you with an incredible expertise in your chosen fields. This program you're enrolled in is open only to the highest achievers."

Joyce almost laughed. These old farts were high achievers? Maybe he was speaking to her, not wanting anyone to feel left out....

"Despite what some of you may think," Don said, "Puff Daddy is not a new brand of cigarette, the Cardigans are not necessarily sweaters, and Fastball refers to something other than baseball."

She knew one out of the three. Puff Daddy was a rapper, right?

He returned to the instructor's position behind the desk. "I'll tell you what makes old age a killer," he said, eyes panning the classroom, "and it's not any kind of disease.... It's a cultural killer called a closed mind … tunnel vision … failure to keep up with current trends—like alternative music."

Joyce shifted uncomfortably in her seat, thinking of the oldies stations she preferred to listen to.

"It's noise," a male voice behind her said.

She turned her head to look at the stocky man with a round face and bulbous nose. He wore a green polo shirt a size too small.

Hanson gave the guy a tolerant smile. "There's a court in Colorado that punishes youthful offenders by making them listen to Wayne Newton and Tony Orlando. To them, *that's* noise."

Actually, Joyce agreed with the youthful offenders.

"I'm sorry," the stocky man said, "it's crap and there's no way I'm going to learn to like it."

Hanson drifted over to the stocky man's seat. "Your name is…?"

"Rick."

"Rick," Don repeated. "I'm not here to change your personal tastes. You can play Mantovanni or the Cowsills, in private, if you like. I'm just here to make you familiar with the rock and roll that's out there that came along *after* Fabian."

Mild chuckles erupted around the room, and even Rick smiled.

Hanson moved to the side of the desk, halfsat on it again. "Let's play out a little scenario, shall we, Rick? Your line of work is…?"

"Architectural engineer."

"Okay," Don said. "You're now a thirty-year-old architectural engineer with thirty-year-old peers in the workplace. But what's this? Rick has never heard of Tori Amos, and he thinks Garbage is something you put out at the curb for trash pickup!"

A few more chuckles; some of these people picked up on the references, Joyce among them—well, the Tori Amos part, anyway.

"How can that be?" Hanson asked, archly. "Has Rick spent his life in a plastic bubble? Suddenly, your coworkers start to look at you funny." The teacher paused, then asked the man, "You familiar with the movie *Dawn of the Dead?*"

"Yeah, sure," Rick said with a shrug. "Zombies are trying to take over the world."

The mall, actually, Joyce thought. A frightening prospect.

"And how is it, Rick, that some of the people keep from becoming zombies?"

Rick thought for a moment. "By pretending to be one of them."

"Congratulations, First Caller!" Mr. Hanson, still half-seated on the desk, nodded. "You win the free Sheryl Crow tickets. That's right, Rick, by pretending to be one of them. And if you refuse to conform ... to become one of them ... they'll start to come after you. And then you'll be putting yourself in jeopardy.... *And everyone else in this program.*"

The room fell silent; all eyes were focused on the engineer. Zombie eyes.

Hanson stood from where he was seated on the corner of the desk. "I think I've made my point," he said, then added, "But fair warning: Tomorrow I bring the boom box."

Gentle laughter rippled.

"No earplugs allowed. And oh, one other thing ... I mentioned that you're going to get to know each other during the next four weeks, but I caution you against forging any potentially lasting friendships. After this session, you won't be seeing each other again."

Hanson wrote on the board, in huge letters: FIRST NAMES ONLY. And he underlined it three times and added a trio of exclamation marks after.

New names, new faces, new jobs. Joyce was almost relieved to have an excuse not to get too close to any of these people.

The instructor reached for some of the papers he had on the desk. "We've got a lot of ground to cover," he said, "so what the hell, kids—let's get started...."

When class broke for lunch, the small group—minus the instructor, who Joyce assumed didn't care to eat the cafeteria food—took one of the winding cement pathways over to the student lounge. The brisk winter air was a welcome slap in the face, waking her up from the drudgery of sitting for four hours.

Hanson was interesting enough, and she was really enjoying the pop culture makeover, but in this effort to turn her into someone younger, she still had the same old ass, and it ached from sitting so long.

Inside the cafeteria, which didn't smell as bad as she remembered, a heavyset facial-mole-sporting woman in a hairnet served up a limited menu of salads and sandwiches. Joyce ordered a small salad with diet dressing, and coffee.

The other women had already gone through the line and were clustered together at a table near the center of the room. Two of the men, pudgy Steve and a lanky guy named Phil, took their food to one corner, where sports news was playing on a big-screen TV. That left Rick all by himself at another table.

Joyce couldn't help feeling sorry for the guy; he had the world-weary look of one who'd suffered too many disappointments in a life that was too soon in running out.

She took her tray over to his table.

"Mind if I join you, Rick?" she asked.

He looked up, chewing a bite of the hamburger held in one hand, and shook his head. She set her tray down and took a seat next to him.

"I'm Joyce."

"Hi, Joyce."

It sounded like the beginning of a particularly lifeless A. A. meeting. This guy definitely needed cheering up....

"I'm hoping to lose another ten pounds," she said, gesturing toward her spartan lunch. "I don't want to go through liposuction. I hear it can be really painful."

He swallowed, grunted. "At least you don't have to have hair plugs stuck in your skull. You want to talk about painful. I know a guy who had it done."

She winced. "Well, I'm not nuts about having my whole face stretched up and tied in a knot on the top of my head."

One of the women at the table not far away said to them, "Do you mind? I'm trying to eat." She was in the process of removing the skin from a chicken breast.

Joyce lowered her voice and looked back at Rick. "I'm too scared to have my ears pierced, let alone my face carved up."

He put his half-eaten hamburger down on his tray. "I'm not sure I'm gonna go through with that slice-and-dice crap," he told her.

"Well you have to," she said, stabbing a piece of wilted lettuce with her plastic fork. "It's required."

"For that matter," he said, "I might not go through with *any* of it."

"What do you mean? Break the contract?"

He shrugged facially.

She chewed the lettuce and thought about that. No, a little discomfort was a small price to pay for the rewards she'd been promised.

He moved his head closer to hers. "Doesn't this whole deal strike you as just a tad bit ... creepy?"

"Not really." She was starting to lose her compassion for Rick. Scared was one thing; ungrateful another.

He shook his head, smirking disgustedly. "I mean, it's like *Damn Yankees*."

"You mean the play? I saw the touring company in Chicago."

"Yeah, well, you ask me, we're all selling our souls to Jerry Lewis."

"Well, just so it helps his 'Kids.' "

He didn't laugh; she thought that had been pretty witty.

Joyce put her folk down. "Come on, Rick—I don't feel that way at all. I think X-Gen is a godsend ... hell! Getting another shot at a job. At a life!" She looked squarely at him. "Do you know where I was when they called me? In the process of committing suicide."

His troubled eyes softened. "You, too?"

"More coffee, miss?" It was the heavyset woman in the hairnet, smiling down at her pleasantly, steaming pot of coffee in one hand.

"No, thank you," Joyce said, and the woman moved on toward those at the other table.

She put a hand gently on Rick's forearm. "Look, if it's the surgery you're scared of ... just ask for extra painkillers. I mean, if our generation knows how to do anything, it's take drugs!"

"I was never into that."

"Yeah, well I've never been into pain. I'm gonna have them put me so far under, they'll have to come looking for me in Australia."

He did laugh at that, just a little. Then he said, "It's not the pain, Joyce—I know I can deal with that. It's just ... what if, in this 'new life,' I ... meet somebody?"

"What if you do?"

"Suppose I might want to get married again, someday?"

"So what? Get married again." What did that have to do with the surgery?

He gave her a strange look. "Well, it's contractually forbidden."

She laughed. "What do you mean, contractually forbidden? That's absurd."

He furrowed his brow. "Didn't you read the contract you signed?"

"Yeah, sure, of course I did." Sort of. Skimmed it, anyway; but she didn't remember seeing any clause that required her to remain single. Not that that was even an issue for her, and certainly wouldn't have been a deal-breaker even if she had seen it.

On the other hand, maybe she'd better reread the contract. Only she still hadn't received her copy....

"Well, Rick—surely the contract doesn't preclude us from *living* with somebody?"

"You can do that. But ... that's not me. I was always a straight arrow. I do things the old-fashioned way. You know what the wildest thing I ever did was?"

"What?"

"This."

Chairs screeched as some of the people got up and began to clear their trays away. Joyce looked at her watch; time for class to start again.

She stood up and slowly took her half-eaten salad to the wastebasket, then headed back over to the Social and Behavioral Building, along the winding path, moving out in front of the others, leaving Rick behind, but wondering nonetheless what else might be in that contract that she didn't know about.

Chapter Five

"TO SIR WITH LOVE"
(Lulu, #1 Billboard, 1967)

The following weeks in Indianola passed quickly, and on the last day of class Joyce was surprised to discover that the thought of leaving saddened her. The experience reminded her of going to church camp as a kid: initially excited, then wanting to get the hell out of there, and finally a growing fondness for her campmates/classmates, who by the third week had bonded together in their collective quest for a brighter future.

Even Rick, who remained somewhat sullen and skeptical, could not help being pulled into the fold. Who could blame him for being apprehensive? Who among them wasn't? Only for Joyce, her sense of adventure outweighed any concerns.

Mr. Hanson never showed her any preferential treatment, even though he'd quietly revealed to her that she'd consistently scored the highest grade on all the tests. And she respected him for that, and made no effort to act upon her lustful daydreams about him.

So she was a little surprised, when—on the last day of class—she turned to the final page of her test paper (subject: Swing Revival; she missed only one—Big Bad Voodoo Daddies recorded

"The Boogie Bumper," not The Squirrel Nut Zippers) and found next to the A minus a notation in cursive: *400 Kelly Street, 7 p.m.*

At first, Joyce wasn't sure how to take the scrawled address. Puzzled, she looked up at Hanson, and their eyes met, and the note's meaning became obvious. Slowly she folded the test paper and tucked it away in her school notebook.

At exactly six-thirty, Joyce slipped out of her dorm room. It had taken her a long time to decide what to wear. At first she put on one of her old power suits with high heels; but, after weeks of coed-ish attire, she was afraid the maturity of the outfit might jolt Mr. Hanson (or should she be thinking of him as Don, now?) right out of the mood of the moment.

And she wouldn't want that, would she?

So she climbed into her tan chinos and put on the plaid madras blouse—tied in a knot at the waist—and slipped on the brown Weejuns. Then she grabbed a brown leather bomber jacket (she'd bought it at a secondhand store in Des Moines) off its dorm-room closet hook, and headed out the door.

The corridor was hushed as she walked quickly along. Most of the other women had already packed up and left, for wherever their next stop was. Only Sally and Joyce were left.

Earlier, when Joyce had just stepped out of the shower, Sally had peeked in.

"You up for pizza?" Sally had asked. "Celebrate bustin' out of this joint?"

Wrapped in a towel, Joyce said, "Oh, that sounds like fun, but I still need to pack, and then I think I'll just walk around the campus and town, a while. Kinda say good-bye to the place."

Which truly was her intent. Only at seven o'clock she'd end her walk at 400 Kelly Street.

Sally tried again. "Want some company?"

"No, thanks."

The woman got a funny little hurt expression, waved and went out. What was *that* about?

Outside, a heavy snow was drifting down from a darkened sky, flakes clumping together to make huge ones, sparkling in their descent in the bright light of the street lamps, covering everything with their soft, white blanket.

It was just so incredibly, storybook beautiful, and Joyce smiled as she strolled the curving paths of the campus, perhaps for the last time, past the Social and Behavioral Building, past the Old Chapel—its Addams Family bell tower looming gothically against the inky sky—past the Administration Building, on her way to the town square.

Digging her hands deep in the pockets of the old leather jacket, she walked slowly down Main Street, pausing now and then to peer at the window displays in shops closed up tight for the night. Only a laundromat, diagonally across the square, and a fifties-style diner, at the end of the street, were open for business.

As she walked by the restaurant, her smile, which had not left her lips since leaving the dorm, broadened as she watched the patrons eating in the diner. Next to the window, a teenaged couple in one of the red plastic-padded booths looked dreamily into each other's eyes; they were seated on the same side of the booth, as if the separation of the small Formica table was more than they could bear.

At the counter, their backs to the street, was a husband and wife and two little girls. The children were happily twisting back and forth on the swiveling seats as they munched on french fries; Joyce could imagine an earlier altercation where the parents wished to sit in a comfortable booth but the girls wanted the stools at the counter, and the doting parents gave in.

And at the cash register an elderly couple was paying for their meal; the man, tall and slender, with gray hair and a thin mustache, was handing the cashier some money. He then turned to help his stout wife into her coat, she flashing him an appreciative smile.

It was all there in the diner, Joyce thought. The road of Life. And she was envious of them and their simple, small-town existence.

She hadn't realized it, but she had stopped in her tracks and was staring in the diner window, like Tiny Tim checking out toys. The cashier, a middle-aged woman who looked like she'd logged a lot of miles taking orders, glanced up from the drawer and gave Joyce a friendly little nod.

Embarrassed by her voyeurism, Joyce waved awkwardly back and moved on.

She crossed the street, the snow still coming down, the accumulation on the ground such that with each step the cold white stuff got in her shoes and stung her feet. But she didn't care; it was a nice reminder that she was alive.

At the end of the square began the one-hundred block of Kelly Street. She picked up her pace; it was almost seven and she had four more blocks to go.

As she hurried along the sidewalk lined with trees, their limbs coated with snow, reaching skyward for more, she couldn't help looking in the front windows of the grand old homes. This wasn't like Chicago, where mini-blinds and heavy drapes kept the prying eyes of the world out. Here each home seemed like a miniature doll house as she passed by; she could see all the way to the back, from the front room where light from a television flickered, to the dining room where families laughed and ate, to the kitchen where dishes were being cleaned and put away.

She was approaching the four-hundred block when there came a sound she hadn't heard since her childhood. She turned and saw an old pickup truck coming slowly up the empty street.

It wasn't the truck's engine, which was sputtering and wheezing as the vehicle chugged along, that made her heart race, but rather the sound of the iron chains on its wheels, slapping at the snow and clanking on through to the cement.

There wasn't another sound in the world like it—it had died with the advent of snow tires—but every kid in the Northern states in the 1950s knew that sound, and loved it. Because that particular clanking meant heavy snow and no school, sleeping in, snug under warm blankets, and spending the rest of the day sledding on golf-course hills or ice-skating on park ponds.

Joyce watched as the truck lumbered on by, her smile fading into melancholy. Actually, the melancholy had come on in small degrees ever since she left the dorm, but until now she'd thought it was euphoria.

Standing in front of the brown brick house at 400 Kelly Street, she considered fleeing. After all, what kind of depressed company would she make, now? All the romance and excitement had left her—only an aching sense of loss remained.

Loss and cold, that is. Her toes felt numb, and Hanson's house looked so warm and inviting.

She trudged up the three cement steps to the wide porch where a wooden swing hung high near the porch's roof, waiting patiently for spring.

She wrapped on the screen door.

And waited.

She sighed, her breath smoking, and knocked again.

And waited some more.

It's just as well, she shrugged, and turned to leave when the front door flew open.

"I'm sorry," Hanson said ... Don said ... pushing the screen door wide. "I was in the kitchen. I hope you weren't standing out here freezing, long!" He was wearing a denim shirt with the sleeves rolled up, and khaki slacks.

"I'll thaw," she said, entering the house. Her Weejuns made squishing sounds as she walked, and she halted in the small entryway. "I'm afraid my shoes are all wet."

"Here," he said, pointing to a pair of his boots on the floor, on a floor register, "you can put them there."

She bent to take them off and when she straightened up, caught her reflection in an oval mirror on the opposite wall of the vestibule. Her hair, which had been perfectly coifed when she'd left the dorm, perched on her head like a drowned yellow cat. Why hadn't she had the sense to wear a hat?

"And maybe a towel?" she asked, feeling stupid, the last remnants of any hope for a romantic evening dashed.

He smiled and helped her out of her jacket, which he hung on a coatrack behind the front door.

"Why don't you go sit in the living room and I'll get you that towel." And he disappeared toward the back of the house.

The living room yawned off to the right, and Joyce went in, tiptoeing on the beige carpet in wet socks, and sat down on a brown leather couch in front of the fireplace, where flames danced a red-hot number, occasionally reaching out as if to greet her.

She stretched out her cold feet, instantly feeling better, and took in the room.

It was decidedly masculine, with dark-wood freestanding bookcases crammed with novels, an elaborate entertainment center taking up one whole wall, end tables stacked with magazines, *Entertainment Weekly* and *Widescreen Review* on top; but here and there a feminine touch betrayed itself: A collection of cornhusk dolls huddled silently on a shelf in one corner, dead eyes staring at her, and a family of ceramic ducks sat on the coffee table, as if its glass top was a pond.

Joyce frowned. What if Don was married? Unbelievably, that hadn't occurred to her. He didn't wear a ring. But, then, there wasn't a law that said a married man had to.

Any moment now, a beautiful, shapely young woman—a former student who'd hooked him—might come bounding out of the kitchen, wearing a tight, short dress with a plunging neckline, waving a spatula, announcing perkily, "Dinner's ready!" Was she prepared for that?

Joyce stared at the crackling fire. Well, then, she'd just have to eat the lousy dinner and go.

Another thought perked her up: Maybe his wife was out of town; *that* she was prepared for....

Don sat down on the couch and handed her a green towel. She took it, and, bending toward the warmth of the flames, rubbed her head with the towel, then ran her fingers through her tousled hair like a comb.

"Better?" he asked.

"Much," she smiled.

"Come into the kitchen, while I finish dinner."

She followed him to the back of the house, padding along a wood floor hallway in her damp socks.

The kitchen was large but cozy, with gray-painted cabinets wearing round silver knobs like big bright eyes, obviously installed in the 1950s. The linoleum, however, with its deco-ish white-and-gray checked pattern, looked new. And here and there were red punctuations in the form of a toaster and coffeemaker. On either side of the window over the sink, shelves displayed dozens of old salt and pepper shakers: ears of corn, cowboy boots, bowling pins.

Joyce pulled out a chair at the round oak table in the center of the room, set for two, and watched Don, standing at the stove, stirring a large, steaming sauce pan, with a wooden spoon....

He didn't exactly look like a salt-and-pepper-collectible kind of guy. But then, she used to collect old thimbles.

"Smells yummy," she said from the table.

"It is yummy—yummy is my specialty." He turned and grinned at her. "Carrot soup."

"Carrot soup? As in, what's up doc?"

"Yeah—good stuff," he said. "I make a lot different kinds of soups in the winter." He set the wooden spoon down on the stove, picking up the saucepan by its handle. "This recipe came from my wife's side of the family."

She nodded. His wife. Which explained the feminine touches around the house. Probably away on a trip. All right. Okay....

He poured the hot, thick yellow-orange soup into the bowl in front of her. "I can guarantee you'll like it," he smiled down at her. "Sherry's favorite."

She smiled up weakly at him; now the wife had a name.

"I'm sure I'll love it," she said.

He poured himself a bowl, then sat down across the table from her, but jumped back up. "Oh, I forgot something.... You like Caesar?"

"I'm way too young to remember Sid Caesar, teach. You taught me to forget, remember?"

"I meant salad, you pretty goofball."

He went to the refrigerator and brought out a wooden bowl brimming with lettuce and croutons and other goodies, and placed it in the middle of the table like an edible centerpiece.

She was taking a sip of the hot soup, which was quite good, tasting a little like squash; she paused to wipe her mouth with her napkin.

He looked at her with the bright eager eyes of a kid. "Verdict?"

"I love Caesar salad," she assured him. "And I love soup."

"The question is, do you like *my* soup and salad?"

"Oh, yes," she said, with a silly little laugh. "You'll find I'm really a soup-and-salad kind of girl. Woman."

Oh, brother, she thought, *did I really say that?*

"Made the dressing from scratch."

Joyce speared a leaf of lettuce with her fork. "Another of your wife's recipes, I suppose?"

"Uh-huh."

She chewed the bite; it was delicious. "Is she away on a trip?"

"Excuse me?"

"Sherry. Is she gone?"

An odd look came over his rugged face, and he stared into his soup. "Yes, she's gone."

Joyce nodded, a spoonful of soup raised to tight lips. So the great teach was just another typical male bastard, fooling around while the wife was out of town. Of course that was a category that even her late lover, Henry, had fallen into, and it had never seemed to bother her, before….

"I'm sorry," Don said, "I thought I'd mentioned it to you."

"What?"

"My wife died last year. Breast cancer."

Joyce choked on the soup, then coughed into her napkin. "Oh … I'm so sorry … I didn't know…."

"Look, I didn't invite you here bore you with my trials and tribulations." He smiled one-sidedly.

But clearly he needed to; it was obvious he wasn't over his wife's death. His eyes told the story, a story of anger and hurt that Joyce was all too familiar with—she'd seen it in her own eyes, in the mirror, after Henry died.

She asked softly, "Was it … a long illness?"

He looked up from his soup bowl at her. "Yes. Long and painful and, in the end, degrading…. Fucking animals get treated better."

Joyce sat back in her chair. "I know what it's like to lose someone you love," she told him. "But thankfully he died instantly…. I don't know if I could have handled a prolonged illness…."

"You could have."

"Do you think?"

"You would've had to."

She leaned forward. "I think in the next twenty years, as our generation grows old, we're going to see a lot of assisted suicides. What we need is a law that supports euthanasia." She paused. "But with or without that law, *we're* gonna leave the party when we've stopped having fun."

He smirked but it wasn't nasty. "We always were a defiant bunch of little assholes."

"Yes, but more than that ... we're *pragmatic*. If death is inevitable, why expend the emotional *and* financial expense? Why put yourself and your loved ones through that?"

"Hope, I guess." He shrugged. "Hope for a medical breakthrough ... or miracle. But I can tell you this much, the method of euthanasia needs to be quick and painless for the public to accept it."

"I'm sure there are plenty of ways...."

He started to say something, but evidently changed his mind. "Hey, I think we can come up with happier dinner conversation, if we try real hard."

She laughed her agreement, and their conversation turned to movies and books for the remainder of the meal. Stephen King and Dean Koontz were mutual choices (and acceptable authors for her upcoming second life, as well) and they both loved screwball comedies.

"But I'd advise you saying your favorite movie is *There's Something About Mary*," he said, invoking one of the films they'd screened last week, "before bringing up *Bringing Up Baby*."

After clearing the table and putting the dishes in the dishwasher, they moved into the living room, where the fire had died down.

"I'd offer you a glass of wine," he said, throwing another log in the fireplace, sparks from the cinders flying upward, "but I don't drink anymore."

She was sitting back comfortably on the couch, feet stretched out; her socks were almost dry. "That's all right, I'm off the sauce myself. It accelerates aging, you know."

He joined her on the couch, legs out toward the fire, next to hers.

"Are you frightened about the surgery?" he asked.

She wiggled her toes, the warmth of the fire now crawling up her legs. "Frightened? No. Well, maybe a little. I don't imagine it will be as pleasant as these past few weeks."

He turned his head toward hers. "You'll be fine. I know Dr. Carver. He's a skilled plastic surgeon ... the best in the business."

"Dr. Carver?"

He laughed. "Yeah, it does sound like something out of Dickens. But it's his name—not a description of the level of his skills."

"That's a relief." She gazed at him. "How did you get involved with this program?"

He was silent for a moment before he turned more toward her, putting one arm on the back of the couch. "I don't know if you were aware of it, but Simmons was in financial trouble a few years ago."

"I wasn't aware of that," she lied. After all, she hadn't sent them any money, back when she could well have afforded to.

"The situation was so dire," he went on, "that the college board decided to close the school."

That made her feel better: a few thousand dollars from her wouldn't have helped, anyway.

"So, believe me," he said, "I know all about being over fifty and out of a job."

"What happened?"

"Well, out of the clear blue, this X-Gen company up and buys the college, pumps all kinds of dough into it.... D'you ever make it inside the new Biology building?"

One day over her lunch period. "State of the art," she replied.

He nodded. "And you've seen the Performing Arts Center, the new football stadium.... It was a miracle—a whole new start. A second chance...."

"I believe I can identify."

He grinned, the fire doing nice things to his well-chiseled features. "But best of all, they didn't can the old faculty. Some new staff came in, sure, but heads did not roll. Jobs were saved."

"That's wonderful ... but how was it they happened to ask you to head up these 'special session' classes?"

He leaned toward her. "That was the neat thing...."

She smiled at the word "neat."

"None of this was a coincidence. These X-Gen guys, they were mostly alumni! The founders of the corporation? They were all former students of mine."

"You must have been a good teacher, to inspire that kind of loyalty."

He studied her with half-lidded eyes. "Don't you think I'm a good teacher? Don't I inspire your loyalty?"

His face was very close to hers; she could smell the musky scent of his cologne.

"Well," she said, putting a hand on his bearded cheek, "there's inspiration, and then there's ... inspiration."

Then his lips were on hers, the kiss awkward, like they'd both been out of practice. But the next kiss was better ... and the next even more so. She felt on fire, as if the warmth of the flames had continued up her legs, spreading to her whole body.

When they finally broke apart, he whispered, "This is the last time, you know."

"Last time for what?"

"To make love with a man who knows your real age, and doesn't give a damn." He gave her a devilish grin.

She couldn't help smiling back. "Ah-huh. That's a line I've never heard before."

He pulled Joyce up off the couch, and taking her hand, led her to the stairs and up them, the steps creaking as they went.

The back bedroom where he brought her was as cold as the living room had been warm, which made her want to dive under the bedcovers. Maybe that was his strategy....

Light from a street lamp poured in through the bedroom windows, and in the dark she could make out an antique dresser, a Queen Anne chair, a bedside table with lace cloth.

This must be a guest room, she thought. Maybe his own room wasn't tidy ... or perhaps he couldn't quite bring himself to make love to her in the same bed he once shared with his wife.

No matter.

He sat on the edge of the bed and pulled her to him, unbuttoning her madras blouse. She reached behind herself unfastening the bra, and both pieces of clothing slid to the floor. He kissed her breasts, cupping them tenderly, and she reached down to undo his trousers.

In another moment they were under the covers, between ice-cold sheets, and they cuddled, hands moving everywhere, at first mostly for warmth, then for other things.

Then he eased himself on top of her, and she spread her legs, arched her back, and he entered her like a red-hot poker, intense heat spreading up to her chest and face like a hot flash—only so much more pleasant.

Panting, moaning, they moved together in desperate desire, until Joyce climaxed, the orgasm exploding outward from ground zero to her fingertips. Then Don shuddered and collapsed into her, nuzzling her neck, nibbling her ear, then eased himself off her.

They lay draped in each other's arms, neither speaking, their breathing subsiding, gradually drifting into sleep.

Sometime later, Joyce awoke with a start; Don, next to her on his back, was trembling, talking incoherently in his sleep. She gently shook him, and his eyes flew open, wide and frightened.

She sat up on one elbow and leaned over him. "You were having a nightmare," she said.

His hands covered his face, and he sighed deeply through them.

"Are you all right?" she asked, concerned.

He nodded, then leaned over and put his head on her chest, holding her tightly, and she reflexively put her arms around him.

"You want talk about it? What was it, Don?"

His shoulders heaved, and she felt wetness on her breast.

"Tell me."

A moment passed before he spoke, his voice muffled. "I ... I helped my wife kill herself." And his shoulders heaved again.

Joyce tightened her grip, moving one hand to his head, as a mother draws a child comfortingly to her bosom, and whispered, "It's all right…. It's all right."

"Doctor Carver…."

"Shhh…. You don't have to tell me," she whispered. You did the right thing. "You didn't want her to suffer. It's what anyone would do, *should* do…."

She kept reassuring him, until his crying subsided, replaced with rhythmic breathing, then gentle snoring.

She could make him forget the pain, she thought, as she lay holding him, listening to the wind outside, rattling the windows with icy fingers.

For the first time since she'd committed herself to this new path, she had doubts. Perhaps she shouldn't be trying to start back down that same old road, in the same old profession; the notion of a professor's wife on this quiet campus that had such meaning to her became a sudden, sharply focused alternative. Could she be happy living here, in this house, with this man, in this town?

Maybe she could. That would be a second chance, too, wouldn't it? Another life? A new life? She could be happy here!

For a while, anyway.

She stroked his hair gently before easing from beneath him, slipping out of the warm bed, finding her discarded clothes on the floor, putting them on, and tiptoeing silently out of the room.

The fire in the living room had died, along with any post-coital thoughts about becoming the next Mrs. Hanson…. A new future beckoned.

She was a professional, wasn't she? Already under contract?

She got her leather jacket and put on the Weejuns, which were still wet, and slipped out the front door, closing it quietly.

The snow had stopped and the temperature dropped, the wind giving her face icy little slaps as she hurried along, as if helping bring her back to her senses; tramping along, she dug her hands deeper in her pockets. Christ on a crutch, it was cold!

Across the town square, a snowplow plodded, scraping the street, breaking the deathly still of the night. Joyce moved into the gutter, where there was less snow than on the sidewalks, which hadn't been cleared, her toes tingling, breath nearly crystallizing in midair.

It stings the toes and bites the nose, as over the ground we go....

She was almost in a run by the time she reached the edge of the campus, cutting across the lawn, the Alice-in-Wonderland paths having disappeared beneath the powdered-sugar snow, when she abruptly halted, sucking in air so quickly that her lungs ached.

There was a light moving in the bell tower.

The phantom of the Old Chapel had returned!

Then someone was laughing, giddily, girlishly: her.

Feeling like Nancy Drew in *The Ghost of Blackwood Hall*, Joyce raced across the snow to the old red-brick Gothic building. She found the front doors locked, but the back was not, and she darted inside, shaking the snow from her shoes as she entered.

Consumed with an adventurous rush of adrenaline, she tiptoed down a long narrow hallway with a red-carpeted runner, eyes slowing growing accustomed to the dark. Then she stood silently in the center of the first floor, a bank of elevators to her right, the grand spiral staircase to her left.

From somewhere high above, she heard an ungodly sound, a moaning or groaning.

The fun drained out of her; the adventure, too. Something really *was* wrong here....

She leaned and peered up the hole in the staircase, which wound all the way to the tower, where a faint light still could be seen.

Wait just a damn minute, she said to herself. This place always had been the pinnacle of pranks on this campus. She smiled to herself. Was Sally in back of this? Performing a final farewell stunt? Or was it one of the returning students, who were due back from break in another day or two?

Like an apparition herself, she glided up the stairs, past the second floor, then third floor, where she stopped and listened. The sound had ceased.

The final steps leading to the bell tower narrowed, and Joyce knew they would creak with her every step, because they weren't carpeted. So she bounded up them, landing on the fourth floor with both feet firmly planted.

"I've got you now!" she said loudly, ridiculously.

But just the howling wind gave her a frosty greeting.

She shivered; maybe that's all it was.

Slowly she moved forward in the small tower room, skirting the center where the old bell used to hang—it had been removed long ago due to incessant pranks—toward a discarded flashlight on the floor, its cyclops eye shining away from her.

"Come on," she chided loudly, "you'll have to do better than this *X-Files* moment, to make it into Old Chapel folklore."

She bent and retrieved the flashlight, stood, then retreated, knocking into something with the back of her head. She whirled and found herself tangled up in a pair of legs. Shrieking, she fell backward on her butt, the flashlight in one hand traveling up those legs to a torso.

A stocky middle-aged balding man in brown pants and white shirt was dangling by his neck, where a bell cable was wound so tight the visible flesh was a sickly purple, bloated tongue lolled out, blank eyes bulging, face a red-splotchy white, head at a hopelessly askew angle that made this anything but a prank.

Rick.

And her terrified scream resonated in the small tower, echoing off the walls—insuring Joyce her own place in Old Chapel folklore—and she stumbled out of the room and down the spiral staircase, losing her footing, the flashlight in her hand creating a wild laser show as she tumbled ass-over-teakettle the rest of the way down, landing rudely in a heap at the bottom.

Frightened and bruised, she picked herself up and hobbled down the hallway to an office door, but found it locked. Using the head of the flashlight, she broke its stenciled-glass panel to get inside, where she dialed 911 on a desk phone.

She sat on the floor with her back to the desk, her legs drawn to her chest, rocking back and forth, sobbing, waiting for the help that would soon come.

Knowing that it was too late to really help.

Chapter Six

"YOU MAKE ME FEEL BRAND NEW"
(The Stylistics, #2 Billboard, 1974)

Waiting at the curb for Joyce outside the tiny airport in Bemidji, Minnesota—where a chartered plane had brought her north from Minneapolis—was a white van that almost blended into the blinding white of a recent snowfall, but for the black letters on its side: *Chestnut Mountain Resort.*

The man in brown parka and tan corduroy pants who took her single small suitcase (she'd been instructed to bring only essentials) had an infectious smile in a well-grooved face, eyes as blue as the clear sky and as sparkling as the sun-reflecting snow, whose whiteness was shared by his full, rather shaggy head of hair. Joyce guessed his age to be in the late sixties.

He held up a little sign that said JOYCE JONES, which was amusing to her, considering this miniscule airport wasn't exactly brimming with limo drivers.

"That's me," she said. She was wearing slacks and a Simmons College sweatshirt with the bomber jacket over it—generally, warm enough apparel, but not for Minnesota weather.

"Jerry Jensen," he said, in a husky baritone, helping her into the front passenger seat.

"How much of a drive do we have, Mr. Jensen?"

"Oh, bout an hour north, pretty near the Canadian border, missy."

She found his Minnesota accent charming, and his manner comforting.

As the van pulled out of the airport and onto the highway, Joyce asked, "Are Paul Bunyan and Blue Ox still standing?" She was referring to Bemidji's most famous attraction, massive statues of the hero of local folklore and his famous pet.

Mr. Jensen gave her a sideways glance. "Poor ol' boy's still waiting for his true love," he said, referring to the statue of Lucette in the town of Hackensack.

When Joyce was eight, she had vacationed with her parents in Bemidji. They stayed on the lake in a cabin and had a wonderful time—or she thought so anyway. She now wondered why they had never returned. Perhaps it hadn't been much of a vacation for her parents, sharing the bedroom with an eight-year-old.

Now and then, as Mr. Jensen skillfully maneuvered the van along the heavily snow-laden blacktop, the two made light conversation.

He told her he was retired from the real estate business, having sold lakefront property for forty-some years; and she told him she'd been in advertising for most of her life. But beyond that, she didn't offer anything else about herself, and he didn't ask.

As the landscape became more desolate and even the tiny towns disappeared, giving way to thick, luxuriously green pine forests, the flat land becoming more hilly, Joyce leaned her head back against the seat's headrest.

She must have fallen asleep, because the next thing she knew they were winding their way up a steep, narrow incline, where signs along the way warned of falling rocks and deep drop-offs.

She straightened up in her seat. "I hope I didn't snore," she said sheepishly.

"I didn't hear anything, missy, 'cept a few trees gettin' sawed down." He gave her another sideways glance, eyes twinkling. "Pretty common in these parts."

She smiled back at him. "Pretty common anywhere I fall asleep—but thanks for the graceful out."

"All part of the service, missy."

Then the land flattened out—they must have reached the top of the mountain—and through the thick pine trees she could see the resort looming just ahead, man's work rising over nature's.

The big, rambling, turn-of-the-century structure, with its gables and towers and spires, added-on wooden wings alternating with stone, emerged like a gray Victorian cliff against the sky, looking both inviting and mysterious. Beyond the sprawling many-storied building, she glimpsed the frozen lake, its surface smooth as glass, though unreflective.

Well, this could be interesting, she thought.

But instead of pulling up to the wide porch that dominated the front of the building—where caned-back rockers sat empty in a row, bobbing gently in the breeze, as if invisible guests were seated there—Mr. Jensen guided the van along another path, explaining, "You're on t'other side of the lake, missy."

The lake, which was rather small by Minnesota standards, was only about a mile long and half a mile across. Joyce made this observation as they traveled the narrow blacktopped road that wound around the water, shading her eyes against the sun as its rays darted in and out of the tops of the pines.

Then the road began to ascend a nature-fashioned cliff that rose magnificently against the back of the lake, and she could see a modern cement building perched on top; the structure looked as if it were a bizarre extension of the cliff, angular cement slabs jutting out in every direction, Frank Lloyd Wright gone just slightly mad.

Mr. Jensen eased the van beneath a cement portico and shut off the engine. He turned to her. "First and last stop on this milk run," he announced cheerfully.

But Joyce didn't know if she liked the sound of that; suddenly Mr. Jensen's folksiness seemed less benign.

And, looking at the burnished-steel front double doors that seemed more appropriate for a vault than a building, she wondered just what the hell she was in for....

"Well, thank you for the pleasant ride," she said, but he was already getting out. She repeated that, as he opened the door for her.

"Pleasure's mine, missy, pleasure's mine," he was saying, giving the building nervous little looks, as he scurried to the rear and got her little suitcase out, nodded to her and scrambled back into the van, before she could even decide whether a tip was called for.

Then the van was whooshing away behind her, tires crunching on the snow, and she was alone—standing by herself, under the cement portico, small suitcase in hand. Drawing in a deep breath, she moved sluggishly forward toward those doors, as if the suitcase weighed a ton, butterflies fluttering in her stomach.

Entering as Joyce—wondering who exactly she'd be when she finally exited.

Inside, a sterile but not forbidding reception area greeted her, though no human did—all cool gray carpet and chrome, light gray stucco walls, black-and-white modular furniture, a waiting area where nobody was waiting.

Nobody but Joyce.

Was she the only patient here? she wondered. Or did patients arrive in staggered schedules, so they wouldn't see each other?

Just ahead, the black marble cube of a reception desk sat empty, like an altar awaiting a sacrifice. It was chilly in here, and she thanked God for the fur-lined bomber jacket.

Then, through a doorway just behind the massive desk, a striking woman in a navy suit entered, a folder in hand. She was perhaps twenty-eight, gorgeous, with long black hair, creamy skin, full red lips, deep blue eyes and a button for a nose.

The woman smiled at Joyce, a smile that looked warm but seemed cold, and extended a slender hand.

"Ms. Jones," the young woman said, "how was your trip?"

"Fine. Lovely, really. What beautiful country."

"*We* like it," the perfect young woman said, as if she were at least partially responsible.

Joyce could not help staring at this woman, who was spectacularly beautiful, as if she had walked out of a Revlon ad. Was *she* a product of the plastic surgery Joyce was about to receive?

"We have the usual papers for you to sign," the young woman was saying, "but that will wait for later. Right now, the most important thing is to get you settled into your room."

Joyce continued to stare. There was something about the receptionist's eyes that didn't jibe with the young face. They sat a little too deep in their sockets, and seemed much too mature and … knowing.

Smiling to herself, Joyce knew that if she was correct, and the receptionist *had* been rebuilt, then she had made the right decision.

"Yes," the woman said, as if reading Joyce's mind, "I am one of you."

"Do you … do you mind if I ask your age?"

A tiny smile tickled full, perfect lips. "Certainly not—thirty-two … now."

The advertising maven in Joyce noted how effective this "ad" was—having your arriving clients, who might be suffering last-second misgivings, immediately encounter a success story like the receptionist.

"The nurse will see you to your room," the young woman told her. "And if you need anything at all, just call the front desk. My name is Sarah."

Suddenly, as if materializing, a woman in white appeared at Joyce's side, startling her. She was as unattractive as Sarah was beautiful—tall and mannishly muscular, dull brown hair pulled back from her face, which was as lumpy as putty and about the same color, tiny close-set eyes, bulbous nose, thin lips set in a patronizing smile, Mrs. Potato Head features stuck haphazardly on.

No ID tag, but her name could only be Broomhilda.

Joyce smiled warily at the nurse.

"Come," Broomhilda said, and pivoted on her heels, walking away from Joyce so quickly that she had to scurry down the unadorned hall to catch up.

They took an elevator—a silent, interminably long ride—to the fourth floor, and then went down another anonymous hall to a white door numbered 417.

With a hand smaller than a catcher's mitt, the nurse opened the door, flinging it wide, and gestured with her head for Joyce to enter.

Joyce did.

The blankness of the hallways did not extend to the rooms, anyway this one, which was almost lavishly decorated, like a really nice suite at the Marriott: cherry-wood furniture in the Chippendale style, navy and gold tapestry drapes and matching bedspread, floral watercolor paintings in gilded frames, and in one corner, a well-outfitted kitchenette.

Joyce smiled, pleased with, and relieved by, her accommodations—she had pictured a dreary little cell—and slung her Vuitton suitcase onto the bed, which was the only telltale sign in the room that this wasn't a hotel suite: It was a regular hospital bed.

The mannish nurse brushed briskly by her to the closed heavy drapes and drew them aside, pointing to the view of the lake below—it was breathtaking!—then opened up a cabinet to reveal a 27-inch television ... no high-up, wall-mounted TV for this hospital room.

Finally, the nurse stood silently, like a bellhop waiting for a tip, before clearing her throat and instructing, "Dr. Carver will see you in his office on the first floor in one half hour."

As the nurse exited the room, she cast Joyce a glance over her shoulder, saying, "My name, by the way, is Hilda."

Then the door closed and Joyce thought, *Well—half-right anyway....*

Joyce waited only a few minutes in a small, spartan outer office, where another lovely receptionist sat—this one a blonde with cheekbones like Julia Roberts but not the wide mouth—providing further reassurance as to the quality of the clinic's work.

The receptionist rose, said, "Dr. Carver will see you now," and ushered Joyce personally to the inner office door, opening it, whispering, "You'll be *so* happy...."

The office was surprisingly small, with a heavy cherry desk and matching files, white stucco walls wearing framed diplomas, a window on the lake, and a wall of reference books and mementos and family pictures behind the desk chair.

And, of course, the doctor himself, who rose from that chair, a formidable figure in a Brooks Brothers gray suit with black and white tie (no white smock for this one!) with his hands spread in a gesture of welcome. Perhaps forty, he was tall, wide-shouldered, sturdily built, with a dark complexion and very dark hair and heavy dark eyebrows—he reminded her a little of the actor Mandy Patinkin, though more slender, brown eyes soothing behind wire-rim glasses.

"Joyce," he said, with a disarming smile. "I've heard so much about you—I've been looking forward to meeting you."

As she approached the desk he offered his hand, which she shook; his grasp was firm and warm.

"And I you, Dr. Carver."

"No formalities between us, Joyce. We're friends—partners in your new life. Call me Stan."

"All right ... Stan."

"Please have a seat." He gestured to the padded burgundy chair in front of the desk.

"Thank you," she said, knees feeling weak, knowing that her fate—and face—were in this man's hands.

He leaned back in his black leather chair; to the right of him, the picture window offered another spectacular view on the frozen lake. "How do you like the accommodations?" he asked, with a tiny smile that said he knew what her answer would be.

"Oh, my room," she responded, "it's lovely."

"I think you'll soon see that we do everything in our power to ensure that your stay here is a pleasant one."

The next ten minutes or so consisted of small talk. Dr. Carver told her the history of Chestnut Mountain Retreat, which had begun as one of the Kellogg brothers' health spas in the early 1900s, then became a ski resort for decades, until several mild snowless winters caused the popular vacation site to fall on hard times.

"The X-Gen people had been looking for a rather remote site to build this clinic," Dr. Carver said. "I was—am—on their board of directors, and called Chestnut to their attention—it was scheduled for demolition. What a tragedy that would have been!"

"I'm surprised it isn't on the register of historic buildings," Joyce said.

"Well, the government didn't recognize Chestnut's value, but X-Gen did. You see, Joyce, that's the specialty of this unique company—possessing the vision to look at something society has discarded and recognize the potential that remains within. X-Gen bought Chestnut, converted it into a health spa and built this clinic, on the resort grounds across the lake. Should a patient need an extended recovery, what nicer surroundings could you imagine?"

"I couldn't." She gazed out at the frozen lake. "I love this country—my family vacationed in Bemidji, but I've never been this far north before."

"You're barely still in America," he said with that disarming smile.

She was beginning to wonder why all the chitchat, when it became clear to her.

"Now, Joyce, I need for you to go into the next room and remove your clothing." He gestured to a closed door next to the bookcase behind his desk. "You'll find a robe, and just knock on the door when you're ready for me to join you."

Obviously he'd wanted some time for them to get to know each other, however superficially. He was about to look her over head to toe, like a classic car restorer checking out every hubcap, taillight and door handle on a '57 Chevy.

Feeling like a '42 Hudson, she nodded and rose from the chair.

The room she entered was even smaller than the doctor's office, a typical examination room: padded table with its white protective paper that had always reminded her of what a butcher wrapped meat up in; a counter arrayed with various jars of tongue depressors, cotton balls and such; blood pressure unit on one wall; and a wall rack of magazines that dated to Clinton's first term.

She took off her things, primly hiding her underwear beneath the other folded items on the counter, and slipped on the white terry-cloth robe with the resort's insignia on the breast pocket, thankful it wasn't one of those ugly thin cotton hospital gowns. Then she rapped once on the door, and went over to the table and sat on its edge, paper crinkling, and waited, legs dangling, wondering if she should lie down.

The door opened.

"I want you to stand here," Dr. Carver instructed, pointing to the center of the room.

She complied.

"Are you ready?" he asked.

"Yes." She let the robe fall to the floor.

He flipped a wall switch, turning on a light in the center of the ceiling, just overhead, bathing her in its brightness. She felt like a fried pie at McDonald's.

His eyes, before so soft and friendly, turned hard and analytical, though his touch remained both gentle and clinical, as he examined her face, forehead, eyes, nose, cheeks, mouth, chin, neck, then her torso, arms, breasts, stomach, his fingers poking, probing, and finally her buttocks, inner thighs, knees and even her feet.

Throughout, she held her breath, taking only tiny gulps of air. Now she knew how a bug under a microscope felt.

At last he said, "You can go ahead and get dressed, Joyce, and, when you're ready, join me in my office, please." Then he flicked off the bright overhead light and slipped out. She reached for her clothes and hurriedly threw them on, vaguely embarrassed, mildly humiliated.

Back in his office, with Dr. Carver once again behind his desk and Joyce seated in front of him, the doctor's warm, friendly demeanor returned.

"You're in excellent condition," he told her.

She smiled a little.

"If most women your age had your figure, Joyce, guys like me would be out of business."

She smiled more, the embarrassment, the humiliation easing away.

"But we do have a lot of work to do," he added.

Her smile faded.

"How much work?" she asked.

"A woman's face ages faster than her body, in many instances. As I say, your body could pass for a woman ten years your junior … but we have to make sure you can pass for *twenty* years younger. Understood?"

"Understood."

He leaned forward in his chair, looking down at a piece of notepaper on the desk. "Brow lift, face lift, blepharoplasty—that's your eyes—neck tuck, breast augmentation, inner arm lift, tummy tuck, thigh and knee liposuction…."

She gasped.

"I don't really think you need cheek implants—sometimes they tend to slide out of place—and, anyway, your bone structure is just fine."

"Well, at least that's something," she said glumly.

He made a tent with his fingertips. "And I might suggest augmentation on your upper lip ... to make it fuller," he said. "I use alloderm instead of collagen because it's permanent.... I make small incisions in the corners of your mouth and thread the alloderm through...."

"Okay," she interrupted. "You're drifting into the more-information-than-I-need area, Doctor ... Stan. Just do it, okay?"

"Okay. But most patients like to know what they're getting into."

"*What* is fine. *How* is irrelevant."

He jotted a notation on the piece of paper.

She shifted in her chair. "Isn't this all a bit excessive?" she asked. "I mean, I like my room, but I don't want to spend a year recuperating there, or am I headed over to Chestnut and the rocking chairs?"

"Neither." He put the pen down and looked at her. "A team of doctors will be performing all the procedures at once."

Her mouth fell open. "Is that possible?"

"Not only possible, but we do it frequently, here, with great success. Oh, I'm sure it must sound a little unorthodox—"

"A *little*? Won't I be in terrible pain?"

"Not at all," he assured her. "You'll be heavily medicated, then gradually weaned off the drugs. Don't worry—our patients feel very little discomfort."

"Well ... all right," she said halfheartedly, not knowing whether to believe him or not: She knew a sales pitch when she heard it. This seemed like one hell of a lot of surgery to have at one time; then again, wouldn't it be nice to have it all over and done with?

"All right, Joyce," Dr. Carver said, bringing their consultation to a close. "I'll see you in the morning. You're not to eat any solids the rest of the day, and you're not to eat or drink anything after midnight tonight. Hilda will give you more complete instructions."

Back in her room, Joyce opened the sliding glass door to the cement balcony and stepped out into the cold late afternoon air; the sun, just beginning to set, was turning the sky purple and pink, casting long shadows over the iced-over lake and the sprawling resort across the way, which from her balcony looked like a child's Victorian playhouse.

She returned inside and got out her flannel gray nightgown and slipped it on, then settled into the hospital bed, elevating it a little so she could watch the TV. In the middle of the national news, Hilda served a less than sumptuous supper of chicken broth, lemon Jell-O and iced tea, little of which Joyce ate.

Nothing on TV seemed to hold her interest and she used the remote to turn it off with a *click* that seemed weirdly loud to her. She reached for a mystery novel she'd set on the nightstand and, settling further in the bed, began to read. Around eight o'clock, Hilda arrived again and gave her two blue pills with a small cup of water, to help her sleep, she said.

Joyce returned to her book, but began to have trouble concentrating on the words, and the next thing she knew, the nurse was shaking her awake, handing her a hospital gown, telling her to put it on.

Groggily, Joyce stumbled out of bed, sun streaming in through the balcony glass door—was it rising, or still setting? She was so confused! She staggered into the bathroom and somehow got into the thin, cotton gown, used the toilet, brushed her teeth and ran a brush through her tangled hair. The face that looked back at her in the bathroom mirror was old and haggard ...

... but she stood frozen there for the longest time, staring at herself, seeing the shadow of her parents in her features, wondering if that shadow would be cut away along with the years, studying for a final time the lines and wrinkles she had worked so hard to earn, bidding herself a bittersweet good-bye.

Then she was on her back, on a gurney, wheeled down the hall, watching the overhead lights glide by until she went through double doors and the ceiling became whiter, brighter. She turned to see a blur of monitors and tubes and doctors in white, so many doctors, too many doctors, heads covered with green hats, mouths obscured by white masks, like bandits robbing her stagecoach.

Two of them gently lifted Joyce off the gurney and slid her hospital-gowned body onto a table; she shivered as her bare backside made contact with cold metal. Someone stuck an IV in a vein on the back of her left hand, expertly—no pain.

No gain, she thought.

Then one of the doctors leaned in close over her; she recognized the kind brown eyes and heavy dark eyebrows of Doctor Carver, which seemed to bore through her like laser beams.

"Are you ready, Joyce?" he asked, his words muffled behind the mask. Or was that the effect of the drug she'd just been given?

Joyce nodded and closed her eyes. *This will all be over soon,* she thought. *It'll all be worth it,* she told herself.

"I want you to count back from one hundred," Dr. Carver was saying; his voice seemed so far away—as if from across that lake....

She began counting: "One hundred ... ninety-nine ... ninety-eight...."

That was as far as she got.

After the surgery, her first sensation was one of panic. Something was making her cough—which was extremely painful—over and over again. The only way she could explain it to herself, in her semi-unconscious state, was that she was trapped in a basic computer program with a loop: START. COUGH. GO BACK TO THE BEGINNING. START. COUGH. GO BACK TO THE BEGINNING. And she would be in pain for all of eternity! She wanted to scream, but couldn't open her mouth, couldn't summon her voice.

Then, inexplicably, her coughing stopped.

And the pain stopped, too, just as inexplicably, and Joyce drifted back into nothingness.

Much later, when she related to the nurse her terrifying experience, Joyce learned that it was Dr. Carver making her cough in order to clear her throat and lungs, and, under the effect of the sodium pentothal, she had diligently obeyed his orders.

After the effects of the anesthesia had worn off, Joyce woke gradually, to find herself back in her room, in her bed, which was elevated so that she was sitting up. She looked down at her body stretched out before her, wrapped in gauze like a mummy, from her feet to her head, and touched her bandaged face, finding little slits for her eyes, nose and mouth.

She ached all over, like she'd been battered with a blunt object. But Hilda showed her how to give herself the pain medication through her IV with a push of a button, and the dull ache she felt went away.

And Joyce—thinking what a lovely, truly lovely woman Hilda was—closed her eyes and slept.

"Well, what do you think?" Dr. Carver asked.

A week had passed since the surgery, and all the bandages and draining tubes had been removed. Joyce stood nude in the examination room, in front of a full-length mirror. A week earlier she had been nervous about baring her body; now she felt confident.

"Amazing," she murmured, staring back at herself. Granted, here and there her skin was black and blue, and her face seemed a bit swollen, but beyond that, Joyce could see a beautiful young woman emerging. "I can't believe the difference."

Standing behind her, Dr. Carver nodded and smiled, obviously proud of his work.

"How much longer before I'm … normal?" she asked, looking at the doctor's reflection behind hers in the mirror.

"Possibly months for the swelling to go down, completely," he told her. "But you can leave the clinic in another week, and we'll transfer you across the lake."

"To the resort, you mean?"

"Yes. It's a restful setting for recovery, for physical and emotional therapy."

"What sort of emotional therapy?"

"Counselors will be working with you. You'll be reading, listening to music, watching videos, in a sort of home-study follow-up to your intensive training at Simmons. In about a month and a half, you'll join the general population at Chestnut."

That sounded like a prisoner getting out of solitary confinement.

"You'll interact with other guests of the resort," Carver was saying, "many of whom are *not* part of our program, just average citizens getting away from it all."

"What's the purpose of that? If I've recovered, physically, and completed the courses—"

"You need to meet and relate to people ... strangers ... as Joy Lerner. It's a sort of practice period, before you're thrown into the challenging work environment ahead. To give you a chance to get used to the new you ... to *become* the new you."

"Oh, I'm already used to the new me." She smiled back at herself in the mirror, then frowned; her face felt like it might crack. Fingers of both hands went to her cheeks. "This is so tight," she complained. "Like a rubber mask!"

The doctor nodded again. "That feeling will go away in time," he explained. "Also, you may experience some numbness, as well, but that, too, will fade as the nerve endings grow back." Then he added, "Any other concerns?"

She cocked her head, still staring at the young woman in the mirror. Never in her wildest dreams had she thought she could look so gorgeous. She had the figure of a Playmate of the Month, better than when she'd really been young.

"No," she said, then, "Yes! Every now and then I get a sharp pain here, and here." She pointed to both sides of her pelvis.

"Ah," Dr. Carver said. "That's nothing to worry about, Joyce. I performed a oophorectomy."

"Excuse me?"

"Took your ovaries out."

Joyce's mouth fell open. "You did *what*?"

"While I was doing the tummy-tuck, I was right there, so what the heck—I removed them."

What the heck?

She turned to face him, eyes wide, too shocked to speak.

He shrugged. "You weren't using them anymore," he said, matter-of-factly.

"Well, I know," she replied, shock now turning to anger, "but ... Christ ... *Stan* ... is there anything *else* I'm missing?"

He laughed at that, but she hadn't said it to be funny.

"No, of course not," he assured her.

Suddenly she felt self-conscious about her nudity, and reached for her white terry-cloth robe and put it on.

"Ovarian cancer is one of the worst kinds of cancer a woman can contract," Dr. Carver told her. "In the early stage, it has no symptoms, and by the time you suspect something is wrong, it's too late." His voice took on concern. "I wanted to spare you that."

Joyce's anger faded. "Well, I guess it will be nice not having that worry hanging over me," she agreed. And he was correct she was no longer using her ovaries: They'd stopped producing eggs a year ago. So losing them really didn't matter.

Dr. Carver patted her terry-clothed shoulder. "You run along now," he said, as if talking to a child. "It's about time for your dinner."

"When can I have solid food?" she asked. She was getting tired of the broth, Jell-O and apple juice that was her necessary post-surgery regimen. Not that it mattered; even the smallest amount of food filled her up. She didn't seem to have much of an appetite.

Which was good.

Dr. Carver had explained that the best way to stay young was to limit calorie intake to almost starvation mode, thus limiting the number of times a cell renews itself, which causes aging.

"You know," Joyce said, happily, "I don't think I'm going to have any trouble keeping my weight down."

The doctor, exiting through the examination door, looked back. "I'm sure you won't, Joyce," he said with a tiny smile. "Not after I stapled your stomach."

And he left her, standing in her terry-cloth robe, mouth hanging open.

Playmate of the Month.

Staples and all.

"BEYOND THE SEA"

(Bobby Darin, #6 Billboard, 1960)

Palm trees, beach, mountains—what was heaven to the tourists could be hell for Ben McRae, and sometimes he roused, deep in the night, in the predawn morning hours, after dreaming of Viet Nam, only to find himself on a sandy slope with scrubby grass and thinking he was fucking back there!

It only lasted for a moment or two, but they were bad moments, and his waking scream would echo down the beach and across the rippling water, as if trying to be heard across that vast sea, beyond which lay that nasty little country that had taken so much from him.

Otherwise, beachfront Santa Monica was proving a good new location for the homeless man. The wide, white beach and the nearly constant sunshiny days, the steady influx of tourists and relaxing locals, made for perfect pickings. The parklike strip high above the beach had public restrooms and plentiful benches, and the cops only did a once-a-week sweep, which was easy enough to duck.

The place had its dark side, sure—and any day of the week a cop, particularly one of those SMPD Harbor Patrol clowns, could yank your ass in for an overnight. But as long as you weren't one of these blatantly slovenly homeless drifters, or some pier rat working a nickel-and-dime hustle, or hooking (more males than females down here—tricks and trade), you could do just fine.

Ben's method was not to wear his welcome out in any one place—he alternated between Main Street, with its dozens of trendy shops and art galleries, and Montana Avenue, which ran a little more to restaurants; and the mall, Santa Monica Place, always tricky, as well as the Third Street Promenade, with some shops but more night clubs, movie theaters and restaurants.

Best of all, of course, was the Pier itself, with its classic carousel and arcades and restaurants and fishin'-off-the-side. The full-scale amusement park, with its Ferris wheel and roller coaster, provided a perfect panhandler's crowd. People throwing their money away are always ready with a little spare change and loose guilt.

Weekends were particularly choice. He'd wander the pier, and in the amusement park—no admission—he could linger around the fringes of the Sea Dragon, the Rock and Roll, the bumper cars. Since he wasn't a dyed-in-the-wool alkie, he would take up the offer of, "I won't give you money, but I will buy you a hot dog." Nothing like a Chicago dog, California style—unless it was the spicy chicken or the Mexican food or those homemade potato chips soaked in salt and vinegar....

Those public bathrooms sure did come in handy.

Ben sat on a bench in the parklike strip, straights walking along, heading toward the Pier, drawn by the thousands of multicolored lights of the amusement park, the nine-story Ferris wheel and the five-story Roller Coaster in particular giving off a gaudy come-hither glow. He never tired of looking at this all-American light show—it reminded him of the Fourth of July, it reminded him of the Missouri State Fair.

Life was good. He had never dreamed he'd get a second chance. But when that awful auto accident started giving him bad dreams again, he had abandoned the block near the Kafer Building and headed for newer, sandier pastures. He had heard that the Santa Monica beachfront was as much a playground for the homeless as it was for the "gainfully employed."

And they hadn't lied.

Tonight—it was midnight, and he'd made out good, bummed a hot dog and had twenty-some in change and dollar bills in his jeans—was as close to heaven as a homeless man could imagine. The hot dry wind, the Santa Ana blowing in off the mountains, was soothing, pleasant, not like the humid Missouri summers of his youth; the smog was clearing off and the sky was a deep blue and the stars were giving the amusement-park lights a run for the money.

"Ben?" a male voice said.

Ben turned. Standing beside him, a hand on the back of the bench, was a blond kid of twenty-five or so, with a buzz cut and a blue T-shirt and black jeans; five nine, maybe, with a muscular build and a roundish baby face that seemed very young despite dark glasses. Midnight and sunglasses—what was he, some soap opera star wanting a B.J.? What the fuck kind of lowlife did he think Ben was?

Ben frowned up at him. "Do I know you, son?"

"No. You talked to my boss, though—Lieutenant Anderson?"

LAPD. Shit.

"Mind if I sit, Ben?"

"No ... free country. Look, I ain't no vagrant. I'm waiting to hear on a dishwashing job."

The young cop held his hand out. "Detective Clemens, Ben."

Warily, Ben shook it. Firm. Maybe too firm.

The young cop continued: "But call me Ed. And I'm not here to hassle you about your ... chosen lifestyle."

"What do you want?"

"You gave a statement a couple months ago. That accident. That woman who was run down right in front of you?"

"I told you guys everything I saw. Everything I know."

The young cop twitched a smile; street-lamp light danced in the blank black lenses of the sunglasses. "Well, Ben, you said you worked that block, that we could always find you there, but then you up and disappear. You shoulda told us you were movin' on. In fact, we told you, give us a call, if you left the area."

"No, you said if I left town. Santa Monica is not leavin' town."

"Well, it sorta is, but let's not sweat the small stuff. The point is, Ben, we have reason to believe that Rachel Wilson—that's the woman who was run down, Ben—may have been murdered."

"Oh."

"You see, Ben, if this were just a hit-and-run, that would be one thing. Oh, that's serious enough, don't get me wrong. But if it's homicide—if she was run down intentionally—then that's something real serious."

"What's it got to do with me?"

He stared at Ben with the blank lenses. "You saw it. Do you think the hit-and-run driver's actions were consistent with a hit-and-run, or could it have been murder?"

"I don't know. Why talk to me? Who cares about my opinion?"

"Ben, *I* care about your opinion."

Ben shifted nervously on the wooden bench. "Can we walk and talk, mister? You got a cop sign hangin' around your neck—people I know, they see me sittin', talkin' to the fuzz, I could get a bad name. A snitch or something."

A faintly amused smile formed on the baby face. "Why, is there something you *could* snitch about, Ben?"

"I see more illegal shit than a Mafia boss."

"Okay. All right. Then let's just walk on down the beach."

Ben held up a palm in "stop" fashion. "Don't walk close to me. I don't want to look gay."

That made the young cop laugh. "Okay. Let's head down the stairs. Talk on the beach."

This time of night, middle of the week, the beach was fairly empty. A few homeless types like Ben were camped out, in the glow of the stars and the pier. The homeless man and the young cop walked toward the beckoning lights. The young cop kept his distance, working his voice up over the rolling tide.

"You testify, there could be dough in it," the cop said. He did look like a soap opera actor, or those *Baywatch* people, who weren't filming here, anymore. Word was they headed to Hawaii.

"Money?"

"The woman who was run down, she was a successful businesswoman. If someone murdered her, we want to know why. We want to know who."

Ben shrugged as he shuffled along the sand. "I got a look at the guy. Some."

"Can you still remember him?"

"I think."

Muffled music from the pier drifted toward them; the Beach Boys singing "Good Vibrations."

The lights of the pier flickered on the black lenses. "Could you sit down with our sketch artist?"

"Yeah. She sure was a pretty girl. Red dress. She was nice to me. Not everybody's nice to me."

"They should be, Ben. I understand you're a vet."

"How'd you know?"

"You mentioned it to the lieutenant…. I admire that. I was in the Marines but I never saw any action. Too young. Too young for friggin' Desert Storm, let alone Viet Nam."

Shuffling, kicking up sand, Ben glanced out at the sea, starlight shimmering on its deep blue. "You didn't miss nothin'."

"What exactly did you see that afternoon, Ben? I'm not asking you to make anything up. We just want the truth."

"Well … it didn't really occur to me at the time. But looking back—I think he sped up."

The cop stopped and so did Ben.

Urgently, the cop said, "Like he was trying to hit her."

Ben nodded. "Yeah—and he did the coldest fuckin' thing, too."

"What's that?"

"Turned his wipers on. To wash the blood away. Never slowed. Never missed a damn beat."

"Jesus … did you get the license?"

"I told your boss I looked at the back of the car, but I don't remember the license plate. I was … I was kind of fucked up."

"Drunk?"

"No, that's not it. I liked that girl. She was nice to me. She just give me a goddamn twenty! I mean, I worked all day today, and barely got more than that."

"So you were upset."

"Yeah … and it … nothing."

"What?"

Ben sighed, and started to walk again, the young cop tagging along. "Ah, it kinda … took me back. It sounds stupid, but … shit, I could hear the damn Medevacs."

"Helicopters, you mean."

"Yeah. Now you think I'm nuts."

"No. Not at all. You served your country. You got a raw deal."

"All I did was my duty. I killed, you know? But it wasn't my idea. I did what they told me. Was I wrong? I got blood splashed on me, twice."

"Over there?"

"No, here. Some protesters splashed blood on me once and called me a baby killer."

"Dirty damn hippies."

That sounded funny to Ben, coming from somebody so young.

The cop asked, "What was the other time?"

Ben swallowed. "When I held that poor girl in my arms, after the car run her down."

They stopped again, simultaneously this time. The lapping waves and the muffled sound of the Beach Boys formed an eerie duet.

The young cop put a hand on Ben's shoulder. "*Did* you get a good look at the back of that car?"

"Yes, but … I don't remember…."

"We have techniques. Hypnotism can bring back details like that. Would you be willing to sit still for that?"

Ben thought about that. They were nearing the bright lights of the pier. "Sure. Why not? Anything to bring the killer of that nice girl to justice."

"You're okay in my book, Ben … listen … can I advance you a few bucks?"

"Of course, you can, but … look, let's do it out of sight, okay? I don't want anybody thinkin' I'm takin' a payoff from a cop."

Or from some homo, Ben thought, but didn't say it.

"Sure. No problem."

They walked under the pier. Sometimes there were people under there, but tonight the tide was too high, up to their ankles, and he and the young cop had the place to themselves. Above them the music and noise of the pier, the amusement park in particular, blared. Oldies music from his high school days—they played that a lot on the pier.

"Freddy Cannon," Ben said.

"What?" the young cop said. He was getting his billfold out, fishing out a twenty.

"That song—it's 'Palisades Park.' '62! I was in junior high. Freddy 'Boom Boom' Cannon."

"Sorry. Never heard of him."

"Hell, son—he never heard of you, either!"

Ben took the twenty from the young cop, and was stuffing it in his pocket when the kid sidled next to him, slipped an arm around his shoulder.

"I appreciate your help, soldier," the cop said.

"Hell, you're okay yourself, Ed."

Then the cop's arm slipped around Ben's neck and caught him in a grip so tight, the world turned instantly red. Knees buckling under him, Ben was held up only by the young cop's powerful grip, although Ben suddenly wasn't sure this was a cop at all....

The kid was saying, "I'm just doin' my duty, Pops. Not my idea ..."

Was that regret in the young voice?

Ben began to flail but his breath was choked off, there was no screaming, and he felt himself being thrust forward, splashing into the water, and the viselike arm around his neck was joined by a hand on the back of his skull as he was held under, face-first, water rushing into his mouth and nose, and he shut his eyes, choking, coughing, gagging, processes that only encouraged the salt water's terrible acrid invasive presence, inundating his lungs....

He thrashed as he died, as had so many fish on the pier above him, and the sound of his own gurgling death brought the Medevac blades churning into his consciousness one last time.

Part Three:

AFTER

Chapter Seven

"CALIFORNIA DREAMIN"
(The Mamas & the Papas, #1 Billboard, 1966)

The woman who exited the Kafer Building on Wilshire Boulevard in Beverly Hills—with her trim, yet amply top-heavy figure, *Baywatch* blond hair, pert nose, full lips and dewy skin—might have been thirty, even a gloriously well-preserved thirty-five years of age; but certainly not fifty-six.

Even in this town abundant with beauties—where waitresses who looked like the *Penthouse* Pet of the Year moonlighted as porn kittens, and the streets seemed littered with Midwestern D-cup beauty queens with C- high school averages, B-movie futures and A-list aspirations—this was a singularly striking woman.

Though she was fairly conservatively dressed in a blue linen suit, Joy Lerner's subtly hip-swinging gait caused men with younger women (younger than thirty-five, that is) to crane their necks as she strolled down the sidewalk and into the parking garage, where her company-owned Jaguar awaited. There she got into the sleek, silver car, to head home after another productive day in a fulfilling, fascinating job.

Life was good.

She'd been at the Kafer agency just over six months, and had loved every minute of it; just today she had had lunch with a Warner Brothers vice president of development, and tomorrow a honcho from Fox TV was on her menu.

And her performance excelled; her new and improved body made her feel more aggressive and powerful, yet at the same time more feminine. Best of all, her peers at the office seemed to marvel at such insight and maturity coming from one so relatively young. Not to mention that among the firm's older clients, *she* was the one they repeatedly asked for, because she connected so well with them.

And from the very first day, she'd been the boss's favorite.

C.W. Kafer himself, the "old man," that tall, slender graying fox with the James Coburn smile and the keenest advertising mind in America....

She had not met him until—at the senior vice president's behest—she made her first formal presentation in the boardroom. All the senior account officers were present, lining either side of the endless conference table, coldly smiling Yuppies and Yuppettes in suits any one of which had cost more than her monthly rent in Studio City.

None older than forty—except for the Gray Fox himself, who was a grandly well-preserved sixty-two.

At one end of the table, next to the VCR and TV on their stand (where she would display the tape she'd assembled), she had stood, making her pitch. Way down at the other end, smiling throughout, arms folded, had been Kafer.

Wearing an outlandishly expensive black Donna Karan jacket, white silk blouse and slim, short skirt—all of which she planned on returning to Saks the next day—Joy gazed down at the shiny table, where her presentation, neatly typed and organized, awaited; and in the table's mirror-finish, the face of a beautiful, young woman looked back, giving her such confidence that she didn't refer to the papers once.

Better, anyway, to look from the corner of her eye at the TV screen, so she could properly time her delivery … one misstep, one point made with the wrong image juxtaposed on the screen, and the effectiveness of her presentation—and the impression she wished to make—would fizzle like a cigarette dropped in a toilet bowl.

"Ladies … gentlemen," she said, in a clear, strong voice, looking down the line of unfriendly smiling faces. "As competition in the drug industry continues to intensify, and pressure mounts for those companies to build profits, a unique opportunity has come our way."

Everyone in the boardroom was aware of the recent decision by the Food and Drug Administration to loosen its restraints on television and radio commercials for prescription drugs.

"In the past, drugmakers never considered using celebrities to market to consumers, because the industry's sole focus was promoting their products to *doctors* who prescribe the medications. But we're soon going to see that change…. And the ad agency who can snag these pharmaceutical companies first will be the one to ride this new wave!"

She pushed PLAY on the VCR. Images tailored to her words popped onto the screen, as perfectly, as gracefully, as a well-rehearsed ballet.

"The use of celebrity product endorsement, of course, is as old as advertising—on the radio, Fibber McGee and Molly extolled the wonder of Reynolds Wax, and Jack Webb hailed the health benefits of smoking Chesterfield cigarettes…." She smiled, nodding at various faces around her, and added, "Though, of course, none of you are old enough to remember the Golden Age of Radio…."

Kafer, in his gently rumbling bass, interrupted. "Some of us are, Joy—that is, *one* of us is."

Everyone laughed, nervously—except Joy, who just returned the boss's knowing smile.

"Then television came along, and Uncle Miltie hawked Texaco Gasoline," she continued, "and the Old Redhead made drinking Lipton Tea *de rigueur.*"

Grainy images of Milton Berle and Arthur Godfrey popped perfectly into place behind her words.

"But the general public understood that these celebrities had to push these products because they were their sponsors. Alfred Hitchcock even made a joke out of it, kidding his sponsors, mercilessly—very hip for its day."

On the TV, Hitchcock's shadow filled his caricatured outline.

"Then came celebrities who were simply paid for their services…. But by this time the consumer had become wise, weary, jaded, and the only products that really did well were those the public believed were really used by the celebrity … like Jane Russell wearing the twenty-four-hour Playtex bra, and Bill Cosby liking Jell-O because he actually ate the damn stuff on the air."

Kafer's smile remained in place, but he was squinting—thoughtfully, nodding, almost imperceptibly.

She continued. "The answer to a successful drug ad campaign lies in celebrity testimonials: firsthand accounts by actors, politicians and sports figures who actually have the disease or affliction that the drug they're being paid to advertise is supposed to cure or contain. Bob Dole and Viagra have opened an important door—now we need a *Dawson's Creek* actress who has migraine headaches, and makes it to the set thanks to her medication, and a star athlete who needs his sinus medication to make it through the big game."

One after another, the faces of current celebrities popped on and she identified them with their ailment: "Diabetes … asthma … hay fever…."

"Herpes," someone interjected.

A smirking young account exec.

"Why not?" Kafer said, and bellowed a laugh. "I'd venture to say this boardroom has seen its share of sexually transmitted diseases!"

The rest of them picked up on Kafer's laughter, once they sensed it was genuine—like the minions around Al Capone's table roaring with insincere laughter, to avoid a blackjack or a bullet.

And then Kafer began to applaud.

As, of course, did the rest of the execs around the table.

Later, when she was called to Kafer's office—a wood-and-steel inner sanctum smaller than a Hilton ballroom—she sat with her handsome boss on a leather couch. His arms were folded and yet his gray Brooks Brothers suit did not wrinkle; he was supernaturally natty (to use a term she dare not speak aloud, except with irony).

"You hit a home run, little lady," he said. He was smoking a Cuban cigar and had not asked her permission to do so.

"Thank you, sir."

"Chuck. Call me Chuck—when we're alone."

Would that be often? she wondered. He did remind her of Henry ... that same elegant, worldly flair only an older man had.

"That's not going to be easy ... Chuck. I have too much respect for you—I've admired you, I've read about you—"

"Yes, I know—since you were a little girl. You know, if I were twenty years younger—or you were twenty years older ... well, to say more would be legally imprudent in these days of sexual harassment."

"You can say more ... if you like."

"I didn't bring you here to seduce you, Joy—or to be seduced. My wife, Linda—my fourth, actually—is thirty years old and has even nicer tits than you do. I ought to know—I paid for them."

She laughed. "Too bad."

"Not really. Better to take the romance out of the workplace; sex, too. I've been looking for someone like you for years."

"You have?"

"A young woman who understands today but still has a grasp of yesterday. The sense of history you displayed ... well, I was goddamn well and truly impressed. You keep at it, Joy. Just watch out for these fucking sharks."

"I will."

He blew a big fat Cuban smoke ring. "You see, Joy, I'm on the lookout for the right somebody to replace me—oh, I'm a good five to eight years away from that ... but I need the right man. Or woman. Today ... well, today you made my short list."

From time to time, Kafer would invite her into the office and talk shop—some mild flirtation accompanied it, but she knew he would be a mentor, not a lover. He made that clear. He loved his wife, or anyway was weary of divorces and the financial and emotional strain they carried with them.

And because she was the boss's favorite, she got her ass (as Kafer would say) well and truly kissed by everybody else. She was so popular with the Gray Fox, no one dared backstab. She had never encountered such a smooth and easy work situation, even at the height of her success at Ballard.

It was only after her workday was over that she felt something missing, as she made the drive each day in bumper-to-bumper traffic over Laurel Canyon and down into Studio City, where she lived in that minuscule rented bungalow. How ridiculous it seemed to have an expensive Jaguar sitting in the driveway; she often hid it away, in the sagging garage, so it wouldn't get stolen.

She had fixed up the ramshackle Hobbit house as best she could, with furnishings from Goodwill, and told herself it was charming. Many who saw it were nice enough to say, "Oh, how wonderful! Retro!" Even so, she could barely afford the rent after she sent X-Gen their monthly check.

After a typically spartan dinner of fresh fruit and/or salad, she would relax for a while, sometimes vegging out in front of her 19-inch portable TV (rabbit ears—no cable), other times heading back into Hollywood to browse the used-bookstores or secondhand boutiques, looking for castoffs from the wealthy. Appearances must be maintained.

On the weekends, she would drive to Santa Monica and spend the day at the beach, using the highest sunblock known to man, or would engage in other activities that were free—a play or concert was out of the question, unless it was an outdoor concert or college theatrical production. She splurged on a movie now and then (a matinee) sans popcorn and beverage (unless she smuggled in her own).

Actually, Joy didn't mind not having much money; it reminded her of when she was first on her own after college. She found herself surprisingly good at adjusting to this new life; with this new face and body, she was, after all, a new person—on the outside, anyway.

But when her old eyes, Joyce Lackey's eyes, looked back at her in the mirror in her tiny bathroom, she was reminded of the one thing she could never adjust to: growing old.

Once a month she paid a visit to X-Gen's health clinic near the Beverly Center, where a nurse drew her blood and gave her another month's supply of "vitamins"—clear capsules, taken twice daily, to keep her skin moist and wrinkle-free. The nameless drug was obviously experimental—this was no prescription, rather a sturdy silver-capped plastic medicine bottle refilled at the clinic itself—but she didn't let that worry her.

The pills worked. That was all she cared about. They were the Fountain of Youth. Life in a capsule.

Not that the wonder drug was without its drawbacks.

Dr. Green—a physician with a round face echoed by round-framed glasses, his skin as unwrinkled as a bisque baby's—had warned her that if she stopped taking the drug, her skin would react with a vengeance, quickly drying up.

"That's the only nasty little side effect of this medication," Green said with a bland, inappropriate smile.

"You mean, I'd be left looking *more* wrinkled than I did before?" she asked. Movie images of vampires hit by sunlight strobed through her mind's eye.

"In a word ... yes."

She would have liked a more in-depth explanation, and had joked, "Then how did you get this stuff past the FDA?"

"We didn't."

She knew Dr. Green wasn't exaggerating about the risks of ending the medication. Once, she had forgotten to take a capsule in the morning and went merrily off to work. By the time she got home in the evening she could see a marked difference in the texture of her skin. After that, she carried the pills in her purse.

While Dr. Green's bedside manner may have been clipped, he did show an interest in, and even concern about, her welfare. When, on the regular visits, the nurse would finish Joy's blood test, Dr. Green—looking too young to be out of medical school—would come in and ask Joy if she was having any personal problems. Because of his tender age, she felt skeptical about discussing anything of that nature with him; and, anyway, would she want that kind of thing recorded in her folder?

But the third time she saw him, and he asked that same question, she blurted, "Yes."

His eyes narrowed to slits behind the glasses and he leaned toward her, stethoscope dangling from his neck, and said, "Tell me."

"Well ... I'm lonely."

A smile appeared in the bland balloon of his face, not making a single dimple or crease. "Is that all?"

She nodded.

He shrugged. "So date, already. You're an attractive woman. We've seen to that."

"I'm afraid."

"Of what?"

"That, well, shit—you know ... that they'll find out how old I *really* am."

He placed a hand on her shoulder, gently; something like compassion appeared in the doctor's eyes. "Just be careful. And don't get too attached to any one man. Remember the terms of your contract."

There it was again…. Terms of that damn contract; the only contract this businesswoman had ever signed before reading it in detail. Which made her furious with herself.

What exactly would they do, if she broke the contract? Sue her for everything she had? She didn't *have* anything! Take away her job?

Now, that *would* hurt.

So, she buried her fury….

Over the next few months, Joy began to date—men in their twenties and thirties she'd met through work, or through friends or in some of the more upscale bars. They were all decent enough guys, and with her looks she was able to land the most handsome among them, and perhaps this was why they were so self-centered and cold; she hated that in people. But it was useful, in a way, because it made becoming attached to any of them no problem.

All they seemed to want was sex. Which was all right with her. She enjoyed making love, especially with her new body. And these younger men, who were much more uninhibited and experimental than those of her generation, took her to new heights … though some of them wanted her to do things that she didn't feel comfortable doing (especially on the first date). But she supposed if a man was going to bring her to multiple orgasm with his tongue, the least she could do was learn to swallow his indignities.

Still, where was the romance of her youth? Even one-night stands used to have a pretense of love, fleeting love perhaps, but love. After the sex she felt lonelier than before.

Then she met someone who would change that.

His name was Jack Powers, which was the perfect name, she thought, for what he was: a private investigator. He ran the one-man L.A. office of a Denver firm that Kafer kept under retainer for running background checks on employees, clients and spokespersons.

He was not at all her idea of what a detective should look like—neither the brawny Magnum or Rockford type, nor the sloppy Columbo or Sipowicz variety. Powers fit neither Hollywood mold.

The fortyish man seated at the round conference table in her office, sipping black coffee out of a china cup, was average in all respects—five eleven, medium build, pleasant features, brown suit and white shirt and brown-and-gold tie—and could have been an accountant or insurance salesman. Her first impression was that if they passed on the street tomorrow, she would fail to recognize him.

Once she'd spent a little time with him, however, she realized there *was* something memorable about his manner, which exuded intelligence, and his slightly tousled dark brown hair, along with the hint of a playful smile in the corners of his mouth, made her think he was completely confident about himself.

And his eyes were a deep, deep brown—gentle and knowing, at once, indicating a compassion that seemed unlikely in a career cop.

"You understand," she said, pouring cream into her coffee, "why our corporate clients are becoming quite skittish about using the entertainment world anymore to promote their products."

"When you spend years and a large fortune polishing your image," he said dryly, "you don't appreciate it getting tarnished by some young drug addict."

"Exactly." She stirred her coffee. "But the beautiful people in the entertainment business are still the fastest way to get the attention of every generation, young or old."

"Pharmaceutical companies skew mostly older, don't they?"

"Not anymore—not when you're tackling allergies, migraine and the like."

Jack had a white legal pad and a Cross pen in front of him, but he wasn't taking any notes. He leaned back casually in his chair. "Dinah Shore selling Chevrolet … Jimmy Stewart slurping

Campbell's soup … it was a lot simpler back then. Now everybody seems to have a skeleton in their closet."

"They probably always did," Joy smirked. "But with the media as hungry for blood and instant scandals as they are, the landscape is very different. It might work for Versace to use Courtney Love in their ads, but can you imagine her associated with General Mills?"

"Not unless it's crack-flavored Rice Krispies."

She laughed. "You seem a little young to remember Dinah Shore hocking cars…."

"What, and a little old to make a crack crack? Well, I used to be an LAPD cop—and got around. As for Dinah, I took advertising in college, but decided it was too boring. No offense."

She smiled one-sidedly. "None taken. It can sometimes be incredibly boring."

The playful smile cropped up again. "Like now?"

"No, actually, I'm managing to stay pretty well awake."

"Nice to hear. Anyway, Chuck told me you had an unusual sense of history for one so young."

"You're a friend of Mr. Kafer's?"

"Friendly acquaintance. He's a hell of a guy."

"Well, I'm just glad you think thirty-five is young. In this town, that's ancient."

They fell silent.

"What were we talking about?" she asked.

He laughed. "I don't remember. But I assume you want some backgrounds checked."

She nodded, and passed him a folder; she had an identical one in front of her, which contained a list of entertainers and sports figures. "These stars are the ones being considered," she said, "roughly in order of desirability to our clients."

The brown eyes narrowed as Jack studied the names with corresponding numbers. "Well, I can tell you right now," he said, "you can scratch number two … unless your client is Betty Ford."

"Really." It wasn't a question. She drew a black line through the name, thinking it was too bad that she wouldn't get to work with the popular nighttime soap star ... but at least he wasn't gay.

Speaking of which....

Jack was saying, "And number five ... forget her. Unless it wouldn't bother your client if she pulled an Ellen."

"As long as she's in the closet, no, we wouldn't want to risk it—the gayness isn't the issue, really, it's honesty." Another black line.

"Number six, also gay."

A male. She crossed him out, shaking her head; those bitches in the bathroom back at Thomas Advertising had been right: all the really cute ones ...

"Surely you know about number eight?"

Joy looked at him warily. "What about her?"

He shrugged. "She was featured in *People* magazine last year, telling the world her father raped her."

"Huh. Must have missed that issue. Still, for certain products ..." Joy sighed. "Hey, this isn't going to be a picnic, is it?"

"Sure it is—heavy on the ants."

She tapped her pen against the table. "You know, if they have a background or affliction that ties into the drug being advertised, that's a plus ..."

"Each has gotta be an exact fit, though. Anyway, off the top of my head, without really goin' to work, those are the ones on the list I can tell you about, right now. So? Want me to start diggin'?"

She nodded. "Get out your Sam Spade."

"Ha! You do know your history."

A muffled ring announced Jack's pager summoning him.

"You can use the phone in here," she said, gesturing to her desk.

Then, to give him some privacy, she exited her office and went over to Susan, her secretary, positioned just outside her door, working at the computer on some letters Joy had dictated.

Joy had a nice rapport with Susan, who was a petite, pretty brunette of perhaps thirty-five, prone to colorful print dresses and funky plastic jewelry. Maybe the woman was a little high-strung and nervous, but the photos on the secretary's desk of two beguiling little boys and an almost-too-handsome husband went a long way toward explaining that.

Anyway, flighty or not, Susan was a hard, highly skilled (and highly paid) worker—an executive on Joy's level required, and received, only the best in the secretarial field.

Approaching Susan—who was hunched diligently over the computer, almost like an air traffic controller in her dictation headphones—Joy smiled at this typical display of dedication; but her smile faded and turned to a frown when she noticed that the secretary was typing with some difficulty.

Joy put one hand on her shoulder, and the woman jumped.

Joy jumped, too.

"Oh, Ms. Lerner!" Susan said. "I didn't mean to startle you!"

"I didn't mean to startle you, either, Susan," Joy said with a gentle laugh.

Susan removed the dictation headphone. "That's all right, I just didn't hear you. Is there something …?"

"I'm going to walk down to the lobby with Mr. Powers."

"Lucky you."

"He isn't hard to like, is he? Anyway, I'll be back in a few minutes."

"All right."

"Susan?"

"Yes?" The woman looked up with big light blue eyes, her expression almost childlike.

"I couldn't help but notice your hands. I hope you're not getting carpal tunnel syndrome. Everyone will think I'm working you too hard."

Susan smiled one-sidedly. "You're not—you're the best. They're just a little stiff … you know, the weather."

"It has been awfully humid. I've been using chamomile, an herbal—free sample from a client? It works as an analgesic. I have some in my purse … why don't you take it?"

"Thanks!"

Jack appeared at Joy's side.

"Thanks for the use of the phone," he said. "I made a few international calls—hope you don't mind."

Joy grinned, enjoying his deadpan humor. "I bet some people don't know when you're kidding."

"That's right. They're called idiots."

And when he turned to leave, saying, "I'll be in touch when I got something," she blurted, "I'll see you out."

He shot her that playful smile. "You think a detective can't find his own way out? Well, you're right."

Susan, rubbing her wrist, said, "Oh, Ms. Lerner! Those herbal pills?"

"In my office," she said. "Help yourself."

Joy and Jack were the only ones in the elevator on the ride down, and when the loud Muzak began to play an absurdly awful version of "Purple Haze," they both broke out laughing.

"Jimi Hendrix is probably rolling over in his grave," she said.

"It's probably just the drugs kicking in," he replied wryly. "But this isn't as bad as what I heard earlier, coming up."

"What was that?"

"Strings and flutes having at 'In a Gadda Da Vida.'"

In the marble, deco lobby, they lingered; she felt like a teenager, grabbing a few precious moments with a new boyfriend in the school hallway between classes.

"Listen … I don't mean to be forward," he said, suddenly schoolboy awkward himself, "and I know the company policy against fraternization…."

"But you're not a company employee. This would be different."

"What would?"

"You asking me out, sometime."

And she stepped onto the elevator, smiling just a little as the doors closed on Jack standing there, half-grinning, rubbing his chin.

On the ride back up, serenaded by an obscenely soft-rock instrumental version of "Revolution" by the Beatles, her smile wilted, and it wasn't just the terrible music.

If his specialty was background checks, she wondered, what was there to prevent him from investigating her?

Chapter Eight

"(LISTEN) DO YOU WANT TO KNOW A SECRET?"
(The Beatles, #2 Billboard, 1964)

By noon the next day, the California sun had finally burned away the morning fog. Light streamed in the windows, turning everything it touched white.

Joy had spent the morning at her spacious desk in her modern, black-and-white, well-appointed office, working on the ad campaign for one of her clients, a pharmaceutical conglomerate moving into the herbal supplement market. But she couldn't seem to get her mind to focus on echinacea or kava or even Saint-John's-wort.

That brown-haired, quietly sarcastic private investigator kept insinuating himself into her thoughts, turning them into daydreams....

"Earth to Joy," a female voice said.

Susan, standing in the doorway, was wearing her usual bright print dress, a sleeveless affair as perky as she was.

"You look like you could use lunch," Susan said, brown hair bouncing off her shoulders. "I'm buying."

The offer blindsided Joy, who had gone out for lunch with Susan only a few times—Secretary's Day and the woman's birthday—and, though she liked Susan, Joy didn't particularly want noon get-togethers to become a habit. Habits had a way of becoming hard to break.

It wasn't that Joy didn't want to spend her lunch hour with Susan; it was that she didn't want to spend it with *anybody*. This was her private time, time to recharge herself by strolling the streets, eating an apple, not stuck in a noisy restaurant ordering food she couldn't consume, or even afford (unless she could expense-account it on a client).

She was comfortable being Joy Lerner—she even relished being Joy Lerner; but there were times when she liked to be herself, and not play the role.

"We could split a shrimp salad," Susan coaxed.

That *did* sound good…. Joy hadn't splurged like that in some while.

Screw the apple.

"You are such a bad influence," Joy said, reaching for her purse.

Eyes bright with her boss's acceptance, Susan said, "I know just the best place."

They walked along Wilshire, which was bustling with noon traffic, and, like life, going by much too fast. A pleasant breeze, with a westerly hint of ocean, tousled their hair and teased the hems of their dresses.

Susan led her boss to a small café on a side street, a recently opened place Joy wasn't familiar with, a typical, vaguely French indoor-outdoor thing; the breeze was just insistent enough that they opted to dine inside.

In the back corner at a small linen-covered table for two—the last available in the noon rush—Susan ordered the shrimp salad from a billy-goat-bearded Sean Penn wannabe, who gave them a disdainful look before he left, when Joy added, "And an extra plate" (as if *he* wouldn't know what it meant to save a few dollars).

Joy leaned forward, putting her elbows on the table. "This is really a nice spot," she said, in an attempt to get the conversation going. But what she really thought was that the restaurant was so mundane, it would be lucky to last the week.

Susan, sitting straight in her chair, like a child reprimanded by a mother, nodded as she glanced at the other tables, occupied mostly by business and professional types.

Susan's perkiness had evaporated. What the hell was this? The woman had seemed so anxious for Joy to come for lunch....

Joy shifted in her seat, and tried again. "How are your boys?" she ventured.

"Pardon?"

"Your boys. Your sons—Robbie and Clint, right?"

"Right, right! Oh ... they're just fine."

All of a sudden getting a sentence out of Susan was like pulling a tooth—an alligator's tooth—with pliers. What was the matter with the woman? The secretary's cheerful chattiness on the walk to the restaurant had disappeared, replaced by a sullen nervousness that made Joy wish she hadn't accepted her subordinate's invitation. That shrimp salad had better be goddamn good....

"And your husband?" Joy asked. "Sorry ... I've forgotten his name."

"Jerome. Great. He's great."

"Uh-huh. What line of work did you say he's in?"

"Construction. He's in construction."

"Well, that's certainly a booming business right now," Joy replied. "Tear something down, build something up, tear something down, build something up. That's L.A. for you."

Joy had never heard herself spout such inanities.

Thankfully, the waiter brought their salad, along with the extra plate, which he set down with a glower and a clunk in front of Joy. Then Susan divided the meal, and the two women began to eat in silence.

Looking over her shrimp-speared fork, Joy studied Susan, who was listlessly pushing lettuce around her plate, and concluded that the woman wanted something from her—a raise, some time off, a recommendation for a promotion, perhaps—but had lost her nerve to ask.

The notion irritated Joy. Why hadn't Susan used company time instead of wasting this precious lunch hour?

Putting her fork down, sitting back, Joy asked somewhat pointedly, "Susan—what is it?"

"Pardon?" Susan's eyes were on her plate.

"What do you want? And don't say extra dressing for your salad."

The secretary looked up, her dark eyes empty—then suddenly they were full: brimming with tears.

And Susan was sobbing into her napkin, as Joy's irritation faded and compassion kicked in.

"Susan, dear," Joy whispered, leaning forward, repeating again, patting the woman's hand. "What is bothering you?"

But Joy—who prided herself on reading people, as it was part of her business—already had a good idea. Did the poor woman really think she could keep that hunk of a husband just by dressing like a go-go girl? A woman should never marry a man who looks like a male model; it was asking for trouble—if they're not gay, they're banging the babysitter....

"Is it Jerome?" Joy asked.

Susan wailed into her napkin.

"It is Jerome, isn't it?" Joy frowned. "Haven't you learned yet that all men are bastards?"

Joy was really starting to hate that cheat Jerome, a man she had never met.

But, surprisingly, Susan shook her head, arcs of brown hair sweeping across flushed cheeks. "No! It's not ... him," she replied.

So what else *could* it be? Joy waited patiently while Susan dabbed at her eyes with the napkin.

Finally, Susan—glancing around the nearby tables, making sure other patrons weren't listening—whispered, "I have rheumatoid arthritis."

By the seriousness of her voice, Joy would have thought the woman had said cancer.

"Is that all?" Joy responded, laughing a little. "Millions of people have arthritis. I'm even stiff in the morning until I get going."

"You don't understand," Susan continued whispering, "my father *died* of it."

Was that possible, Joy wondered, in this day and age? "Surely there's some kind of medication you can be taking."

"There is. It can slow the process, but it won't stop the disease. And the shots are very expensive."

"You've seen a specialist, of course."

Susan shook her head.

"Why not?" Joy sighed. "If something's wrong, you see a doctor, you get the best care possible. Hell, Kafer's insurance will pay for it."

Tears returned to Susan's eyes, and desperation to her voice. "But then everyone will know and I want to keep working...."

"Well, you can ... you can...."

"If you could just be patient with me, with my work..." The woman was pleading.

"I will ... I will..."

"... And cover for me."

Cover for her? Now wait just a damn minute. Joy could certainly be patient with Susan's disability and slowness of work ... but "cover"? Cover, exactly how? As much as Joy liked the woman, as much as she sympathized with her illness, Susan had just crossed a line....

"You were so sweet, yesterday," Susan was saying. "Sharing your herbals with me ..."

"A little over-the-counter remedy ain't gonna cut it," Joy told her sternly. "You *must* see your doctor."

Susan swallowed, not replying; then she reached in her purse and withdrew something, fingers closed over whatever-it-was; then she gazed gloomily down at her tight hand, resting it on the table.

Weird.

"If that's my herbals," Joy said, "keep them."

"It's ... not your herbals."

"Susan," Joy said firmly. "If you don't have a doctor, you can find one easily enough—"

The secretary continued to stare at her hand, which formed a tight, rather fat fist on the table, and Joy's eyes traveled to it.

And slowly, so only Joy could see, Susan opened her hand, revealing something in its palm. Something that made Joy gasp.

A prescription bottle with a silver cap.

"Oh, shit," Joy murmured.

Then Susan's fingers closed around the bottle and she withdrew her hand from the table, slipping the pills back in her purse.

"Now you know who my doctor is," Susan said.

Swallowing, shaking her head, Joy began, "How did you—?"

"Find out you're Dr. Green's patient, too? When I got in your purse for the herbals, yesterday."

Ever since that day Joy had forgotten to take her pill, she'd been carrying them with her. In future she'd have to be more discreet.

"But ... but you have a family," Joy said, thoughts tumbling. "Those photos on your desk ..."

Susan smirked. "They came with the frames."

"No Jerome? No Robbie? No Clint?"

Susan laughed, once. "I'm glad you can remember their names, 'cause I have trouble, sometimes."

Someday Joy might laugh at that, too; right now she didn't seem to have the capacity.

"Look, Susan," she began, "you know I'll do whatever I can for you. But you really should tell Dr. Green and get on *some* kind of medication—even if just to ease the pain."

"No."

Joy leaned forward. "For Christ's sake why not? I would."

"He'll … he'll put me out to pasture."

And the woman blubbered into her hanky again.

Susan's self-pitying stubbornness was exasperating. How could Joy help her secretary, if this fucking woman wouldn't help herself?

"Don't you see, Joy?" Susan asked, dabbing with the hanky. "I *have* to work. I don't have enough built up in matching funds with X-Gen to retire on."

"How long have you been … *you*?"

"A little over a year."

Joy gestured dismissively. "But Kafer's insurance …"

"I'd have to report to somebody other than Dr. Green. What if Kafer's insurance-company doctors discover that a fifty-seven-year-old woman has been living in a thirty-four-year-old's body? They may not pay. Maybe I'll even be charged with some kind of fraud. Maybe it'd risk exposure for X-Gen, and … who knows what *they* might do?"

"Don't be ridiculous," Joy replied. "X-Gen knows the risks in recycling the likes of us. What do you think they'd do? Toss us on a trash heap?"

Susan stared at her, then, finally, said, "Maybe."

"That's crazy. No, it's silly." Still, Joy knew Susan just might have a point: Everybody in the program could have their covers threatened if any one of them were found out.

The Sean Penn waiter brought the check, interrupting their conversation.

Now he was charming. "It's been a pleasure serving you, ladies."

"Fuck off," Joy said, and as he wheeled away wide-eyed, she leaned in and took Susan's hand, asking conspiratorially, "How many are there of us?"

Susan winced, not understanding at first, then asked, "At Kafer, you mean?"

Joy nodded.

"I don't know. You're the only other one I'm sure of. You know, I don't exactly go around rifling purses...."

"What's your guess?"

Susan shrugged. "Quite a few, I think. More than just us, anyway."

"Humm. Well, it does make sense that if Kafer was satisfied with the results of a headhunting outfit like X-Gen, they'd keep using 'em."

Then she released Susan's hand and drew away, saying, "And if there are others ... of us ... at Kafer, I don't want to know who they are. I don't even want to know about *you*, understand? I'll go crazy wondering if everyone I meet is another ... bride of Frankenstein."

And Joy dug in her purse for loose bills.

"I said I'd pay," Susan said.

"No—Dutch treat, Susan. We're each of us on our own, understand?"

Back on the street, in front of the restaurant, the two women paused as Joy put on some lipstick, using her reflection in the storefront glass. Susan was watching luxury cars and limousines glide by, their windows tinted—movie stars or drug dealers or both could be within, advertising executives or gun runners or movie producers.

"You know," the secretary commented, "this town is the perfect place for us."

Joy turned to look at her.

"L.A., I mean," Susan explained. "Hollywood-land—where everything is one big fake-out."

"It's a one-industry town," Joy admitted, "and that industry is illusion."

"That's right—and nothing is what it seems."

Back in her well-appointed office at her big desk, Joy was again having trouble concentrating on her work; but this time it wasn't the hunky P.I.: Now her thoughts, her troubled thoughts, were of her luncheon conversation with Susan.

Maybe she should intercede on behalf of her secretary and enlist the help of Dr. Green; after all, Green had access to powerful new drugs—like the one both she and Susan were taking—untested but effective drugs not yet on the market. Perhaps he knew of something that could stop or even reverse Susan's condition.

She owed that much to Susan, and to herself, and, really, to X-Gen, too, the benefactor of both their new lives.

Joy was considering her plan when Susan—suddenly a businesslike zombie—announced that Jack was in the outer office to see her.

Springing from her chair, Joy tripped over her purse on the floor by her feet, regained her footing, shaking her head, silently admonishing herself for acting like a lovesick schoolgirl. Then she smoothed her skirt and walked casually out to meet him.

Jack, his back to her as he chatted with Susan, turned as Joy greeted him. He wore a tan suede sport jacket and a yellow sport shirt and darker tan slacks, casual yet somehow very professional—maybe it was the small brown attaché he carried like an oversize purse.

"I was just in the neighborhood," he said, with a goofy little smile, "and was gonna see if your secretary would make an appointment for me."

"I'm not the dentist," Joy said, faintly teasing, arms folded.

"I can come back. I mean, if this is a bad time."

"It's a good time," Joy said with a smile. She instructed Susan to hold her calls, and would she mind bringing them some fresh coffee, and scones, if any were left?

Susan nodded.

As Joy closed the door, Jack turned and gestured toward it. "Is she all right? Your secretary, I mean?"

"Why?"

"I don't know—she's always been so friendly. I don't wanna get her ass in a sling or anything, but she seemed distracted, almost … rude."

"Do I have to explain the facts of life to you, Jack? Women do have certain moods tied to biology.…"

"Oh. Well. Most women I know seem to be retaining water thirty days a month. I'm always lookin' for that one 'normal' day between post-menstrual and pre-."

She grinned at him, shaking her head. "You do have your nerve, Jack Powers."

"You know, I love that."

"What?"

"When a woman calls me by both names. It's a cross between having your mom bawl you out, and the way they talk in some old movie … some movie before your time."

"I have a sense of history, remember? Please sit." She gestured to the round table in the corner.

She took her seat, arranging herself rather primly; but Jack made himself at home, crossing a leg, ankle on a knee, running a hand through his thick brown hair—he didn't use "product," like the younger guys.

"You're not going to be happy," he told her, placing his brown attaché on the table.

"Really."

"I haven't done the athletes yet, but the actors …" He tapped the attaché with one finger. "Only one came out clean on the rest of that list you gave me."

Joy groaned, then asked, "Who?"

He gave her the name, adding, "Hottest gal in Hollywood … ten years ago."

Joy grunted a small, humorless laugh. "And she was my last choice."

"Next time give me a bigger list."

"I'm already working on that … but damn. I didn't see this coming. You were right—finding actors in Hollywood without a past isn't going to be easy."

"Worse than politicians, though they got a lot in common, both bein' professional liars."

"Have you always been this cynical?"

"No. It didn't start till that doctor slapped me on my baby ass."

Shaking her head, laughing, she said, "Are you *sure* about your research? I mean, can you really be that thorough overnight?"

"I wouldn't touch that line with a rake." He gave her a comically reproachful look. "You want to see chapter and verse, lady? Did I ask to see your college diploma or your portfolio or anything? You're good at what you do, I'm good at what I do. Have a little faith."

She gave him a mock-offended look, touching her chest. "Oh I'm sorry … sorry to have questioned your work, impugned your integrity, when we've established that Hollywood is a place where you're safe to take everything on face value. Please accept my apology!"

He grinned, shrugged. "Yeah, sure."

Susan entered with a silver tray. "No scones left," the secretary informed her boss, placing the tray with thermos pot and cups on the table. Then a touch of perkiness returned to the secretary's voice as she added, "They're just too good."

"Figures," Joy said.

"I can run out and get some," Susan offered.

Joy glanced at Jack, who said, "Not on my account. I won't be here that long. I don't even like scones."

"As in real men don't eat scones."

"Not real American men."

"Thanks, anyway, Susan," Joy said, and the boss and secretary traded small smiles of truce.

Joy poured the aromatic coffee from the pot into a cup, which she handed to Jack. "Well, get back to me on those athletes as soon as possible," she said. "I mean, I can't exactly go to the client with a single name … and I'll keep going on that second list."

He took a sip of the steaming liquid, then said, "Well … I do have a stupid idea, if you'd like to hear it."

"Hummm … I had a hunch you might have a stupid idea or two. Please—fire away."

He set his cup down, shrugged. "We could work together."

"Checking backgrounds?"

"No, making the list. I could head you off on the obvious 'no' choices."

"Well, I see … that does make a certain amount of sense…."

With a shrug, he said, "Just thinking, it could save you some time, is all."

He was right about that. "When could you start?" she asked.

"I was thinking, dinner. Or supper. Whatever the hell they call it out here."

"Dinner? Supper?"

"You *do* eat, don't you?"

"Yes." A little.

"You know Le Perroquet on Sunset?"

"Yes."

"Meet me there at six. That early, seating shouldn't be a problem."

He gave her a little wink, picked up his attaché and sauntered out. Cocky bastard.

Cute cocky bastard …

She poured herself another cup of coffee, stirring in extra cream, and wondered just how much work the two of them could do—if they really put their heads together.

Chapter Nine

"YOU CAN'T HURRY LOVE"
(The Supremes, #1 Billboard, 1966)

A little after six that evening, Susan drove Joy to Le Perroquet on Sunset.

"You sure you don't mind?" Joy had asked her secretary, who was seated at the computer. "Easier to find a virgin walking Hollywood Boulevard than a parking space on the Strip, y'know."

"True … but then there's always valet parking," Susan said, with a roll of her eyes, "for the independently wealthy."

Despite the strained way their luncheon had ended, the two women now shared a secret—they knew the hidden life they were both living, including the financial hardships. They were sisters under the skin—under the plastic-surgery-snugged skin, that is.

So it was no surprise to Joy that Susan—not privileged with a company car, like her Jag—drove a little red Hyundai.

"You really don't mind, then?" Joy asked. "That way, I could just leave my car here and catch a ride back with Jack."

"No, no, it's right on my way home."

In the cramped little car, they chatted, Susan as perky as ever, exchanging the latest in office gossip, with no mention of X-Gen.

Jack was waiting in front of the restaurant as the two women pulled up.

"Try not to get pregnant," Susan said to Joy with a knowing little smile.

"I just may be able to manage that."

"Remember—on Monday, I want details!"

"You wish," Joy said, and the women exchanged warm glances, as Jack opened the door for Joy and took her hand, helping her out.

"Have her home by ten!" Susan called out to Jack.

"Whose home?" Jack asked.

"That's between the two of you."

Susan laughed, and drove off.

"*She's* in a better mood," Jack said, watching the little red car disappear down the strip in a neon-kissed dusk.

"I think she has a crush on you."

He shrugged. "Everybody does."

As Joy entered the posh restaurant through an etched-glass door held open by Jack, boisterous laughter and pounding dance music assaulted her senses from the open, rather expansive bar, which included a dance floor. The bar was wall-to-wall with twenty- and thirty-something patrons, the restaurant filled to capacity, too.

"So much for beating the crowd," he said, taking her elbow.

After checking with the maitre d', Jack returned and told her the wait for a table would be an hour. "Let's have a drink in the bar," he suggested.

Joy didn't want a drink, however; with her stapled tummy, she could easily fill up on a glass of wine and tempting bar nuts, then have no room left for any of the rich, French meal. Also, she wasn't sure how long she could take the frantic music and the shoulder-to-shoulder company. Couldn't they play something more soothing than this techno-crap—whatever happened to romantic background music, like the Association, or the Carpenters?

But instead, she smiled and said, "A drink sounds fine!"

They squeezed through the crowd of meat-market singles and cheating spouses, commandeering two stools at the sleek deco bar, sandwiched between a tall, thin woman with a diamond in her nose and short hair as shiny and black as wet tar, and a man in an Armani suit whose sniffling signaled something more lingering than a summer cold.

Everyone in the bar was already high on one thing or another, and having far too much fun for Joy's liking. It bummed her out—she could never catch up to their level of gaiety, so why bother trying? She may have looked just as young, and just as good—*better*—than the rest of them, but she simply didn't have the energy anymore, not after a hard day's work.

Joy gazed into the mirror that lined the wall behind the bar, still shocked to see herself looking so young and fresh. Inside her head she was still the old Joyce; could she ever banish that ancient image?

"What do you want to drink?" Jack asked, raising his voice above the din, and the THUMP-THUMP-THUMP of the bass line.

"Red wine," Joy shouted back.

Jack ordered her a glass of burgundy and a gin and tonic for himself from a blond Tom Cruise in tux shirt and vest, who clearly had acting experience the way he kept his cool in the midst of the madhouse about him.

Joy leaned her head toward Jack. "Popular place," she said. "Been here before?"

"I heard good things about it." He gave her a one-sided smile. "So much for my great background checks."

The bartender delivered their drinks. "Run a tab?" he asked.

"Pay as we go," Jack said, and did.

Then Jack downed his gin and tonic, quick, like medicine. "It's been a long day," he pronounced.

Joy nodded in agreement, but took only a dainty sip of her wine.

And as she did, the tar-headed woman shrieked brittle laughter at some unknown witticism, poking a bony elbow in Joy's back, spilling the red wine on the front of Joy's cream-colored silk blouse.

Before Joy could curse or think of the dry-cleaning bill, or do anything other than just be astonished, Jack grabbed a bottle of club soda from the bar's sideboard, poured the clear liquid on his napkin and began dabbing at the scarlet spot on her right breast.

He repeated the process until the stain was completely gone, his eyes focused only on what he was doing, oblivious to the calamity around him, his only agenda being to get the damn spot out….

And in that moment, for his simple act of chivalry, Joy fell in love with him.

"Is that better?" he asked.

His hand was poised at her breast, the damp napkin at the ready.

"I don't remember telling you to stop," she said.

He grinned, and she grabbed his other hand and pulled him off his stool and through the noisy crowd into the cool twilight, as other cars pulled up in front of the busy restaurant.

"Take me someplace quieter," she said, relieved not to have to shout anymore.

"We can wait out here and not have to miss the food. They say it's really something … you *do* like French food?"

"I don't like French anything," she said, then qualified her statement with. "Except clothes, and perfume … and kissing."

He smiled sheepishly. "It was pretty bad in there, even for a Friday night. Where would you like to go?"

Joy thought for a second—and that was all it took. "Cantor's," she said.

Jack raised his eyebrows. "If it's deli you want, Jerry's is a nicer joint."

"But not better food. And it'll be more crowded."

"Okay, you're the boss. Cantor's it is."

The valet brought Jack's car around, a late-model dark-green Lincoln.

A short time later, they easily found a parking space in the open lot next to Cantor's. They got out and made their way along the beverage- and gum-stained sidewalk that paved an appropriate way to the venerable establishment.

Inside, assorted food smells delighted Joy's senses as they passed by the long glass deli counter filled with breads, meats, salads, pastries and other delicacies, many of which a gentile girl like her didn't recognize. An elderly gentleman in an inexpensive but dapper black suit perfect for a mortician led them to a cozy booth on the periphery of the large dining room.

The restaurant was bustling, but pleasantly so, the sounds of clattering dishes mixed with the murmur of other patrons—locals who refused to abandon the place for a more trendy spot; no movie stars here, at least not young ones—reminding Joy of the comforts of her favorite Chicago eateries, like Gino's East, or the Berghoff, or even the late-lamented George Diamond's.

She slid into the cracked and worn red-leather booth as Jack took his place across from her.

He looked around at decor that hadn't changed in an eon, and said, "I think the last time I was here, they'd just remodeled—that must've been sometime in the Kennedy Administration."

"Isn't it just the best?" Joy asked, elated with her choice. "Talk about a sense of history … I'll bet more power deals went down here than anywhere else in town."

"Maybe. Remind me to take you to Musso and Frank's sometime."

A portly matron in a white cotton blouse and black skirt and with more miles on her than a '57 Chevy rolled over to take their order. She had short, thinning hennaed hair, sketched-on eyebrows and clown-bright lipstick. Poised with pencil to order-pad, she wore the stern expression of a mother who might admonish a child for not eating his vegetable.

"What can I get you?" she asked, words clipped. They may well have been her millionth customers.

It would have taken a week to read the extensive menu, with all its orders, half-orders, and combination orders. Could they really have all that stuff back in one kitchen? But Joy already knew what she wanted.

"Matzo ball soup, please," she told the waitress.

The woman grunted her approval, which—when Joy said nothing further—quickly turned to disapproval. "That's all?" she asked Joy, frowning.

"Regular coffee with cream," Joy said, then added to appease the woman, "and maybe some dessert later."

The waitress shifted her stare to Jack.

"I'll have the same," he said, "but add half a Reuben on rye and potato salad."

Mother smiled, pleased that her son was eating so well, then left to turn in their order.

Joy settled back in the comfy booth. "Where did you grow up?"

"Midwest."

"Me, too! Where?"

"Omaha. How about you, Joy?"

"Chicago, mostly." Thankfully the background story X-Gen had given her was consistent with her own past—made it easier to convincingly fake. On the other hand, she realized she was sitting across from somebody whose specialty was checking out people's stories....

But Jack didn't look like much of a threat right now, as he picked out a dill pickle from a selection in the little silver bowl on the table, and bit crunchingly into it. The dill looked so good and sounded so crisp ... but Joy was saving what little room she had for the soup.

"You like it out here, in Phonywood?" Jack asked, chewing the dill.

"Very much. You suppose I fit in?"

"You don't seem phony to me, Joy. And believe me, I can smell it. You do look like you belong—California girl if I ever saw one."

"Maybe so, but sometimes I miss the cold and snow."

He gestured with half a dill. "Hey, I've been in Chicago in the winter, and you're crazy. The one thing I don't miss about Omaha is the snow and the cold."

"That's two things."

"Oh, so you're gonna drive me nuts with details, huh?"

The waitress brought their food. The half-sandwich in front of Jack was no thicker than Stephen King's *The Stand* (unabridged). Joy took a sip of the steaming aromatic soup, which was delicious.

"How did you come to be in your line of work?" Joy asked, dabbing her chin with her napkin.

Jack put down his half-Reuben. "I spent a few years as a detective on the LAPD," he told her. "Until my marriage went south."

"Oh. I'm sorry...."

"Don't be. It was an amicable split ... casualty of my line of work." He paused and added with a shrug, "How can you have a relationship with someone who's never around, and on the rare occasions when he is, brings his work the hell home with him?"

Joy nodded. It was an old, old story—and it reminded her of her own sad sorry tale, and the relationships that had never fully blossomed, and why she'd never married.

"So I decided to take my expertise into the private sector, and found a good job with Mile High Investigations—I'm a partner, you know."

Joy put down her spoon. "When I first started in advertising, I overheard two men in pinstriped suits discussing what they felt was important in life. One of them said, 'First comes work, then comes love, then comes food.' The other man agreed. I remember thinking that the order was skewed. But as time went on, I learned they were right."

"Pretty girl like you? Never married?"

"No. I did have one serious relationship, with an older man … but he died a few years ago."

"Sorry. That's rough."

"Yes." She looked down at her bowl, swirling the half-eaten yellow liquid with her spoon, poking at the big doughy dumpling, then looked back at him, cocking her head to one side. "And since work comes first—and food's been taken care of—what about the reason we got together tonight. The client list, remember?"

"Oh, I can't work here."

"No?"

Somewhere, as if one cue, a busboy dropped a load of dishes, clattering, shattering.

Jack shook his head. "Way too distracting."

"You wouldn't happen to have someplace quieter in mind."

"Why, actually I do … my place."

"You know, there are probably half a dozen frustrated screenwriters sitting in here, if you'd like to get some help putting a new spin on that old line."

"Can't you tell? I'm an oldies-but-goodies kind of guy. I was glad to hear you like older men…."

"You're not that much older."

"What are you, thirty, Joy?"

"Thirty-five. What are you, Jack—forty?"

"Forty-five. My place … we don't have to go far."

"Just keep that in mind."

His "place" turned out to be a beige Mediterranean-style home built high along the hill of winding Beverlycrest Drive. The house sat close to the narrow street, its front door just yards away, but protected by a beige wrought-iron fence.

Unlike her modest home, this near-mansion was worth millions.

Jack pulled his jade-green Lincoln sedan through an electronic gate and into a single-car garage, which was next to the house.

"Something you might be interested in," Jack said, as they made their way to the front of the house, "being as you're a student of history and all—Clark Gable and Carole Lombard lived here."

"You're kidding! Oh, I love them both…. Sucker for old movies…"

"Yeah, well, somebody famous has lived in every one of these houses. You know, I had a young actress up a few weeks ago … interviewing her for work …"

"I'm sure."

"Anyway, I told her Clark Gable used to live here and she said, 'Really! That's so cool—I *love* Superman!' "

The sheer stupidity of that got Joy laughing, laughing hard, as he opened the heavy wooden door and a high-pitched beep sounded, signaling an alarm had been set. Joy quickly stepped inside so Jack could shut it off.

As he punched in a code at the keypad behind the front door, Joy looked around the small but elegant, round marble-floored entryway, where nude maiden statues stood guard on the periphery next to exotic plants elevated on Grecian columns.

An image of a shocked Jack coming in the front door of her painfully humble abode entered her mind, but she pushed the unpleasantness aside. Tonight was tonight, now was now, and tomorrow might never come….

The focal point of the entryway, though, was in its center: a large urn stuffed with canes.

"What's this about?" she asked. "I didn't notice you limping!"

"I once dated a woman who insisted on taking me to her aerobics class," he explained. "Eileen Mumy taught it—she's married to that guy who was in *Lost in Space*, the 'danger danger' kid? Anyway, I sprained my damn foot in the first ten minutes…. Eileen felt so bad she sent me a cane." He pulled out a stick with a gold handle the shape of a duck's head. "I used it instead of crutches. Then everybody and his brother started giving me canes. Friends. Clients." Shaking his head, Jack put the cane back in the urn. "I guess you could say I'm set for my old age."

Joy smirked. "Tell me about what happens when people find out you collect things. I ended up with a drawer full of troll dolls. Somebody gave me one as a joke, and I put it on my desk. Then somebody else thought it looked lonely. Before long there was a whole clan of those ugly little bastards."

He laughed. "I promise I'll never give you a single damn troll."

"And I promise, even if you break both legs tonight, I won't buy you another damn cane."

"Deal."

And they shook hands.

For a moment they stood in silence, smiling at each other, knowing something was happening, her eyes and his holding a separate conversation.

Finally Jack asked, "Can I show you around?"

"I'd love to see the rest of the house.... I assume this is just the guest house. Surely the main house must be more impressive."

"Oh, yeah. This is strictly for the poor relations."

He led her to the left, through an archway that opened into a formal dining room, with crystal chandelier, dark mahogany dining table, thick beige area rug, around whose edges were the names of movie stars (all old-timers), in gold Roman lettering.

The kitchen, through a swinging door, was modern and dazzlingly white; it had a breakfast area that looked out over Beverly Hills, the lights belonging to the stars below, putting those in the sky to shame.

They doubled back to the entryway through a den decorated in tan Berber carpet, walls lined with leather-bound books and expensive Asian and African knickknacks, a modern mahogany desk, Jack's familiar leather attaché tossed casually on it. The desk faced a series of windows, some of them open, providing a delightful breeze, along with another glittering, breathtaking Hollywood view.

A sharp feeling of envy shot through Joy like a sudden chest pain. Sitting at that desk, with that view, she could come up with a million brilliant ad campaigns, compared to where she worked at home now, at a scarred-up little desk, looking out on a tiny, parched lawn.

Money might not buy happiness, but it sure could buy creativity, or at least an environment in which creativity could flourish, and that was more important.

Then down a spiraling staircase they descended, to a lower level (there were three others, she discovered), past the master bedroom (very masculine, with a zebra bedspread) and two other bedrooms that looked unused. A floor below the bedrooms sprawled a workout room with all kinds of equipment, a whirlpool and sauna, looking out on a small outdoor pool built on a cement platform. The final floor was for the live-in help, Jack said, which at the moment was empty.

"Do you use the workout room much?" Joy asked, as they began their ascent back up, admiring his tight buns.

Jack, leading the way, said with a wry laugh, "Very little. I get all my exercise climbing these goddamn stairs."

"I guess if you build on a hill, you can only go down."

"The more modern houses have elevators."

"I'd rather have this one," she commented; they were standing in the foyer once again. "I'd much rather have Gable and Lombard than an elevator. This place has so much character and history. You can just *feel* it."

He was staring with open affection. "Funny, coming from somebody your age."

She shrugged. "Guess I'm a sucker for somebody else's era. I mean, I grew up in the '70s—how bleak is that? You got *The Honeymooners*—I got *The Brady Bunch!*"

Yes, those classes at Simmons did pay off at the darnedest times....

Jack gestured to the right of the entryway, to the only place they hadn't been yet, the living room, which seemed small by Hollywood standards, but had a high vaulted ceiling, and was richly decorated with white leather furniture, a leopard-print rug and an extensive collection of African artwork. Pottery, paintings, masks, sculptures had taken up residence in every nook and cranny.

She stood in front of a white marble fireplace staring at two huge elephant tusks that stood guard on either side.

"I bagged those on my last safari," Jack's voice came from behind her.

She turned and gave him a wide-eyed look.

"Just kidding. I couldn't kill a rabbit." He stood at a liquor cart, removing a silver wine stopper from a bottle.

Joy was relieved; overtly macho men put her off. They were always compensating for something—buying and shooting guns because nature hadn't given them much of a gun to shoot.

"You can almost see Gable and Lombard," he was saying, handing her a glass of wine, "can't you? On the sofa, sipping wine—well, him straight whiskey, her wine." He tapped his glass with hers. "To Clark and Carole?"

"To Clark and Carole," she repeated, wondering if the two icons would have stayed together if Lombard hadn't died in that plane crash.

Seated on the leather couch, which was white as a marshmallow and damn near as soft, they talked in hushed voices about movies and music and books, finding out they had similar tastes, despite the ten-year difference in their ages (of course, he didn't know she was the one ten years older). A deco clock on the mantel read nearly midnight, when Joy remembered something.

"Hey!" she said, turning her face toward his. "I thought you were going to help me with that list. It's getting late, you know!"

"You're right," Jack said, feigning surprise. "It is late ... too late to do any constructive work, anyway." His face came closer to hers. "Tell you what, I'm busy this weekend, but I will call you Monday afternoon. We can do it then."

"Over dinner, I suppose?"

"I work best on a full stomach." He put his fingers under her chin and lifted her face to his. "You know, Joy, if you want something done right, you can't rush it."

Was he talking about the list of names, or their relationship?

He kissed her hard, his lips unyielding; she submitted completely, though unable to match his intensity. Then he drew away, and before she could reciprocate with a kiss of her own, he gently pulled her to him, putting one hand in her hair, laying her head on his chest.

"Let's not rush it, sweetheart," he whispered.

Later, after Jack had driven her back to her car in the parking garage at work, and while she was making the fifteen-minute commute home across winding Laurel Canyon, she could still feel his warm, provocative kiss on her lips.

She wasn't offended, or even puzzled, as to why Jack hadn't tried to sleep with her. In fact, she was touched by the courtliness of a man who could call her "sweetheart" with neither embarrassment nor irony. She sensed, as he must have, that this relationship was special, more than a one-night stand, and neither wanted to compromise it by being in too much of a hurry.

Joy felt a youthful glow that, for a change, did not come from the clear capsules in the silver-capped plastic bottle.

Chapter Ten

"DOCTOR MY EYES"
(Jackson Browne, #8 Billboard, 1972)

A week slogged by and the only contacts she had with Jack Powers were business-related, quick, friendly phone calls adding names to their list of prospective spokespersons, with follow-ups telling her his background checks were coming along fine. By Friday she was thinking she had somehow blown it, when Jack called her just after lunch and asked her out again.

For their second date, he suggested another expensive restaurant (men *never* learned), so Joyce had carried the ball, by saying, "Do you know what would just hit the spot?"

"What?"

"A hot dog down at Santa Monica pier. With ketchup and relish. And onion rings. The greasier the better."

"You can't be serious."

A little hurt, she stuttered, "Well, if, uh …"

"Mustard, not ketchup! Have you no refinement, woman?"

That evening, walking along the sand, the wonderfully gaudy lights of the pier dancing in the darkness, a full moon watching high from a star-flung sky and a balmy California breeze running its fingers through her hair—and his—they kissed, tentatively, like teenagers, as if it were the first kiss either had experienced.

Over the next two weeks they saw each other often—more walks on the beach, evenings at coffeehouses, and matinees at neighborhood second-run theaters and classic-movie houses.

"You know, a client of mine gave me a couple of tickets to the Smashing Pumpkins concert, Saturday," he said over coffee at a vintage diner. "It's sold out ... it's a hot ticket, everyone says they're great...."

She stirred creamer into her coffee. "Can I share a secret, Jack?"

"Well, of course."

"I think their music sounds like their name."

"Oh. Well, so do I, actually ... I just thought...."

"I saw in the paper something about an outdoor oldies concert, up the coast...."

"I read about that," he said. Almost to himself, he said, "I think I know somebody I can sell these tickets to...."

That seemed a slightly peculiar comment, from someone as well off as Jack. After driving her back from the concert—at which the Turtles, the Grass Roots and Bobby Vee performed—he was about to leave her at her door, when she asked him in.

"I don't think anybody famous ever lived here," she said apologetically. She'd hidden the Hobbit house from him long enough. "Except maybe Bela Lugosi."

He had his brown attaché with him—the plan, or anyway the pretense, had been, after the early evening concert, to work on the list (a list they actually had been adding to)—and he set the slim briefcase near the small desk in one corner of her tidy living room with its secondhand furniture.

"I like it," he said. "Funky in the best sense."

At least he didn't comment on the place being "retro."

They sat on the gold sofa (the only non-secondhand piece she owned) in front of her small fake fireplace and began to pet. There was no other word for it: It was as if they were in the backseat of a Chevy at a drive-in movie, as he caressed her breasts through her blouse, taking forever to slip his hand under and around to undo her bra strap.

Her new breasts had never been too responsive before; under rougher hands, they had seemed lifeless lumps, but Jack's sensitive touch brought them alive, and when his lips found their erect tips, he nuzzled them with such loving tenderness that she shimmered with delight, wept with bittersweet happiness. He seemed surprised when she got down before him, on her knees, and unzipped him and took him into her mouth, and he liked it all right, but he wanted more to be inside her, and soon he was, the two of them half-dressed, fumbling on the couch like kids, washed in the artificial glow of the fake fireplace, as masterfully atop her, he brought her to a slow, endless climax that sent youth radiating through her.

When she returned from freshening up in the bathroom, she found Jack asleep on the couch, sprawled out in an ungainly masculine fashion that only made her more fond of him. She went to the desk, hauled his attaché up on it, snapped it open and took out the rather thick manila folder.

But something caught her eye, tucked away in the top snapped-shut compartment—something strangely familiar....

She unsnapped the compartment and there it was: a silver-capped plastic bottle.

Frowning, Joy popped open the cap and familiar clear capsules within confirmed a suspicion she had never allowed her mind to form.

Joy returned the plastic bottle to its hiding place in the attaché, put the file folder back inside too, placed the briefcase on the floor, where Jack had left it.

And, in the dim light of the desk light, she looked down at her reflection in the glass protecting the desktop: Her face stared back at her, the young face with the old eyes. The face had no expression at first; but then, slowly, a smile formed.

"What the hell," she said to the two women in the glass.

Then she returned to the living room, where Jack was rousing, looking pleasantly rumpled.

"You look like the cat that ate the canary," he said.

"Not a canary exactly," she smiled, then leaned closer to him, a hand stroking his thigh.

She snuggled with him on the couch, wondering if she should tell him—or would that spoil his fantasy of being with a younger woman? She had already shared her secret with Susan, a violation of the X-Gen contract. Perhaps she should keep what she knew about Jack to herself … at least for now….

"What are you thinking about?" he asked.

"Nothing. Nothing. Just reflecting on …"

"What?"

"How much nicer it is to be with an older man. All that experience …"

This time she was on top, and as she rode him, they were ageless, not young, not old, two passionate people in love, screwing their brains out.

The following Saturday marked the first time Joy would not spend most of her weekend with Jack.

"Kafer isn't my only client, you know," he'd told her over the phone, midweek, when she was at work.

"Just so your other 'clients' aren't getting the same TLC *I* am, buster," she said.

He laughed. "It's just a quick couple of days in the Midwest for some insurance checks. I'll be back by Sunday evening—I'll call you."

"Okay. Stay away from those corn-fed cuties, all right?"

"I'll try to resist. There's something about the scent of hog-slop on a girl that drives me wild."

"Go away, you goof," she laughed. "Fly away! See you Sunday."

And she made a smooch sound for the phone to pick up, so far gone she didn't feel foolish doing so.

Now it was Saturday morning and Joy was sitting on the edge of the examination table in Dr. Green's office. Wearing snug blue jeans, a white designer T-shirt and silver futuristic-looking jogging shoes, she kicked the air like an impatient kid, waiting for the doctor to come in.

She hoped he wouldn't be long, because she wanted to get home with a walnut plant stand she'd found discarded in an alley on the way to her appointment; her Jaguar, cruising the realm of the rich and famous, was never looked upon with suspicion.

It was amazing what some people considered useless and just threw the hell out! The stand would look perfect in her living room with the right plant on it … a little worse for wear, perhaps, but still functional. Besides, old-and-distressed had become fashionable—too bad that didn't apply to how her generation was viewed.

So she was pleased when the door opened and Dr. Green stepped in, her medical file in his hands.

She flashed him a bright smile, because today she was feeling happy.

"Well, aren't we chipper," he commented, returning the smile.

"Yes, we are."

"Ah, well. Good … good." He studied her a moment, as if to determine whether she was telling the truth, before setting her file folder on the white countertop next to the examination table where she perched.

"And how have you been?" he asked. "Any complaints at all?"

"None."

"Excellent."

He proceeded to check her blood pressure, her ears and throat, looked in her eyes with a bright light, tested the strength of her fingers, and her reflexes, by tapping her knees with a little hammer.

Then Dr. Green reached for her file and, pulling a three-legged stool over in front of her, sat down.

"Last month," he commented, reading her file, "you had some depression about your personal life." He looked up. "Is that any better?"

She didn't want to tell him she was madly in love—it was none of his business—so she said casually, "I have a friend whose company I enjoy. But we're not serious."

Her words came out stilted, sounding false; like the time she'd fibbed to her father about having "just a platonic relationship" with one of their married neighbors. She was never good at lying, except in the context of her work.

Dr. Green was jotting something in her folder. Was everything she had ever uttered to the baby-faced physician recorded in there?

After a moment, he said, "We need a bone density test so we can adjust your estrogen replacement as time goes on. You can make the appointment with the nurse."

"Is that for osteoporosis?"

He nodded. "But not to worry—you're in fine fettle."

Not to worry? Fine fettle? Green wasn't old enough to be spouting phrases like that ... or was he?

Green gave her the perfunctory smile that signaled the end of their appointment. "Anything else?"

"I don't think so."

"Then the nurse will be in with your monthly pills." He patted her knee. "You're doing fine, Joy."

Like she'd gotten an "A" on a test. "Thanks."

He stood.

"Doctor? I guess I do have a couple questions. That is, if you have the time."

"For you, always." He seemed sincere enough, returning to the stool. Behind that blank professionalism, did an actual human being lurk?

This was her first checkup since she and Susan had shared their secret—and since she'd learned of her secretary's health problem.

Joy cleared her throat. "I have a client who gave me some samples of herbal supplements. Are they okay to take? I mean, with the capsules."

The query was a smoke screen for what she really wanted to ask. She wasn't really interested in taking much, if any, of that garbage; she only promoted it.

"What kind of supplements?" he asked.

"Valerian."

"Ineffective, in my opinion."

"Ginkgo."

"There's something wrong with your memory?"

"No, I just understand it's a good source of Vitamin B."

"We can give you a monthly shot of B if you feel you need that extra zip."

"Maybe next month. How about ginseng?"

A short laugh vibrated his plump lips. "Poppycock."

Poppycock? Again, an expression at variance with his unformed, bisque-baby face.

"Anything else?" Dr. Green asked patiently.

"What can you tell me about rheumatoid arthritis?"

"I can tell you you don't have it."

She forced her own little laugh. "Well, I know I don't have it. I just want to know about it."

He raised his eyebrows, shrugged, and launched into a clinical description of the disease, followed by the prognosis in layman's terms.

It wasn't anything she already didn't know from recent research on the Internet in her office.

"And there's no cure?" she asked after he'd finished.

"No."

"Nothing … at all?"

Now he seemed to understand. He cleared his throat. "There is a drug that's been successful in stopping its advancement—and in some cases even reversed the effects of the disease—but it's not available here."

"In the States, you mean."

"Correct."

"But it *could* be obtained," she ventured.

He nodded slowly, then said, "But you won't be needing it, Joy, if that's what you're worried about."

"I just … it's just … I've had a little stiffness of my joints. Nothing serious, but when it gets damp…."

"In this dry climate, I wouldn't worry." He gestured with one hand. "Oh, as you get a little older, you'll get the common type of arthritis that most everyone has. And when that happens, I'll give you something that works a lot better than anything that's been FDA-approved today."

Dr. Green stood, clutching her file folder to his chest. "Just let me know when your joints begin to really get stiff—when it's chronic, not just on rare occasions."

"You'll be the first to know."

His eyes hardened; they seemed to bore through her. "I'm here to help you," he said. "We're on the same team. *My* job is to see that you can do *your* job … and I can only do that if you're honest with me about your aches and pains and *any* health-related concern." His eyes softened, his voice, too. "Understood?"

She nodded. "Understood."

"All right, then. See you next time."

An hour later, in Studio City, with another month's supply of the clear capsules tucked in her purse, Joy pulled her car into the narrow driveway adjacent to her bungalow. She got out and, with some difficulty, removed the heavy walnut plant stand from the back seat of the Jaguar. She set it down on the cement, marveling at her find. The piece, which stood about four feet tall, was shaped like two hourglasses on top of each other, with a thick round top, and a matching round base that had three little claw feet to hold it steady.

To be sure, some of the wood, especially on top, was badly weather-damaged; but with a little mothering, it could be brought back to life and serve a useful purpose.

Joy carried the furniture in through the front door and put it on the carpet to one side. She was looking forward to an afternoon of dragging the piece from one room to the next, one corner to another, until she found the most aesthetically pleasing spot for her newfound treasure.

But before she could fully enjoy this simple furniture ritual, she had to take care of another piece of business, something she'd been thinking about on her drive back from the doctor's office.

Removing her appointment book from her purse, she leafed to the back of it and found her secretary's home number. Then, using the phone on the end table by the couch, Joy placed a call to Susan. She wanted to tell her secretary about her conversation with the doctor.

On the sixth or seventh ring, an answer machine picked up, and Susan's voice, sounding worklike efficient, told Joy to leave her name and number, which she did.

With that in motion, Joy's attention returned to the plant stand.

The California sun, now low in the sky, shone through the open blinds in the living room, cascading in yellow ribbons across the walnut plant stand, which stood proudly before the front windows. It was the first place Joy had tried it several hours ago, before moving it around the entire house, just to be sure.

Joy was sitting cross-legged on the couch, sipping a rich cup of Starbucks French roast—she'd be damned if she'd cut costs on her coffee—admiring the stand, basking in her luck, when the phone rang shrilly next to her.

"Joy, it's Susan," her secretary said.

For a moment, Joy forgot why she'd called her. "Oh, hi," she responded, then remembering said, "Listen, I went to see Dr.

Green this morning, and he told me something interesting about your type of disease."

"I know. I just got back from seeing him, myself."

Joy was shocked. "Susan … I never mentioned your name—I never specifically said …"

"I told him," Susan interrupted. "I got to thinking about what you've been advising, when we go out to lunch …"

Lunching together had become a ritual for these two who shared a secret.

Susan was saying, "… how I needed to level with Dr. Green, and get some help. So I made an appointment for this afternoon."

"What did he say?"

There was a sigh over the phone. "You mean after he bawled me out for not disclosing rheumatoid arthritis was in my family, when I filled out my original questionnaire?"

Something made Joy clutch the phone receiver, tight. "You're not in trouble with X-Gen?"

"No, no, not in the least. Dr. Green was nice enough about it. Said he had a new drug I could take."

"Oh! Well, that's what I was going to tell you about. That's great news, isn't it?"

"Beyond great. I'm so relieved not to have to hide it anymore. You can't imagine the weight that's off my shoulders …" And Susan added sheepishly, "I guess I was foolish to wait."

"Well, you've done the right thing now."

There was a pause.

"Look," Joy said suddenly, "would you like to come over for dinner? Jack's out of town, and I make a great veggie salad: It's more than I can eat."

"Oh, that's sweet of you," Susan responded, "but I'm driving to Bakersfield tonight. Sort of a date."

"Really?" Susan had never mentioned any man in her life, other than the mythical husband, Jerome (that bastard); and Joy had never really been interested enough to ask. Until now.

They were sisters of a sort, weren't they?

"We met in a chat room," Susan explained gaily.

Joy suppressed a groan. "You're going to see a man you met on the Internet? Get real, Susan!"

If it had been Susan questioning Joy's judgment, Joy would have gotten testy; but Susan's enthusiasm continued unabated. "Oh, Paul and I have been trading E-mails and chatting online for *weeks*, Joy. He really is nice. And, besides, we're just friends ... for now, anyway."

When had she heard that one before? "Get a grip, Susan—your online 'friend' is gonna be married, with a wife just made for *Jerry Springer* and a horde of bratty kids...."

Light laughter came over the line.

Joy kept at it: "Or he's really a twelve-year-old kid, holding his one-inch pecker in his sweaty palm."

"You're terrible!" Susan said, but she was laughing. "I'll tell you what, you can have Jack check him out, top to bottom, dental records, family tree, whatever.... But could I *please* just meet him first?"

"Now having Jack check him out is a great idea," Joy said. Another legitimate excuse to call Jack from work. "But I don't know about meeting the guy first...."

"What's it gonna harm? Hey, I gotta run. See you on Monday."

"Bye," Joy said. "Be careful!"

But the line had gone dead before she got out her last two words.

Joy put the phone down, leaned back on the couch. She hoped Susan's Internet "pal" would work out. But she didn't give it much credence; those people were always such fucking losers....

Joy's attention returned to the scavenged walnut stand and what kind of plant to put on it.

On Sunday, after a typically meager breakfast of grapefruit and toast, Joy drove back over Laurel Pass to Hollywood, then down La Brea to a rather "seedy" plant shop that would have better prices than in Beverly Hills.

For several hours she roamed the outside nursery in the warm sun, poking at all kinds of plants, from the exotic to the mundane, inquiring at length about each one to the manager—a dark middle-aged man named, inevitably, Raoul—who eventually could not conceal his exasperation with her.

No matter; she'd never be back. Even at these lower prices, this would be her one and only plant.

Finally, after lining up three semi-finalists on a sunbaked workbench, Joy chose the winner: the tried and true Boston fern.

After getting detailed instructions on its care (not too much water or sun; mist once a week) and inquiring about a refund if it died (a firm no—even if she followed the instructions), only then did she lay out her hard-earned cash for the plant.

Joy put the fern in the front seat of her car, under a piece of plastic Raoul had provided—the plastic would come in handy if she ever decided to refinish the stand—and, as if the leafy thing were her precious child, carefully put the car's seat belt around it.

Then back over the pass she went, glancing at the plant every now and then like a worried mother checking her baby in its car seat, once nearly rear-ending a Toyota.

At home, she ceremoniously placed the green fern on the top of the stand, a crown for a queen, and stepped back to assay her choice.

Perfect.

The only thing that could make her happier at this moment would be a call from Jack, saying he was back … but it was way too early.…

For the remainder of the day, Joy busied herself hand-washing some of her business clothes in the bathroom sink.

Dry-clean only, my ass! she thought, as she gently scrubbed the cream-colored silk blouse Jack had gotten the wine spill out of with club soda. Club soda was wet, wasn't it? And the blouse didn't get ruined.

There was a conspiracy between the clothes manufacturers and dry cleaners to bilk the poor consumer! Cold water and a little mild detergent would clean any garment as well, if not better, than dry-cleaning—and with no chemical smell.

Joy, smiling smugly at her cleverness to save money, hung the wet clothing on padded hangers over the tub. (Except for a black Tricot sleeveless blouse, which had shrunk to a size-two toddler. But that was the only casualty.)

Then Joy curled up on the couch, waiting for Jack's call, with a book on furniture refinishing she'd found in a bargain bin; as the afternoon darkened to dusk, Joy got drowsy and decided to just rest her eyes....

Sometime in the early morning hours, she woke from a nightmare that left as bad a taste in her mind as the one in her mouth.

In the dream she'd been back at Simmons College, in the bell tower. Rick was hanging by the rope, his face purple, his neck scraped raw and bleeding; only he wasn't dead yet. And this time his wide eyes were staring directly at her, his mouth moving, tongue lolling grotesquely. He seemed—in his last choking moments—to be trying to tell her something. But she was just screaming and screaming, so loud she couldn't hear him but couldn't stop herself....

Joy forced herself to wake up.

In the movies, people always woke from nightmares by bolting upright, soaked with sweat. But Joy, on her side, curled fetally, felt cold, gathering a quilt around her, from where it had been folded over the back of the couch; and it took her a while to shake the dreadful feeling, and even longer to fall back to sleep, which was fitful at best.

In the morning, she overslept, causing instant panic, making her dress in a frenzied hurry. Gone was the serenity of Sunday. She gulped some orange juice, the clear capsule her only breakfast, then rushed out of the house.

The early morning air was an unpleasant cocktail of haze and smog, and the traffic heavy, adding to her misery. *Why hadn't Jack called last night?* she wondered, half-irritable, half-concerned.

At the advertising agency, when Susan wasn't at her desk to handle the calls, Joy's irritation grew; Mondays were usually hectic. It was one thing for a boss to be late, but a secretary should always be punctual. Where was the considerate phone call from Susan saying she was sick, or otherwise detained?

Though barely half an hour late, Joy found her answer machine blinking frantically with messages. She just had time before the Gray Fox's Monday morning staff meeting to listen to them, all but one related to various clients.

But one, thank God, was Jack.

"Sorry about last night," his voice said. "My flight was postponed and then finally canceled—too late to call you. Anyway, I took advantage of the layover to do a little more work, here—I may not be able to get back till tomorrow. Love you."

Love you too, she told the machine.

By one o'clock, with no sign of Susan, Joy's irritation with her secretary turned to concern. And still later, her concern became worry after calling Susan at home and only getting the machine.

Terrible thoughts began to race through Joy's mind. *What if Dr. Green had given Susan the experimental drug, and she'd had a terrible reaction? Or what if that Internet "friend" was a psycho ... a serial killer, even?*

Skipping a three o'clock departmental meeting, Joy stopped by accounting and asked for Susan's home address, then rushed out of the building.

It was nearly four in the afternoon by the time Joy parked the Jag in front of the run-down stucco mission-style apartment complex in a questionable neighborhood in West Hollywood. Turning off the car, hoping her hubcaps were safe, Joy felt sorry for Susan; her own bungalow was a palace compared to this....

A rusted iron gate creaked opened to a small courtyard with a postage-stamp swimming pool that hadn't been cleaned in some while. The dwellings surrounding the courtyard looked more like motel rooms than apartments.

Joy walked down a dreary row of them, stopping at number five. She opened a patched screen door and knocked on the warped, paint-peeling front door.

She waited, then knocked again, this time putting her face close to the door. "Susan! It's me, Joy! Are you home?"

Ear pressed to the wood, she could hear nothing inside.

She tried to peer in the front window, but the curtains were drawn tight.

Turning, Joy wondered if she'd have any luck around back, when she noticed the last apartment across the courtyard. Below the number "10" on the door was the word "Concierge."

If she hadn't been so worried about Susan, she might have laughed at such a grand designation for a slum super.

Hurrying across the courtyard, she banged on the super's door. This time someone answered: a short, stocky woman in a cotton housedress with a cartoony paw-print print.

"Have you seen Susan today?" Joy asked anxiously. "Susan Henderson—in number five!"

The concierge shrugged, bringing up a pudgy hand with a burning cigarette in it. "You may find this hard to believe, but my clientele and me don't socialize all that much."

"I think she may be sick. She didn't show up for work."

"I'll call Geraldo," the woman said, the cigarette dangling in her lips now, as she started to close the door in Joy's face.

Joy grabbed the doorknob and held the door open. Exasperated, Joy asked, "Can you let me in her apartment?"

The woman's eyes narrowed.

"I'm her boss!" Joy explained. "Please ... do you have an extra key?"

"I forget."

Sighing, Joy dug into her purse, handed the woman a precious five-dollar bill.

The woman smiled, cigarette bobbling, and turned, disappearing into the black hole of her apartment. A moment later, she returned and, with thick fingers, held out a key.

"Bring it back," she said sternly.

"For my deposit, you mean?" Joy said, with a sneer.

Joy hurried to Susan's apartment, unlocked and opened the front door, and stepped inside.

The air was heavy with that stale apartment smell—the combined odors of everyone who'd ever lived there. And it was pitch-dark in there.... All the curtains closed, shades pulled. Joy left the front door wide open to allow a shaft of light in.

"Susan?" she called.

No answer.

Joy moved slowly through the cramped living room, which was—as best she could see in the dim light—filled with a depressing array of eclectic furniture. It was apparent Susan hadn't even tried to make the apartment cheerful; no feminine or homey touch, no matter how pathetic.

The kitchen, off the living room, was even more dismal: ghastly, Pepto-Bismol-pink cupboards, a tired dinette set and a yellow linoleum floor that may once have been white. Joy stuck her head in just long enough to see that Susan wasn't there.

Then down a short, narrow hall to the bedroom, where Joy— suddenly shivering with dread—was certain she'd find Susan, either comatose or dead....

But to her great relief, Joy found the bedroom empty.

This, the most pleasant of all the rooms, was probably where Susan spent her time. A stack of used paperbacks—historical romances—was piled high on the floor near an old rocker draped with a patchwork quilt. A stereo arrayed with ancient L.P.s (Monkees, Ronettes, Bobby Rydell) sat atop a dresser. In here, the air did not reek of houseatosis, rather redolent of the floral perfume Susan wore to work.

Joy moved on, to the only room left: a bathroom at the end of the hall. As she approached the half-open door, she could hear the *drip, drip, drip* of a sink or bathtub faucet.

Again the fear, the dread gripped her. She reached a hand out to push the door wide, and her heart began to pound. An image of poor Susan flashed through Joy's mind: jilted by her Saturday night date, unable to cope with her disease anymore, lying dead in the tub, wrists slashed....

The door creaked open, and as the entire bathroom came into view, Joy held her breath, eyes darting from the floor to the toilet to the sink to the tub.

No Susan.

Joy sighed in relief. But where could her secretary be? Maybe Joy was worrying for nothing. Maybe Susan would show up at any moment, with some silly, inconsequential explanation, and they would both laugh at Joy's overreactive concerns. Joy crossed the bathroom, to the ruststained sink, to shut off the annoying drip so she could think.

It was then that she caught a motion in the cabinet mirror, behind her.

She shrieked as hands grasped her shoulders, whirled her around, and backed her up against the cold hard sink, flailing at the man in the blue suit, who reached in his breast jacket pocket.

Was he going to shoot her?

"Who are you?" she shouted, and it echoed in the little bathroom.

The man, tall, tanned, with a rugged face and Indian cheekbones, pulled out an identification wallet.

"Sergeant Ryan, LAPD," he said. The face on the ID was the same hard face looking at her. "Now let's move on to who *you* are? Which for starters isn't Susan Henderson."

as a moment before Joy could speak, before she could get her heart out of her throat.

"Joy Lerner," she said. "I'm a friend of Susan's—actually, her boss." Anger replaced fright in a knee-jerk reaction; she slapped at his forearm. "What the fuck d'you have to scare me for?"

"The door was open," he shrugged, as if that were an adequate explanation. "You have a reason to be here?"

"Do *you* have a reason to be here?" Joy snapped. But as soon as she'd asked it, she realized the implications of her own question.

"Oh, my God, has something happened to Susan?" The words came tumbling out. "Please … I told you. I'm her boss and I'm her friend … do you know where she is?"

The eyes in the hard face softened.

"You'd better come in the other room, Ms. Lerner," Sgt. Ryan said, "and sit down."

Chapter Eleven

"BEEP BEEP"
(The Playmates, #4 Billboard, 1958)

In the living room of Susan's apartment, in the halfhearted yellowish illumination of a secondhand floor lamp with a threadbare shade, Joy settled uneasily down on a sagging blue sofa. Sgt. Ryan took the worn gray arm chair across from her, sitting on its edge, his expression that of a priest doing his best to explain God's role in a meaningless, malicious world.

Leaning forward, elbows resting on the knees of his blue suit pants, hands together as if in prayer, Ryan told her—as gently as possible—that Susan's body had been found in the trunk of her car Sunday afternoon along a remote stretch of highway leading to Bakersfield.

She had been strangled.

Susan's purse, he said, minus any wallet, was found in the front seat; but a prescription bottle bearing her name, and that of a physician, a Doctor Vernon Green—to whom Ryan had placed a call in Beverly Hills—had led him here, to Susan's apartment.

Joy, tears sliding slowly down her cheeks, informed the detective about Susan's Saturday night date.

"She met him on the Internet," Joy said, sniffling, digging for a Kleenex in her purse. "I warned her to be careful. Tried to, anyway ..."

"You need something...?"

"No," she said, finding the tissue. She wiped her face with it, adding bitterly, "This Internet 'friend'—he's your killer."

Ryan reached in his jacket pocket and brought out a small spiral notepad, flipped it open. "Paul Kundell. Works in a strip-mall computer store—assistant manager."

That perked her up, just a little—not that justice, speedy or otherwise, would do Susan any good. "You've found him already?"

"He notified the highway patrol early Sunday morning," Ryan explained. "In fact, he was the reason we knew your friend was missing. Kundell said a woman he was supposed to be meeting hadn't shown up ... that she was driving a red early-'90s Hyundai and he was afraid it might have broken down ..."

"Sounds to me like he was covering his tracks—trying to look good in your eyes—"

Ryan shook his head. "I wish it were that easy. I've already spoken at length with Mr. Kundell, and everything he says checks out. At this juncture, at least, we don't consider him involved. But we're checking him and his background in depth."

Joy, dismayed by this apparent dead end, thinking she would have to get Jack involved, stammered, "Th-then ... then what happened to Susan?"

Ryan shrugged with his eyebrows. "Highway robbery," he said.

The term sounded silly to her; childish. *This is highway robbery!* the childhood phrase cried out to her, mockingly.

Ryan was saying, "A woman, alone, in the wrong place at the wrong time ... happens all too frequently."

"She wasn't raped?"

"No. No signs of sexual assault whatever."

Joy sighed, shaking her head. "Susan couldn't have been carrying much money."

"Do you know that for a fact, Ms. Lerner?"

"Yes." But she didn't explain why. "Sergeant, something's wrong here ... puzzling. Why would any thief bother to stop a cruddy little car like hers? My Jaguar I could understand."

"Now you're trying to make sense out of a senseless act of random violence," he said, with a faint, weary smile.

He had a point. She remembered those three women on a sightseeing excursion to Yosemite, brutally murdered, bodies stuffed in the trunk of their car, vehicle set on fire....

"Does it matter, Ms. Lerner, whether it was a junkie needing fix money, or some pervert who gets off on hating women?"

"Only if knowing that helps you find who did it."

"That's exactly right. Now—do you know of any family I can contact?"

Joy shook her head. "She didn't have anyone."

"You're sure about that?"

"Yes." At least, no family that would be able to recognize the "new" Susan. "I'm familiar with her job application, after all, as her boss."

There was no reason to bring up the fake husband and sons.

"And you were friends?"

"And we were friends."

"If you don't mind my asking, Ms. Lerner ... you mentioned your Jaguar yourself, and I can see how you're dressed ... and I see how Ms. Henderson lived. What turned your boss/secretary relationship into a friendship? What could you have had in common with the murder victim?"

Joy hesitated.

Finally, she said, "We liked the same music."

Ryan considered that for a moment, then shrugged.

A stray thought sent a sudden chill through Joy. She leaned forward on the couch. "I ... I won't have to identify Susan, will I?"

The idea of having to look at her secretary's stiff toe-tagged corpse on a cold steel autopsy tray, or pulled out in a refrigerated vault, black rubber sheet yanked back, made Joy's stomach twitch nastily.

"I just couldn't handle that," she said pleadingly, "I really just couldn't...."

Ryan shook his head. "Her doctor's already taken care of that."

The baby-faced Dr. Green; she wondered if that blank face had registered anything approaching sorrow....

Still, Joy had to sigh in relief; the dead image of Susan would have forever eclipsed the live one in her memory.

Ryan was standing. "We may need to talk again," the detective said, handing her a business card.

Joy gave him a card of her own, and told him her home phone number, which he jotted onto it.

"I'm very sorry about your friend," Ryan said.

"Thank you."

"Sorry about before—startling you." He nodded toward his business card, which she was holding by the fingers of both hands, as if it were a much larger, weightier object. "If you think of anything else...." His words trailed off.

She wondered how many times in his career he had said that.

Leaving the detective behind, Joy exited the apartment, moving on rubbery legs, passing the scum-surfaced pool where little twigs and dead leaves floated. As she went out the iron gate, she turned and looked back. The light remained on in Susan's place, as if someone were living there, and not just a cop searching the place for clues, for reasons, why someone might have wanted to murder a good-hearted, innocent soul like Susan Henderson.

Numbly, Joy returned to her car, dusk descending. Magic hour, the movie business called it. But with her friend and coworker gone, Joy could see nothing very fucking magical about it, at the moment.

She turned the ignition on and slowly eased her Jaguar out into the street. She wasn't sure where she was going, but knew she didn't want to go home. She drove aimlessly, swept along with the other cars, letting them dictate her path, until she found herself back in Beverly Hills.

Jack! She'd forgotten about him. He could well be back by now. She used her car phone to try his number, but only got his machine; this was his office number, which he checked fairly regularly, but she left no message. She felt like driving, like doing something, so that was where she'd go ... to his house. If he wasn't back from the airport yet, she would wait.

Only Jack could make sense of what happened; he'd make her feel better.

Joy turned on Laurel Pass, driving now with purpose, up winding Beverlycrest, peering through her windshield at the darkening homes, trying to remember which one was his.

Then it appeared on her right, the beige house that once belonged to Gable and Lombard. She pulled over to the curb, parking behind a shiny blue Ford truck, its back loaded with gardening tools.

She got out of her Jaguar and went around to the ornate beige wrought-iron gate, but found it locked. She looked for a buzzer or intercom, but didn't see one. How was Jack to know she was there? Or anyone, for that matter? He *was* in the security business ... but for Christ's sake, did he have to be as paranoid as everyone in California?

Joy cupped a hand to her mouth. "Jack!" she called, her need to see him overriding how silly she felt.

A light was on in the living room, but the rest of the house was dark. Maybe he wasn't home.

She called his name again.

Then around the right side of the house appeared a woman, long blond hair pulled back with a white scrunchy, tight navy shorts and red tube top barely covering her tanned, shapely body.

Looking very patriotic, she was dragging a garbage bag with one hand, sticks poking through one side, a hedge trimmer in the other.

The woman must be making a killing in the male-dominated landscaping business, Joy thought. Especially when husbands did the hiring.

"You want something?" the yard worker asked, her voice cordial, but with a guarded edge to it.

"Oh, hi," Joy called out, working to put a friendly tone in her response. "Is Mr. Powers home?"

The blonde, advancing across the lawn toward Joy, cocked her head to one side. "Mr. Powers?"

"Yes. I'm a friend of his. Joy Lerner."

The woman hoisted the hedge trimmer to rest on one muscular shoulder, eyed Joy with what seemed to be suspicion. Was the shapely blonde being protective of Jack's property ... or Jack?

"I'm an ad exec. With C.W. Kafer?" Joy said it like the woman should have known that.

"Uh-huh." The blonde, now planted on the other side of the front gate, seemed unimpressed.

"Would you please open this, so I can wait inside?" Joy gave the gate a little impatient rattle. "Or is Jack home? If so, I promise you, he'd want you to tell him I'm out here."

"I might," the woman responded with just a hint of a smirk, "if somebody named Jack lived here. You must have the wrong address, ma'am."

Ma'am? They were the same age! Or, anyway, looked it ...

"What do you mean?" Joy asked. "This is Jack Powers' place— I've been here! *Inside....*"

"Well that's real interesting," the blonde said, "considering who I work for."

And then the blond yard worker told Joy the name of a household-name female movie star, a prominent entry on their prospective list of spokespeople.

Now it was Joy who shook her head. "You must be mistaken...."

The blonde had opened the gate and was passing through, bag of refuse in tow, and quickly shut and locked it again before responding. "I've worked for her, oh, three or four years. And before that, I worked for her late husband."

And now the blonde yard worker named a well-known Hollywood producer, who had been famously married to the female star previously invoked as the mansion's current owner.

Joy looked desperately toward the house. It *was* dusk—could she be mistaken, could this be the wrong place?

No. This was where Jack had brought her. She remembered the front door, and the windows and the way the trees grew next to the garage....

"There was a green Lincoln...." Joy said, glancing toward the closed garage door.

The blonde, tossing the bag of sticks into the back of the truck, turned. "You mean the boss lady's car? Yeah, she bought it after her last picture. Sure beats the hell outa this pile of junk ... Look, nobody's home."

"Well, I guess I got some wrong information," Joy said casually. "Sorry."

"Sorry if I seemed a little cold." The woman opened the truck's cab door. "Fans are always coming around, bothering."

Did she look like a fan?

The woman climbed into her truck. "And, of course, thanks to those stupid movie-star maps," she remarked before slamming the cab's door, "the gawkers know Gable and Lombard lived here."

Did she look like a gawker?

Joy stared after the departing truck. Well, at least Jack wasn't a *total* liar, she thought with disgust. Clark and Carole had lived there, at least, even if *he* didn't! Joy went back to her Jaguar, got behind the wheel, and gave her own door a good slam.

How could Jack have deceived her? What a fool she'd been.

She turned her car around in the narrow, dimly lit street, wrenching the gears back and forth, tires squealing, her emotions accelerating with the speedometer, careening like the spiraling road she was driving down, as she went from disbelief to shock to despair to anger.

Magic hour had darkened to night. At the bottom of Beverlycrest she turned right onto Laurel for the trek over the mountain to Studio City. With rush-hour over and traffic light, Joy pushed her car over the speed limit, headlights cutting through the dark, as she hurried to get home where she could nurse her wounds.

Ascending the winding road, Joy was consumed with questions. Was Jack living with this actress? Did he think Joy wouldn't find out? Then again, what if this actress was only a client of his, possibly out of town, and he was just using her home as a love nest?

Somehow the latter seemed creepier to Joy than the notion of Jack cheating on some unknown lover.

Or had Jack merely been trying to keep Joy from seeing where he really lived? After all, he was an X-Gen client, too; she had assumed—as a partner in the successful investigation agency, and as someone who'd been in the program longer than her, years longer—that he was making big enough bucks to afford the good life.

She was living a lie; and so was he—maybe, within the twisted existence of the X-Gen clientele, there was an innocent explanation … so why was she still angry?

Lost in these unanswered questions, Joy wasn't sure just when the white compact car, a GEO, came up behind her. But it was following a little too close for her comfort. Reflexively, she sped up, wanting to put some distance between her and it, knowing that on the twisting two-lane highway there was no way the other car could pass.

But the white compact increased its speed also, sticking right with her—how could that little bug compete with her powerful

Jaguar?—which irritated her to no end. She glanced in her rear-view mirror and cursed at the unknown, inconsiderate driver.

Halfway up the mountain, taking each curve at an unpleasantly precarious speed, she considered pulling into one of the dirt driveways that appeared now and then, to let the maniac pass; but she was traveling too fast to maneuver that safely.

Instead, she hit her brakes for a second, lighting up her rear end, sending the car behind a message to back off, which it did, or risk running into her. But when she resumed her speed, it, too, sped up, once again tailgating her.

They were on a stretch of the road where a deep chasm to her left yawned into blackness. What the hell was the driver of the compact trying to do? Run her off the mountain?

Suddenly, her fury became fear.

Was this what happened to Susan? Driven off the road, robbed and murdered?

Was someone after her now?

Mulholland Drive loomed just head, at the top of the mountain, intersecting with Laurel, giving Joy a chance to maneuver.

She wondered if she should turn off. If the car behind her was just some idiot racing over to Studio City, late for an appointment with an agent or producer, she would be free of him.

But what if he turned *with* her? She wasn't as familiar with the twisting Mulholland, and could see herself sailing over the cliff at notorious Dead Man's Curve.

She had only a few seconds to decide.

Joy pressed ahead. And to her dismay the compact went with her. Now on the downward slope, she found it more difficult to keep her Jaguar under control at such a speed. At every turn the tires squealed, and once, at a particularly sharp curve, her right fender scraped the metal road guard, sending sparks flying. She gripped the steering wheel tighter, clenched her teeth until they hurt, praying she'd make it to the bottom in one piece.

Her pursuer began flashing his brights on and off, blinding her, obviously wanting to try to make her crash. She slapped the rearview mirror with her right hand, sending it off kilter, and the bright lights out of her eyes, and (she hoped) into the eyes of her pursuer.

Then around a final curve, the road straightened out, signaling she'd reached bottom—the finish line of a harrowing race—and she floored the accelerator, zooming ahead of the compact. At Ventura, she turned right on red without stopping, causing the driver of a Cherokee jeep to slam on his brakes and honk and curse, before speeding away.

Her bungalow was in the other direction, but Joy wasn't about to lead her stalker there. She needed the safety of lights and people … and bustling Ventura was just the right venue….

Weaving in and out of four-lane traffic, she drove only a few blocks before spotting a family restaurant on the right. She'd had breakfast there once or twice; now it would save *her* bacon….

Wheeling her car in the parking lot driveway of the diner, Joy misjudged and caught a back wheel on the curb, bumping over it, noisily scraping the bottom of her Jaguar, making a mother who was entering the restaurant grab for her young daughter, fearful the child would get run over.

For a moment, Joy considered abandoning her car in front of the restaurant, but then she spotted a parking place not far from the front entrance, and accelerating ahead, pulled into it. She turned off the ignition and jumped out, not bothering to lock the doors.

Heels clicking on the cement, she dashed across the parking lot, her eyes on the restaurant door, where inside bright lights burned, and people chattered … and help waited.

She was within twenty or thirty yards of safety, when the white compact tore into the lot, cutting her off, coming between her and the diner. As the car came to a screeching stop, she froze in her tracks with fear…. And astonishment.

Jack was behind the wheel.

With the car idling, he leaned out the driver's window. His expression seemed tortured.

"Joy, what the hell's the matter with you?"

She couldn't believe he had the nerve to confront her like that.

"What's the matter with *me*?" she shrieked. "What's the matter with *you*, you fucking jerk! Trying to run me off the road!"

A gasp of disbelief huffed from his dropped jaw. "Trying to run you off the road? I was trying to signal you…. didn't you know it was me?"

Oh, he was smooth, she thought. She'd better be good and careful….

But with the safety of the diner just yards away, and a middle-aged couple coming out, laughing, lighting up cigarettes, Joy's apprehension dissipated. She put her hands on her hips, defiantly.

"No I didn't know it was you," she snapped. "I thought you drove a green Lincoln … not a white GEO. Oh, and I also thought you lived on Beverlycrest Drive."

She didn't wait for his reaction, instead walking around the front of the little white car, quite certain he wouldn't dare run her over in front of the other people. Entering the diner, she said fiercely over her shoulder, "Just stay the hell away from me, Jack—stay away!"

Inside the restaurant—the decor a '70s study in mauve and turquoise and hanging plants—Joy ignored the PLEASE WAIT TO BE SEATED sign, sliding into a booth near the cash register. Badly shaken, she slumped, eyes closed, head bowed, held in one hand, fingers massaging her forehead, the endlessly long day finally catching up with her.

"Will you please let me explain."

She looked up. Jack was seated across from her, her Jack—casual in the same brown sport jacket and yellow polo he'd worn on their last date; the same Jack—only now the rugged planes of his face twisted into a pained expression.

"You do have brass balls," she said. "I'll give you that much. But you know what? I want to hear it—I want to hear what you could *possibly* say that could undo the damage you've done—that might change the way I feel about you now. Which is betrayed and used, by the way."

"I don't blame you, Joy, I really don't." He gestured with both hands. "I wanted to tell you that wasn't my house ... but there didn't seem to be an appropriate time...."

Joy leaned forward, testily. "How about when we first entered. 'This isn't my house, this is my girlfriend's place.' "

"She isn't my girlfriend...."

A waitress appeared to take their order, causing an awkward silence. Joy asked sullenly for a cup of coffee; Jack, politely, a Coke.

The moment the waitress turned her back, Joy continued on bitterly: "Oh, and that cute, cute story about the canes ... Did you make that up on the spot, or is that something you tell all the women you bring there?"

"I've never brought any other woman there—just you. And a bunch of those canes *were* mine. I gave them to the lady of the house, 'cause her late husband collected them too, and she kind of had a thing for them."

"For them or you?"

"Them. Not me."

Joy smirked, unconvinced.

Jack leaned toward her across the table, his dark eyes intense. "Joy, I have a tiny apartment on Doheny Drive, but I hardly ever stay there anymore. Many of my clients are actors, like the owner of that house—and they go off on shoots for extended periods of time." He paused, turning his palms up. "I house-sit for them. Even though they've got a security system, what's better than having a real security man around? And I like the arrangement because I don't have to spend time in my depressing apartment."

That was what he could possibly say to undo the damage he'd done.

"But I thought you had…." Joy said.

"Money?"

She nodded. "You're a partner in your agency…."

He looked down at his hands, then back up at her, saying, quietly, "I don't have money for the same reason you don't have money. My company is financed by X-Gen. I work for them…. I'm one of them. One of you."

Joy leaned back in the booth. "I know."

He studied her for a long time; then he laughed, wryly. "How long have you known?"

"Since you fell asleep on my couch…. How long have you known about me?"

"Not long … but I've suspected. Hell, anybody working at Kafer might be an X-Gen client, considering the relationship between our two agencies."

"How did I give myself away?"

"No one thing. It's just … after we hit it off so well, your … 'sense of history.' I started suspecting—after all these shallow young bitches I've been with, none of whom I could relate to worth a damn—funny."

"What is?"

"That was one of the things I wanted out of my 'new' life—younger women. What a joke. It took you to tell me what I really wanted…."

"Which was?"

"Someone I could relate to. Someone who'd lived through some of what I'd lived through. Someone with the same … values. Someone … someone I could fall in love with."

She reached out and touched his hand.

"How did you find out?" she asked. "Sneak a look in my purse?"

"Hell, no—what if you caught me at it? Nope—I broke into Doc Green's office one night. Had a look at his files."

"You didn't!" She'd never have the nerve to do that.

He nodded, eyes gleaming boyishly. "It was easy. Who do you think handles his security?"

She couldn't help smiling. "You really are a private eye, breaking in like that...."

The waitress arrived with their coffee and Coke; set them down with a clatter, and left.

"I'm sorry I scared you tonight," Jack said. "I was just trying to catch up with you ... afraid to let you to go home."

"Afraid?" she asked. "Of what?"

He glanced over his right shoulder, at the table behind them where a family of four were wolfing down dinner. He lowered his voice further.

"I know about Susan," he said solemnly. "When I called your office, the girl you had filling in for Susan said you were worried about her, and had gone to her apartment...."

The mention of Susan's name brought moisture to Joy's eyes.

"I must have come along about a half hour after you left. Detective Ryan was just leaving—I know him from way back—he told me you'd been there. I had a hunch you might go looking for me."

Joy nodded. "I *was* trying to find you." Her words came out in a rush. "I was so upset. Then this woman built like Xena says you don't live there ... and this car starts chasing me ... freak me out, why don't you...."

Jack took both of her hands in his. "I'm a moron—the last thing I wanted to do was frighten you—I didn't think about you not recognizing me in my own car—I just *had* to stop you from going home."

"But why?" she asked. "What's to be afraid of at home?"

He lowered his voice. "The same people who killed Susan."

She squinted in disbelief. "What people? That was a highway robbery!"

"Right," he laughed harshly. "Highwaymen. Brigands … Listen, the people who killed your friend are very likely in the process of zeroing in on you—and me."

"What the hell…?" She leaned forward, eyes narrowed. "Jack, that detective said Susan's death was just a random … occurrence." She couldn't make herself say killing. "It has no connection to me or you, unless maybe we're foolish enough to drive alone on the same desolate highway in the middle of the night."

Jack looked thoughtfully out the restaurant window toward the darkened world beyond. Joy followed his gaze, but all she could see was her reflection staring back.

His words were barely perceptible. "That's why every death is different. They're good at that."

"You're not making any sense," she sighed, digging in her jacket pocket for a tissue to dry her eyes. "What deaths? 'They' who?"

Her fingers hit something cold and hard. She pulled out the apartment key.

"It's Susan's," she said in a whisper. "I forgot to give it back to the super."

Jack leaned across the table and plucked the gold key from her palm. He looked at it, then gave the key a little toss in the air, before clamping his fingers around it.

Like George Raft in an old movie, flipping his coin …

"Let's get the check," he said brightly. "Then I'll show you just who 'they' are."

Chapter Twelve

"MIDNIGHT CONFESSIONS"

(The Grass Roots, #5 Billboard, 1968)

Taking Jack's car, leaving the Jag behind in the restaurant parking lot, they headed back over the pass. As he navigated the curves, Jack told Joy about his past.

In his former life, he'd been a cop in Council Bluffs who'd left to take a position as a private investigator with an agency whose major client was a large insurance company in nearby Omaha, Nebraska. After a few years, he'd gone to work for the insurance company itself, lured by an increase in salary and the promise of an executive position. Only the former became a reality; time after time he'd been passed over for promotion by increasingly younger men.

His wife Helen had died at age fifty-five, after a long struggle with breast cancer; medical bills consumed most of their retirement funds. Then their only son, Andrew, was killed in a motorcycle accident, the summer after the boy graduated from college. And as if that hadn't been enough, the insurance company forced Jack into retirement.

"Sixty," he said, the angles of his face highlighted hauntingly by the GEO's dim greenish dashboard lights. "Out on my ass—no family, no retirement, nothing."

Desperate for money, he took a job at a fast-food restaurant, working alongside pimply-faced high school students—"The McDonald's cradle-to-grave plan," he said with a humorless laugh. A few months into this bleak period, X-Gen approached him.

"I was a good prospect," he said. "Kinda rare for a cop—never smoke or drank. Played ball in college and always stayed fairly fit."

X-Gen got him a job with the Los Angeles Police Department— after retraining and surgery, of course.

"It was a good job, too," he said. "Detective Division—X-Gen devised a hell of a background for me. I think it was important to them to have somebody on the inside at the LAPD."

"But you didn't stay?"

"I couldn't take the stress and I couldn't take the politics. You can't come into a structure like that and be anything but an outsider. So I bailed."

"You just up and … quit," Joy said, breathlessly, as they wound round Laurel Canyon Pass. "You actually broke the X-Gen contract? What did they do?"

Jack shrugged, eyes on the dark road. "What *could* they do? Sue me, and reveal their sick fraud? That's not a legally binding contract, Joy—it's too seeped in criminality. They had to find me something else—particularly after everything they'd invested in me. I told them I could only be happy in business for myself. I wanted my own company."

"And they set you up? But, Jack, that's great!"

He gave her a greenish sideways glance. "Great? I wouldn't exactly say that. They made me a partner in an existing firm out of Denver, running my one-man office in L.A."

"That doesn't sound so bad …"

"Oh, I have a pretty long leash … but a lot of what I do is X-Gen's bidding—like for Kafer. Plus, I'm into them up to my eyeballs. They take one hell of a bite outa my earnings … but you know all about that."

"Still, Jack, you're happy," she said, trying to sound cheerful, keeping her voice up over the noisy little car. "Doing what you want … largely your own boss. Nobody to answer to but yourself."

He arched an eyebrow, gave her half a grin, face washed in green. "Nobody?"

"Well …"

The half-grin vanished; his expression turned grave. "Joy, if you pay no attention to anything I say, if you ignore all of my warnings, come away with this one fact: These people are not our friends. Not yours, not mine."

Weren't they? It seemed to Joy that—without X-Gen—Jack might be saying, "Fries with that?" right about now. But she kept that thought to herself.

"You should also know," Jack was saying, "that I'm not their favorite client."

"Well, you have made waves, Jack," she said. "You did break your contract…."

"Oh, yeah—what's that, business ethics? Listen to yourself, Joy. You know those staples they put in your stomach?"

She smirked. "Like I could forget …"

He grinned over at her, devilishly—a bad, bad boy. "I had mine taken out."

She turned in her seat toward him, mouth dropping open, eyes popping, grinning in amazement. "You *didn't*!"

Proud of himself, half-smirking, he nodded. "Took a little day trip across the border. You can get more in Tijuana than just blewed, screwed and tattooed, y'know."

Suddenly she felt flushed with admiration for her trouble-making boyfriend. She slapped him on the shoulder. "So *that's* why you've been able to eat so much!"

"Nobody's gonna restrict Jim Petersen to a half a hot dog and a Diet Coke."

"Jim Petersen?"

He thrust his hand toward her. "That's the name ... pleased to meet you—and you are?"

"Joy ... Joyce Lackey."

"Who were you, Joyce?"

"The same person—a different name, a different town. I just got too old, that's all."

"Maybe that's the way it's supposed to be. Maybe we were supposed to make room for the new kids."

"I don't believe that."

"Neither do I ... any other goddamn fucking culture would venerate our asses."

"Look ... Jim ... Jack. Let's stay with our new names. All right? This is the life we're in, now. It's a dangerous ... bad habit ... please?"

"Sure, Joy—for now."

"Something else ..."

"Yes?"

"Maybe you could take me there, too."

"Where?"

"Tijuana."

He looked blankly at her for a moment, then roared with laughter. "Everything I've told you, and what you focus on is getting your staples removed?"

"Even just the thought of a thick rare steak *and* baked potato with butter and sour cream and chives ... but what about Dr. Green?"

"What about the bastard?"

"Well ... does he know what you did? I mean, he's bound to find out, the next time he takes an X ray...."

"I don't give a rat's ass if he does," Jack said, with a dismissive snort. "They didn't ask me to have the damn things put in, I didn't ask them to have 'em taken out. Did you have any idea they were going to do that to you?"

"No."

"Hell, if I'd had any notion they were going to do that, if I'd known about any one of fifty things they kept from me … from us … I would never have never signed the hell up. Never!"

She said nothing.

"Jesus, Joy! Do you know what they did to me while I was under? They gave me a fucking vasectomy! Why didn't they just cut my balls off while they were at it…."

She was covering her mouth.

Face still bathed in sickly green, he frowned sympathetically. "Don't tell me—what did they take from you?"

"My … oh … oh …"

"Your ovaries. And you rationalized it away by saying you were past your birth years anyway, right? Like I rationalized it by saying I didn't want any more kids, anyway, not at my real age…."

"Ovarian cancer … it's a real risk for women my … my real age…."

"A risk to *them*. You get cancer and die on 'em, X-Gen doesn't get their monthly bite, right? These are our *bodies* they fucked with, Joy! Joyce? Are you listening?"

She nodded, feeling numb, suddenly.

She guessed it *had* been rather presumptuous. But if she followed Jack's lead, and—for example—had her staples removed, how could she hope to get away with it? The occasional steak and potato wasn't worth risking the enmity of Dr. Green and X-Gen. Maybe Jack took pride in being X-Gen's worst client, but she had liked to think she was one of their best.

She hadn't gotten where she was in the advertising game by defying the powers that be. And her one major misstep—with the new management back at Ballard—had only reinforced that assessment.

They were entering West Hollywood, and Joy asked with trepidation, "Do we have to go back to Susan's?"

"Yes."

"*Why*, Jack?"

"You need to see this."

"Just tell me, Jack. Just tell me what you think is going on." The thought of re-entering her dead friend's home sickened her somehow—as had the thought of identifying the body; she had already put this behind her....

He shook his head. "I have to show you. Then you'll believe me. Then you'll know how much exposure we both have in this thing."

Jack pulled up along the curb a block down from the run-down apartment complex. He shut the motor off, dug the gold key from his pocket.

Trembling with fright, Joy asked, "Won't the police have that yellow tape on everything...?"

"Naw. It's not a crime scene. Maybe a sticker over the front door lock."

"Well, then, won't they know somebody's broken in? And somebody might see us—"

"I'm your back-door man, baby," he said, reaching across her and opening the glove compartment, removing a rectangular leather case about the size of a motel bible.

"What's that for?" she asked.

"It's good that you ask questions," he said, slipping the case in his sport-jacket pocket. "It's the only way you'll ever learn."

Then Jack gave her a stupid grin—as opposed to an answer—and got out of the GEO. With a sigh, so did she, and tagged along-side him as he walked silently down the alley behind the shabby housing complex, until Joy pointed to one of the units and whispered, "I think that's hers."

Jack vaulted a four-foot-high wooden fence, and after a moment unlatched a back gate, where Joy waited on the other side.

Joy entered, groping along in the dark, stumbling on a cracked cement walk and knocking into a pair of garbage cans, rattling them.

She froze, as did Jack, who was a few steps in front of her. Chagrined, she raised her palms in surrender, whispering, "I'm not cut out for this P.I. stuff ... why don't I just wait out here...."

Jack took hold of one of her outstretched hands and pulled her up three cement steps to the back door.

No police sticker or tape covered the backdoor lock and Jack inserted the key, turning it. But before he opened the door, he turned to her, his lips close to hers, as if about to kiss her.

Instead he whispered, "Once we go in, not a sound ... understand?"

"Why? No one's in there, are they?"

He put two fingers on her lips and gave her a look.

She nodded. Not a sound.

But the door sure made a sound, opening inward with a *creeeeak*, which made her cringe—seemed to make Jack cringe a little, too, for that matter. Then they were inside. Jack shut the door, which this time thankfully made less noise. Joy huddled against Jack, in the pitch black of the tiny kitchen, unable to make out even the dinette table and chairs. She'd only been in here that once, earlier today, and wasn't sure she remembered the geography of the place....

From his pocket, Jack produced a pen-type flashlight, its beam powerful for its size. Pointing it toward the floor, he lighted the way as they moved slowly along, through the narrow hallway and into the living room; the stale apartment scent seemed even worse than before—oppressive, even, like the smell of death.

Jack motioned for her to sit on the couch, which she did. Then he withdrew the leather case from his sport-coat pocket, snapped it open and brought forth a black rectangular object about the size of a handheld tape recorder. She started to ask what it was for, but he shushed her.

He began passing the object over the front of the couch, as if prospecting for uranium with a Geiger counter. He did the same thing above one end table and a lamp, then came across the back of the couch to the other end table where the answering machine sat. But now a red light began to blink on the black object in his hand.

Joy slid off the couch onto her knees and watched as Jack moved the gizmo below and beneath the end table, the red light flashing faster.

What the hell did that mean?

As Jack beamed the flashlight on the underside of the table, she bent and looked, too. At first, she didn't see anything except the expected cobwebs and spider eggs. Then the flashlight beam focused on a small round silver object about the size of a dime.

She knew instantly what it was: a miniature wireless microphone.

Jack grinned back at her, arching an eyebrow, his expression saying, *See?*

And she saw, all right: Somebody had bugged Susan's apartment.

But who—and why?

In the bedroom, Jack found another one on the backside of the headboard—which Joy found especially creepy, adding a voyeuristic touch to the surreptitious surveillance—and a third one in the kitchen ceiling light.

They left the microphones undisturbed and exited the apartment as quietly as they'd come—quieter, the door cooperating, this time, and not creaking—and walked back in side-by-side silence to Jack's little white compact.

Inside the cramped vehicle, Joy was the first to speak. "Would you mind telling me what the fuck is going on?" she asked. "Who would want to bug Susan, for Christ's sake? She's just a lowly peon—a secretary!"

"Well, it's not industrial espionage—exactly."

"What is it, Jack? Who did this?"

"The same people who bugged my house... and yours."

"My house is bugged?"

"You can bet on it. And probably your car."

Head reeling, she asked, "But why in hell would—?"

"They're keeping tabs on us, kiddo. Making sure we're keeping up our end of the bargain—stickin' to the contract."

"X-Gen, you mean."

"Bingo—to use an expression we're both old enough to understand."

"That's just ludicrous ... ridiculous. Do you know how silly you sound?" She nodded out the car window, in the direction of the apartment. "I don't understand what those bugging devices were doing there ... but I'm sure there's a reasonable, logical explanation."

He arched an eyebrow. "You think so, Scully?"

She sighed. "Maybe Susan was involved in something illegal, like drugs or something ... you were a cop, surveillance is typical in cases like that...."

Jack shot her a smirky look as he started the engine. "Do you know how silly *you* sound?"

They headed west on Sunset Boulevard, the most famous street in the city, maybe in the world. Approaching midnight, traffic was light for a change, as they chugged along, the scenery shifting from seedy to mundane to opulent—capitalism in its every shape and form, its best, its worst.

Jack was right. It was silly to think of Susan involved in anything illicit—Susan a drug dealer, Susan an addict ... borrowing over-the-counter herbals from Joy's purse? Perky as she was, Susan had an underlying timidity, your classic case of afraid-of-her-own-shadow....

There had been, Joy recalled—as they passed Nichole Miller, a trendy store Joy loved but couldn't afford to shop at—something else Susan had been afraid of: Dr. Green finding out about her illness.

"Where are we going?" Joy asked alarmed, as the too-familiar Beverly Hills Hotel sign loomed up ahead, already knowing the answer. "To the clinic?"

"That's would be another bingo."

"But, why? You can't get in, it's after hours, it's closed…."

One hand on the wheel, he pointed to himself, grinned at her. "*I* can't get in?"

She groaned, slumped in the seat, put a hand on her forehead as if taking her own temperature. "Jack, Jack—you're gonna get us in a *lotta* trouble…."

His grin faded; both hands were on the wheel. "We're already in a lot of trouble, baby."

Though what he'd said was troubling, she found herself smiling. It was so nice, so old-fashioned, so … Bogart of him to call her that: *baby.*

"Don't you get it?" he was saying. "The kinda hot water we're both in?"

She slumped further down. "Well, I won't be any part of this— you can leave me in the car."

"Come on, Nancy Drew, where's your sense of adventure?"

"I think it was removed with my ovaries. Jack, we're not young anymore, however good we may look—why are we rocking the boat?"

"It's already rocked. We're already targeted. Too late to just play along with these bastards."

"Jack, stop it—you're frightening me."

"Good."

"But … what are you looking for … what do you hope to find?"

Jack was pulling the car into a parking spot on the same block as the clinic, one street over.

"Answers," he said, turning off the engine. He looked at her, pointedly. "Wasn't that what we were about, our generation? Bringing down the establishment? Seeking truth and love and enlightenment?"

"Not me," she said, shaking her head. "I was in a sorority."

He let out a single laugh. "Yeah, well, I was kind of a toga party guy myself. But when this is over, we'll find some love beads and maybe try smoking a little grass—all my crowd says it's outa sight."

She laughed, too.

"All right, then," he said. And he sang a line from an old song, "Are you ready?"

"Yes, I'm ready," she sang back, feeling silly. And young. And, unlike Jack, singing in tune …

"Then let's go," he said.

As they walked down the street of commercial businesses, glittering art galleries and high-rent expresso shops, a few of which were still open despite the lateness of the hour, Jack put an arm around Joy, nuzzled her neck.

"See, we're undercover, now," he whispered, "and I'm pretending we're lovers."

She stopped and kissed him. Then she looked into the dark eyes and said, "Who's pretending? And I can't wait to get you under the covers."

His arm around her waist, they walked on. "You got to trust me on this, Joy. I know what's best."

"Now you sound like our parents' generation."

"Well, they did some things right. People even fell in love and stayed in love and lived together till they died."

"Not always."

"No, but more often than not. More often than now, anyway."

They stopped walking. He put his hand under her chin, tilted her face up to his; his dark eyes were deadly serious. "You can trust me, Joy."

"Why should I, Jack?"

"It's an old reason—no generation has a lock on it. Because I love you."

"I love you, too," she said softly. The last man she'd said that to was Henry. "It's just … well, can you blame me for being afraid?"

"None of that—not with me around. You don't ever have to be afraid." And he kissed her again, soft and warm, a kiss she felt down to her toes.

Suddenly, in his arms, with his lips on hers, she wasn't scared anymore. Suddenly she was Nancy Fucking Drew and when their lips parted, she said, "Okay, Big Boy. What's the plan?"

At a service entrance at the back of the clinic, Jack and Joy huddled; the bright street lights in Beverly Hills made their presence far more noticeable than in the gloomy back alley behind Susan's apartment. But quicker than Joy could say "breaking and entering," Jack had picked the door's lock with a pair of slender metal tools from the leather case.

They stepped inside the sterile modern building, into a dark entryway with a carpet runner and a coat rack that contained a few unclaimed umbrellas. A push broom leaned in one corner as if resting between sweeps.

Joy looked at Jack, eyebrows raised. "No alarm?"

He gave her a one-sided smile. "Only the room with the narcotics cabinet."

"No bugs?"

"Just us cockroaches."

"You're *sure*...."

"I handle their security, remember?"

Another door loomed just ahead, to the right, but this one was open, leading to the clinic's back waiting room, a smaller, cozier one than the reception area up front. This was where Joy would be inevitably situated upon her arrival, and—after her monthly consultation—the way through which she would be shown out; she assumed this procedure was to keep her and other X-Gen clients apart.

Fingers of light filtered their way in and around the blinds of the windows in the back waiting room, providing just enough illumination for Jack and Joy to move toward the connecting hallway with the examination rooms, supply and drug room, and the doctor's private office.

The doctor's door was, not surprisingly, locked, but Jack deftly remedied that with the same pair of picks. After a faint "click," they went inside, where heavy curtains made moving about impossible without a light of some kind.

Jack withdrew the small flashlight out from his sport-jacket pocket and sent its bright if narrow beam darting around the room.

"Turn on a light," he whispered.

"It's safe to?"

"It's safe to."

Joy reached for the wall switch, but he stopped her with a hand on her wrist. "Not that one ... the one on the desk ... won't be so bright."

In front of the curtained windows was an oversized cherry-wood desk, and on its top, next to some meticulously stacked papers, sat a banker's-style reading lamp with jade shade and brass base. She went over to it and pulled its little gold chain, illuminating the room softly, giving Joy a better look at the doctor's quarters.

She'd never been in this surprisingly homey office, all of her consultations taking place in a cold examination room. As she glanced around at the doctor's personal things—brown leather couch, art-book-arrayed coffee table, walls displaying academic certificates along with idyllic oil paintings of the ocean—she found herself smugly pleased. Now it was *Green's* private life being pried into.

The doctor even had his own private bathroom. She poked her head in, noticing that in addition to a shower there was also a little whirlpool tub—she'd always wanted one of those. Well, maybe in her next life ...

Behind her, she heard a scratching sound; across the room, Jack was using his picks on the lock of a three-drawer file cabinet.

"What is it we're looking for?" she asked sotto voce, edging up next to him.

"Susan's file. What was her last name?"

She had to think for a second—Susan was just Susan to her. Then she said, a little too loudly, pleased with herself for remembering, "Henderson."

Jack bent over to pull open the middle drawer, labeled "H-M," and crammed with manila files.

"Good God," Susan breathed. "Could all the folders in these drawers be relocated Boomers?"

"Sure—and these are just Green's patients. There's a 'Green' in New York, in Chicago...."

Her clinic in Chicago!

"But there have to be hundreds of files here, Jack...."

"No. Thousands."

Jack thumbed through the front third of the drawer, then plucked a folder out. He marched the folder over to the desk, placing it under the light of the desk lamp.

"What are you expecting to find in there?" Joy asked, joining him by the desk, adding archly, "A great big rubber-stamp mark on her file that says, 'Terminated'?"

Jack flipped the folder open and on the first page was Susan's name, photograph, current employment information—and boldly stamped through Susan's name was that very word: TERMINATED.

"Good call," Jack said.

She covered her mouth with a hand, muffled through her fingers: "Oh, shit ..."

"Ready to start taking this seriously?"

Drawing her hand away, she gestured toward the folder. "But ... but that doesn't have to mean anything sinister—she died, they closed her file."

"Her death wasn't discovered until today. This is dated day before yesterday."

"That date could be a typo—or maybe she was going to be fired, and hadn't been notified yet—"

"You trying to convince me, or yourself?"

Jack was examining the contents of the folder, which as far as Joy could see were test results, some personal correspondence and notes made during examinations.

So Dr. Green *did* write down everything his patients said in their consultations! Joy wondered what he'd written about her....

She went back to the cabinet, pulled the middle drawer out again and fingered through the folders till she found her own file. She brought it back to the desk and the light, next to Jack, and opened it up—thankfully the word TERMINATE didn't appear.

"Jack," she said slowly, "what does this mean?" She pointed to the inside flap, beneath her name, where the initials T. D. came before a five-digit number. "Dr. Green's first name is Vernon, so ... and, I ... no, this isn't my X-Gen client number...."

Jack stared at where she was pointing. "You really want to know what I think?"

"Do I?"

"I think T. D. represents 'termination date.'"

"The day our job ends."

"You wish. That's the date they're going to kill you." He said this as calmly as if telling her the time of day.

Joy slapped the folder shut. "Will you stop it?" she huffed. "Now you're scaring me again! That date just means how long they estimate I can keep working." She opened the folder again. Now the number did look like a date to her. She did the math....

"Oh, my," she exclaimed, almost giddily. "I'm going to be working until I'm eighty-two."

"And that makes you happy?"

"Of course it does. I think it's great ... I just hope I'm up to it."

"And if you're not, you wind up like Susan."

"Stop it." But she was fascinated, and couldn't keep her eyes off the date on her folder. "How do you suppose they calculate that?"

"I'm sure they've got some wonderful scientific equation based on medical test results and current longevity stats." He interrupted his sarcasm to shrug. "Of course that means the equation can change every month, with every checkup."

Joy cocked her head, her file held to her chest. "Are you miffed at me?"

"Watch your language—'miffed' dates you, baby."

"You are, aren't you?"

He sighed. "No—just frustrated. Just wishing to hell I could make you believe me."

"I'm trying, I really am. But the whole thing sounds preposterous. To me everything X-Gen has done is designed to give us a second chance, Jack—a second life. We should be grateful, not … sneaking around their offices, spying."

"Then maybe we should go." He plucked the file out of her hands, and put it back in its place in the middle drawer, Susan's, too.

"Well, as, uh, as long as we're here in the principal's office," Joy said, breaking the silence, "why don't we sneak a peek at *your* school records?"

Mock childish, he said, "Let's not and say we did."

"Something you don't want me to see?"

"Why bother? It's an evaluation that says I'm insolent, arrogant and untrustworthy, or words to that effect…."

"I could have told them that," she said, kneeling and pulling out the bottom drawer. "Maybe X-Gen should come to *me* for background checks." She quickly found his name and withdrew and opened his file. She looked at the inside cover, her smile fading.

"Four more years…. that's all?" Joy looked at him wide-eyed.

Jack grabbed the folder. "What? It was fifteen, last time I checked ..."

Beyond the office windows, something slammed shut.

"What's that?" Joy whispered.

"Sounded like a car door ... outside in back ... we better skedaddle...."

"Now who's dating himself?" she gulped.

Quickly Jack stuffed his folder back, closing the drawer.

Joy was turning off the desk lamp, eyes frantically checking the desk for anything they might have left there, when keys jingled out in the hall, behind the closed office door.

Now in the dark, Joy reached out frantically for Jack with one hand, while pulling him toward the bathroom with the other, even as a key was being inserted into the lock, turning in the lock....

As they fled to the bathroom, Joy could hear the office door open behind them, then a click of the wall light switch, and the thud of footsteps on carpet—all mingled with the wild thumping of her own heart. There hadn't been time to close the bathroom door completely, and as the outer room flooded with light, they clung to each other, backed in the dark corner behind the bathroom door.

Terrified of being discovered, she looked up into Jack's eyes, which seemed amazingly calm; if he was at all frightened, he was hiding it well. She tightened her grip on him.

The desk chair creaked, its leather squeaking as someone sat down and began punching in a phone number.

After a moment a male voice beyond the bathroom door said, "Larue? Green." The doctor's voice had an edge to it. "No, I stopped by the office.... Yeah, another goddamn charity event.... Look, what the hell happened? I thought it was supposed to look like an accident."

Joy looked at Jack, whose tight eyes seemed to ask, *Now do you believe me?*

Green's voice became more agitated. "Yeah, well some cop, uh, Ryan, came around asking questions about her.... No, he's not one of ours.... Because my name was on the goddamn prescription bottle, that's why! Jesus Christ, do those backwoods morons have shit for brains, or what...? Oh, they say they *missed* it, well, that's different. Look, Larue, I know it's been cost effective, but they're idiots, we need to do something *else*.... Oh, I'm glad you agree—like I'm not still twisting here in the wind.... Easy for you, I've got this fucking thing leading right back to me...."

Joy, feeling sick to her stomach, leaned her head against Jack.

Green was saying, "Yeah.... Yeah.... Well, doctor-patient privilege ends when the goddamn patient *dies*, Larue. I can't seem uncooperative or we're all.... Okay, okay—I'll change the file.... Bye."

The phone slammed down. Then a file drawer opened. Had Jack put Susan's folder back in the right place? He'd done it so quickly! Joy did something she hadn't since childhood: She prayed....

The file drawer shut. Footsteps sounded on the carpet. *Oh, please don't be coming to use the bathroom*, she thought, looking anxiously at Jack, who seemed to be thinking the same thing.

But to her relief the overhead light out there clicked off. And the office door opened, then slammed shut.

Trembling, Joy released a jagged lung full of air.

"Let's wait a while," Jack whispered in her ear, still holding her tight, which was good because she felt her knees might buckle.

They stayed in the corner of the bathroom forever, or a good three minutes anyway, clutching each other in the dark; the only sound now was Joy sobbing quietly against Jack's chest.

Chapter Thirteen

"WE GOTTA GET OUTA THIS PLACE"
(The Animals, #13 Billboard, 1965)

Seated on the edge of a lumpy bed in the Sunny View Motor Lodge at Sunset and La Brea, Joy was almost pleading with Jack.

"Let's go to the police in the morning—it's the best thing, the *smart* thing—"

Coca-Cola can in hand, Jack was slumped nearby in a nubby turquoise chair, his stockinged feet stretched out, heels on the bed; he was in his T-shirt and slacks and he did not have the physique of a man his real age, chest beneath the flimsy T-shirt beautifully well-formed, arms heavily muscular, and he bore only the slightest potbelly courtesy of his unstapled stomach.

They were sitting in the dark because Joy was terrified of turning on a light, the plastic paisley curtains only partially open, letting a little street light leech in to enable them to see each other, in the shadows of cheap furniture and fixtures.

After they had fled the clinic, Jack suggested they hide out somewhere safe for the rest of the night, until they could come to a mutual decision about their futures.

In response to her suggestion, Jack was shaking his head. "Baby, give it a couple more days—then I'll have the evidence we need to be taken seriously. And we'll go to the authorities together."

"I think we should tell our story now, *right now*, no matter how crazy it may sound. What if something happens to us in the next few days? Like it did to Susan, and God knows how many others? Then no one would ever hear our story!"

He was shaking his head. "We can't go to the cops."

"Why not?"

"Do you think I was X-Gen's only plant in the PD?"

"Jesus! Then where *do* we go?"

"One of us goes to the media, the other to the FBI. I doubt X-Gen has anybody in the latter, and the former is our backup. We do it coordinated, with taped statements in safe-deposit boxes, and letters in the hands of attorneys…."

"My God … it sounds like launching D-Day."

"Well, it's a war, all right, Joy—us against them. As for tonight …" He nodded toward the bedstand, where a .38 revolver lay next to her unfinished can of Diet 7-Up. "Tonight I'll protect you."

"That thing makes me nervous."

"You'll like it better if somebody comes barging through that door."

"Oh, you really know how to make a girl feel secure…." She flopped back on the bed, muttering, "What's going to become of us?"

It was not a question, really, not posed to Jack anyway; and it was no whine. She had just been struck by the realization that her comfortable world—and she had made it comfortable, despite the circumstances, regardless of limitations, and was proud of herself for it—had once again come crumbling down around her. How many times did one woman have to hit rock fucking bottom?

Feeling the self-pity descending, she fought it, refusing to feel sorry for herself … except maybe a little, tonight, in this dreary little motel room. But starting tomorrow she would pick herself up, dust herself off, and go on about her business the best she could.

After all these years, Joy had learned that the one and only thing she could always count on about life was how capricious it was: One minute you're flying high, the next crashing down … only to rise from the ashes once again. Wasn't it only a few hours ago she had feared and hated Jack? Now she loved him again, and he was her comfort, her protection, even her future.

Life was crazy. And that gave her hope.

Jack got up from the chair and came over to the bed, sat next to where she lay, took her hand in his. "If you're wondering what will likely become of us, we'll probably end up in a witness protection plan."

"For how long?"

He shrugged. "Till after the officers of X-Gen have been fully prosecuted, and convicted."

"Years?"

"Years."

"Does that mean I won't be going back to Kafer?"

"Not until it's all over. It would be too dangerous."

She hadn't thought about that. But what about her clients, her meetings with celebrities?

"Why am I even bringing it up?" she asked, glumly. "Once ol' 'Gray Fox' Kafer finds out I'm not who he thought he hired. I'll be out on my butt."

"Maybe not. I know Chuck Kafer pretty well—and I know his high opinion of you. It'll only get higher when you stand up and do the right thing, here."

"You think so? You really think so?"

"I really think so."

"I don't know…." Joy swallowed, her gaze careening around the shabby motel room, dizzily. "This is all happening so fast—"

Now she *was* whining….

Jack settled in next to her, put an arm around her shoulders. "Baby, trust in me, trust in *us*, and it'll all work out…. And we'll be together, that's what's most important."

She nodded numbly; despite her concerns, fatigue was overtaking her. Resting her head on a pillow, she lay on her side, facing Jack, who was studying her lovingly.

Her eyes closed but her mind wouldn't shut down. "Jack … what made you suspicious about X-Gen, in the first place?"

"You mean besides them snipping me down yonder, without my go-ahead?" He sat up, one elbow resting on the bed. "There was a woman, a talented, very nice woman … her name was Rachel … who had your job before you. I did business with her, just like we have."

"*Exactly* like we have?"

He grinned a little. "Well, no—Rachel and I were only friends…."

"This woman died in a car accident, didn't she?"

"Yes."

"Susan mentioned her…." So had X-Gen's Larue, actually.

"Hit-and-run," Jack said. His face had turned stony. "They never caught the son of a bitch."

Joy raised her head from the pillow a little. "But it *was* an accident, right?"

He frowned and bitterness edged his voice. "Of course it wasn't an accident! Wake up and smell the autopsies, Joy."

She swallowed. "What makes you so sure?"

"Because I read the police report, and an eyewitness—a homeless man—saw it go down. From what the witness said, it was an intentional act."

Now Joy lifted herself on one elbow. "But Jack, really … you're going by a homeless man…."

"Because a homeless guy was the only witness, he can't be believed?"

"I didn't mean it like that. But many of them are drug addicts and schizophrenics. You have to admit—"

Jack was almost scowling. "He was a Viet Nam vet, for Christ's sake, down on his luck...."

"Probably trying to get a little money from the police for, what do they call it? Snitching?"

"Jesus, Joy! Listen to yourself!"

"Okay, okay! I believe you."

"Sorry. Guess I'm just tired...."

She stroked his forearm. "Me, too. But go on, go on ... the homeless man?"

He sighed. "Anyway, a few days after the accident, I tried to find that homeless guy, to talk to him about what he saw ... and he'd disappeared. I asked around and word was he'd gone looking for greener panhandling pastures, and I sort of forgot about it. Shouldn't have."

"Why?"

"About two months later, he turned up dead, drowned—washed up under the pilings of the Pier, at Santa Monica."

That made her shiver, particularly thinking of the fun times she and Jack had spent on the nearby beach....

But she said, "Probably drunk. That kind of terrible tragedy must happen all the time."

"Terrible tragedy? Is that sarcasm?"

"No ... no ... it's a human life. What kind of monster do you think I am, anyway?"

He sighed a laugh. "I don't think you're any kind of monster ... but there is something else."

She waited for him to go on.

Jack's expression grew pained. "Rachel was failing, mentally—I could tell it the last few months we were working together. She was forgetting things, simple things, names, mostly, appointments...."

"How old was Rachel?"

"She was supposed to be forty. I'm guessing she was at least sixty."

"She was one of us."

He nodded. "I believe Rachel was suffering from Alzheimer's. And Dr. Green discovered this, in his monthly exams, and X-Gen 'terminated' her."

Joy drew in a quick breath. Ashen, she asked, "To ... to make room for me?"

"To make room for some X-Gen client, sure. But mostly to get rid of deadwood—and prevent some insurance-company doctor from taking too close a look at her."

"It's horrible ... unthinkable...."

He touched her arm, petting her. "You see, they want to keep us working as long as we *can* work ... but once nature takes its inevitable course, we're eliminated. We're workhorses to them. And when we break down, there's always another aging Boomer to step in—and for us, always room at the glue factory."

"Break down," Joy said softly.

"What?"

"At my special training session, in my class, there was a guy that had a mental breakdown ... hell, a meltdown." She shook her head, remembering that ghastly night in the bell tower. "His name was Rick...."

She told Jack about finding her classmate hanging in the belfry during her session at Simmons. "I mean, I thought he'd gone into a full-blown nervous breakdown, you know? Couldn't face the future, but now ..."

"Now you're wondering if he wasn't murdered, weeded out, because he'd washed out of the program."

"Yes ... and, like all of us, he knew too much to be let out. My teacher, Mr. Hanson, told me X-Gen was founded by some of his students...."

Jack averted her gaze. Suddenly he swung off the bed, and wandered over toward the window, as if the closed plastic curtains were providing a view. His expression was grave—even in the dimly lighted room, she could see that the blood had drained out of his face.

"Jack—what is it? What's wrong?"

"Joy, there's … there's something I haven't told you. Something I wasn't … well, I wasn't sure if you were ready to hear this."

She sat up. Threw her hands in the air. "Hit me with your best shot, Jack! What the hell else is there left that you could shake me with?"

He turned, his hands in his pockets, head lowered. "You know I was out of town for a few days—in the Midwest. Well, I saw your teacher this weekend."

Astounded, Joy said, "You saw Don?"

Jack nodded. "He was my teacher once, too—back then, Simmons was the only college where the special session was taught. There are half a dozen locations now, all over the country, more all the time, but … that's not the point, really."

"What is the point?"

"I stopped by and told him I was in Des Moines on business and just came by to say hello…."

"You don't think *Mr. Hanson* is part of the X-Gen conspiracy, do you?" Joy couldn't imagine Don being so cold as to make love to her, knowing what fate awaited her….

"No, he wasn't." Jack sighed. "And I don't think he realized what hatched out of a lively discussion in his economics class six years ago, about the repercussions the Boomers would have on Social Security, Medicare, the job market … not to mention our sheer numbers giving us the upper hand in any major decision. Think about it, Joy…. We'll have the voting power to give ourselves anything we want."

"That's true," she admitted. "We're going to be very unpopular with the younger generation."

"We already are. Or haven't you noticed?"

She had, starting back with how disrespectfully she'd been treated in the bathroom at Frank Thomas's agency by those two younger women.

"I told Mr. Hanson ... Don ... everything I know, everything I suspected," Jack was saying. "I told him about you, and me ... and he told me about you and ... well, he told me he also thought highly of you. I believe his heart was in the right place, I really do, that he wanted to help people like us, our generation, our confused, selfish generation...."

"Why do you keep talking about him in the past tense?" A chill was coursing through her. "Like he's ... dead?"

"Because, Joy, he is."

She gasped; covered her mouth and the tears came in a terrible rush. Then Jack was holding her, whispering the horrible truth. "Don 'killed himself' ... slashed his wrists in the tub. He left a note and the police say it was in his handwriting. It said since the loss of his wife, his life had been empty, a sham. And that he'd gone to join her."

She hoped they *were* together; she did hope that....

"We know he was murdered, Joy, you and I, don't we? I told him on Saturday, all my suspicions, and he was livid with rage, he was going to do something about it. I warned him to be careful, asked him to work with us to expose X-Gen, but he said *he* would do something about it ... and the next day he was found dead."

"They ... they must've had his house bugged, too."

"Oh, they did—but when we spoke, it was outside, on a bench on that lovely campus. I knew there was a good chance his house would be wired. Believe me, I took precautions."

Joy curled her legs up, hugged them to her. "You know he did love his wife ... and missed her. After what you told him, he could have chosen to take his own life. It's possible."

"No. It's another X-Gen termination—a classic one. Built-in motive. That's why I stayed over, Joy—so I could nose around campus a little, talk to the police."

She was shivering. "Th-these former students of Don's who started X-Gen ... you don't think they planned from the start to ... use us up, and then ... get rid of us?"

Jack pulled the blanket up over her. "Maybe. Or maybe some enterprising young lad in financing came up with a nifty new cost-cutting tool."

Joy's mouth felt thick; her brain seemed to throb. "This … this can't be just about money."

"Yes … and no."

"What do you mean?"

He lay down next to her on his back, elbows winged out, as he stared at the ceiling. "Do you have any brothers or sisters?"

She shook her head. "I was an only child."

"Me, too. But there was a family that lived across the street from me when I was growing up … two brothers, one quite a bit older than the other. The older brother ignored the younger one … really treated him like shit-on-a-stick. Parents liked the older brother better, too—he was smarter, friendlier, the chosen son. Then one bright sunny day, the younger brother shot the older one. Killed him dead as Janis Joplin."

Joy cocked her head. "You're going to have to interpret that one for me...."

Jack propped himself up on one elbow, looking at her. "Don't you see? This *is* about something more than money! It's about one generation pitted against the other. They've been living in our collective shadow … forced to grow up listening to *our* music, watching *our* movies, wearing *our* clothes … they're the ignored, put-upon little brother." He paused. "Only little brother isn't so little anymore, and isn't the least bit intimidated by the aging likes of us. He's growing stronger, beginning to see the cracks in our foundation—and believe me, we have our share—and he's starting to see the threat we pose to the bright future of little brothers everywhere."

"I never thought of it that way...."

He let out a hollow laugh. "It's ingenious, really, X-Gen's plan … preying on the two things our generation holds most dear—work and youth."

"Where's love in that equation?"

"A distant third maybe. Sad, isn't it? But true."

Suddenly Joy was more frightened than ever. She put her arms around Jack. "Please hold me," she whispered, clutching him tightly.

They fell back on the bed.

He ran a hand through her hair, kissed her forehead. "We'll go somewhere," he told her soothingly, "disappear together. Live happily ever after, Snow Fucking White and Prince the Hell Charming."

"Where?" she asked, playing along.

"I dunno. How about Colorado?"

"Oh, I love Colorado! Such a beautiful state. Denver?"

"Too big. Maybe Golden, or how about Boulder?"

"Boulder is good." She thought about that. "It's a college town—that would keep us feeling young." If not looking it.

"Of course, we'll have to settle for lower-level jobs, but what the hell—we'll get to keep all of what we make, and won't that be a nice change of pace."

Joy lifted her head, looked into Jack's eyes. "What about our pills? Do you think we could find them someplace else? Mexico or something?"

"Probably not."

"We could have one analyzed … find out what's in them."

"I don't think we should take that chance," he said, with a dismissive head shake. "We can finish out what we have, but then … it's back to nature, baby."

She lay her head back down. "We'll start to look old," she said, words muffled against his chest. "Right away …"

"I don't give a damn." He tightened his grip on her, turned his face to hers. "Anyway, would that be so bad? Growing old together? Isn't that what God or somebody had planned for us in the first place?"

She nodded and laughed, just a little, and smiled at him. "Sounds like it."

"Here's what's really important, the only thing that's important—I love you, Joy."

"Oh, Jack, and I love you."

"For richer and poorer, better or worse, the whole nine yards."

"Whole nine yards," she purred.

He kissed her full on the lips, a hot, passionate kiss. And she kissed back, desperately wanting him, wanting the feeling of youth that only making love could bestow....

Afterward, as they lay entwined beneath the bedcovers, they made plans for the morning.

"I'll keep the room for a few days," Jack told her. "Until we're ready to go to the FBI and the media."

"Okay ... but let me go home, pack a few things. If I get spooked, I'll come back here. I'll take the extra room key."

Jack thought about that. "You should call in sick to work."

"Not sick. I'll take a week of personal leave—I've got it coming. That shouldn't draw suspicion."

Eyes narrowed, a little doubtful, he said, "Okay. But be careful. Meet me back here in two days. Say, two o'clock in the afternoon."

"Will that give you enough time to substantiate our story?"

"It should, and if not, I'll know how much more time I need, and we can proceed from there."

"I don't know if I like the idea, you off breaking and entering without me."

He laughed. "Nancy Drew ... we're going to be fine, you and me, you'll see." Suddenly his voice sounded very far away. "We'll grow old together, two of us...."

"Umn ... umn...."

And she drifted off to sleep in his arms.

The following morning, just before noon, Jack drove Joy back to the restaurant on Ventura where she'd left her car the night before.

"Why don't I follow you home," Jack suggested as they sat in his little compact, motor idling. "Sweep the rooms for bugs."

She shrugged. "Why bother? I'll be out of there in a couple days. And I'd just as soon not know where the damn things are … it would only make me nervous. And removing them would raise suspicion."

He raised an eyebrow, nodding. "You've got a point. Just be careful what you say. Don't go around singing, 'I'm leaving on a jet plane,' okay?"

Joy laughed. "How about 'We gotta get outa this place'?" She leaned over and kissed him, a peck that turned into something serious.

"Now we are going to attract attention," she laughed, pushing him gently away.

Jack grinned at her. "Sorry, baby."

Then she opened the car's door and stepped out, and with a little wave, blowing him a kiss, headed toward her Jaguar.

And they drove off in two directions.

Chapter Fourteen

"TIME IN A BOTTLE"
(Jim Croce, #1 Billboard, 1973)

How odd it seemed to Joy, returning to the tiny bungalow she'd worked so hard to make livable, knowing now that soon she'd walk away from it all. She wandered through her Hobbit house, touching things, as if bidding farewell to special friends: the walnut plant stand she'd found in the alley; the Fire King jadeite dishes she fought a fat lady over at a neighborhood garage sale; the nonsecondhand gold couch she'd flirted so outrageously to get at cost from that odious furniture store manager who would be forever waiting to receive a phone call from her ... not that he ever would have gotten one ...

Joy plopped down on that couch, and on her portable phone punched in the number of the advertising agency, getting put through to C.W. Kafer, the Gray Fox himself.

"I'm sorry to bother you, sir," she said.

"On the phone it's 'Chuck,' dear."

"Chuck, I'll let Stephanie in Human Resources know, but I thought I should tell you I'm taking a week of personal time. I know you were counting on me for that confab on Wednesday, but I'm afraid I'm really terribly stressed out over this awful news about Susan—"

"I can understand that," Kafer said, his voice touched with sadness. "You get close to the people you work with—workaholics like us, Joy, those are the relationships we forge … that we value."

"Thank you for being so considerate…."

"Don't be silly. Of course, you're aware that Susan didn't have any family, so the company is arranging the interment. There will be a small memorial service in the company chapel."

"Oh … of course." Joy hadn't really thought about a funeral or anything for Susan—events had been such a tumbling ongoing jumble. She also was unaware there was such a thing as a "company chapel" at Kafer. Live and learn.

Kafer was saying, "The service will be Thursday afternoon, at two p.m. I hope you will be able to come in for that."

"Oh, definitely." Unless she and Jack were already long gone…

"Would you like to say a few words, dear? You were her closest friend in the world."

"No … I don't think I'd be up to that."

"Of course. We have a retired Presbyterian minister on our advisory board—he'll handle the service. It will be brief, dignified. Do you know what faith, if any, Susan practiced?"

"No … no I don't."

"That's life in the modern world for you—we can't even ask an employee's religious 'persuasion' on our applications now. So how the hell are we supposed to bury them properly?"

"It, uh, is a problem."

"So you wouldn't know what kind of music she might have liked to have played?"

Joy thought back to the old L.P.s on Susan's dresser.

She said, "This may sound kind of weird, but … why don't you have them play 'Daydream Believer' on the P.A. system."

"I don't believe I know that hymn."

"It's not a hymn. It's by the Monkees."

She hung up and began to cry. She wasn't sure why she was crying, or whether it was for Susan, or herself, or just the very idea that that tiny relationship she and her secretary had "forged" had made Joy the dead woman's "closest friend in the world."

For the rest of the day Joy—in Lakers T-shirt and jeans, hair pinned up under a bandanna—busied herself packing as much as she could into her two Vuitton suitcases, then cleaned the bungalow one last time so no one could say she was a slovenly housekeeper, even if she had disappeared without paying the last month's rent.

With the California sun streaming in the windows, and the sounds of young children at play floating in through the screens, the terror and, yes, adventure of the night past seemed to fade, like the memory of a bad dream—had there *really* been a boogeyman under her bed?

This thought had barely danced through her mind when a knock came at the door—two knocks, actually, crisply businesslike.

She gazed through the peephole and saw someone from Joyce Lackey's life on her doorstep.

And she wasn't surprised, really—after all, Jack had said that her house was bugged, her calls monitored. And consciously, or unconsciously, she had counted on that.

Jason Larue had come calling, impeccable in another black designer suit with black-and-gray tie and pale gray shirt, hands clasped before him in fig-leaf fashion, dark curly hair tipped with bronze, his boyish, stubble-bearded Brad Pitt good looks only mildly undercut by tired-looking eyes. Even in Chicago those pale blue eyes had been bloodshot; but now dark circles hugged them and he frankly looked a little wasted—evidently the stress of his key role in such a profitable and ever-expanding business was taking its toll.

She opened the door.

"Sorry to drop by announced," he said.

"Not a problem," she said, gesturing. "Come in. Please."

Bloodshot eyes or not, he still had an ingratiating smile. "Why, thank you. Joy, you look terrific. Like a movie star."

Closing the door, she laughed humorlessly, pointing to her pinned-up hair. "Yeah, Hattie McDaniel ... but that's before your time, isn't it?"

"Not really. I have *Gone With the Wind* on DVD. In my business, it pays to have a ... sense of history."

She said nothing for a moment, then gestured toward the gold couch. "Can I get you something? Sparkling water? Starbucks?"

"No ... no, thank you. I'm not here to impose."

"Why are you here, Jason?"

"I think you know."

"And I think you know *I* know. Shall we skip the bullshit, this time?"

He frowned. Was he going to bawl her out for her language, like that fucking Tyler Hurst back at Ballard?

"Joy," he said, sitting on the gold couch, "what's the matter?"

She stood in front him, arms folded, quietly defiant. Why wasn't she afraid?

"Are you unhappy at work?" he asked gently. "Kafer would seem absolutely tailored to your considerable talents."

"Kafer's fine."

"Sit down, please."

Swallowing, she sat on the couch, but not next to him, leaving space, like a high school girl warning her date not to get fresh.

Larue shrugged one shoulder. "I would think you would be very pleased with the placement we arranged."

"Kafer is fine, I said.... I love it at Kafer."

And, out of nowhere, emotion swelled within her, tears were beginning to fill up her eyes, spilling out, sliding down her cheeks.

"What is it?" he asked quietly, something like compassion in his tone, turning toward her. "You can tell me, Joy."

"No ..." She was dabbing her eyes with the sleeve of her T-shirt.

His voice was soothing: "You're my very best client, Joy, did you know that? One of X-Gen's proudest placements. And your satisfaction ... your happiness ... is important to X-Gen ... and to me."

She looked at him through her tears, forced her voice past the lump in her throat. "You know 'what's the matter.' It's Susan.... It's Don.... It's ... it's Jack. It's everything...."

"Jack Powers," he said, voice calm, reasonable, "is a dangerous man. An unbalanced man."

"He says you had Susan and Don and a lot of people killed.... He says you're killing us, when we've ... worn out."

Now it was out in the open. Tears dry, she gazed at him coolly, waiting for his reaction, his response.

Larue sighed, rubbed the tired eyes.

"Joy," he said as if he had some affinity for her, "before you make any more of these accusations, would you do me one favor? Would you think back for me? And try to remember what your life was like—just before I called you? You had no job, no money, no prospects. When we first met, I sensed you were moments away from suicide. Isn't that true?"

After a moment, she swallowed and admitted, "Yes."

"So in a sense, X-Gen saved your life—in a way, *I* saved your life ... or am I overstating?"

She had never thought about it that way, but she guessed they had caught her at the edge of the precipice.

"No," she said, "you're not overstating."

Larue continued, his voice as placid as the sunny after-noon outside her bungalow windows. "We have saved many lives, Joy, in our company's short existence ... and we want to continue to rescue those deemed unjustly worthless by society, giving unfortunate people like yourself, abandoned by society, betrayed by the world of business, a renewed reason for living."

He leaned toward her, without invading her space. "A win-win-win situation, remember? And, if a few of those people have to be dropped from the program in order for others to benefit, well, it is unpleasant, but necessary." He paused, then added, "Am I making sense?"

"You're killing people."

"When clients come to X-Gen, they are ... at the end of their ropes. They have, in a sense, already lost their lives—we've given them new ones. Occasionally, we have to ..."

"Send the grim repo man?"

He sighed. "People like Susan, like Jack, are a handful that endanger thousands ... thousands like yourself. They represent a small statistic."

With a sneer, she almost spat, "Is that what Don Hanson was to you? A small statistic? He was *your* teacher, too, wasn't he? Your *guru* ..."

Larue lowered his head, and his face seemed gripped with something genuinely like ... regret. Even sorrow.

"We did *not* ... eliminate ... Mr. Hanson. We revered him. Venerated him. He killed himself.... We must take partial responsibility, because when Jack Powers filled Mr. Hanson with these ... vile exaggerations, it added to the grief he'd been carrying for his wife's death, and ..."

"You expect me to believe that?"

"I hope you will. Your classmate, Rick—he took his own life, as well."

"Is this where you tell me Susan strangled herself?"

"No.... Susan was in fact terminated. So was the woman who held your job before you—I'm not here to lie to you, Joy. When serious health problems crop up unexpectedly—rarely—in one of our clients, we may in extreme cases make the decision to terminate."

"Business is business, you mean."

"You say that as if it's a bad thing."

"All Susan had was arthritis! She could have worked for years with that, particularly with the experimental meds you people have at your fingertips!"

"Susan's health was not the only issue.... She told several people, yourself included, about X-Gen."

Joy frowned. "Who else did she tell?"

"Jack Powers, for one. Or possibly, Powers manipulated her into telling him. He's a man obsessed with bringing us down."

"So I suppose he's next on your list? Or am I?"

"Joy, you are not on any such list. Nor is there any truth to the ridiculous accusation that we murder our clients once they have been 'drained' of any usefulness. Could any business exist in such a ... psychotic manner?"

"But you don't deny what you did to Susan."

"No. And others, a small handful whose sacrifice protects the greater number."

She covered her face with a hand. "If I could even bring myself to accept your twisted logic ... how could you justify being so ... *brutal* about it?"

Larue sighed, his eyes clouding. "I could not agree with you more. That is exactly what I have been saying to my partners, that this kind of thing is way out of line.... They insist that these eliminations, terminations, must be carried out in varied manners. But I have insisted—and Dr. Green, who thinks very highly of you, by the way, agrees with me—that we've been inhumane, that these were our clients and we need to have a little compassion and decency about our practices."

"Yeah, I guess I would call strangulation inhumane. You may be onto something there, Jason."

"I don't blame you for being sarcastic. You see, we sub-contracted this work through a militia group out of Montana—reasoning being that, should they be caught, their own militant agenda would take any blame, and heat. But I have maintained that they were enjoying the job a little too much. Anyway, that's all about to change now ... we're about to fire their sorry asses—excuse the language."

"And now what? Replace the militia with a street gang? Mafia rejects, perhaps?"

"We deserve that. No ... no more brutality." Larue dug into his suit-coat pocket. "And we've come up with a new procedure that's virtually painless, thanks to Dr. Carver."

Joy looked at his open palm, which held a clear capsule.

"Our pills?" she asked. "I don't understand...."

"Looks like your pills, but it isn't," he said.

He put the pill back into a bottle filled with identical capsules. And placed the bottle on the couch cushion between them.

"You have a decision to make, Joy. Do you understand?"

She understood.

He was saying, "Jack Powers is a threat to us—to you. He is, I repeat, a dangerous, unbalanced man. He has manipulated you, used you.... He's convinced you, hasn't he, that we have 'bugged' your house, tapped your phones...."

"I know that's true. I saw as much at Susan's place."

Larue shook his head, smiled faintly. "Jack put those there—that's his business, after all."

"Why on earth would he do that?"

"To sway you, Joy—you and Susan ... to bring you over to his side, his distorted way of thinking. You know what his plan is? To expose us—to be the great detective who brought an evil empire down ... and regain what he thinks is his proper place in society."

"That doesn't sound like Jack."

"X-Gen is a business and Jack Powers is a liability. You, Joy, are an asset—one of our greatest successes. Are you aware that you are C.W. Kafer's chosen successor?"

"No ... I had hoped...."

"Well, you are. And he will be retiring within five years, if his chronic heart condition doesn't take him out of the game earlier, of course. You are aware of the kind of money a CEO generates, even factoring in our commission—and you can easily see how you and X-Gen stand to mutually benefit from your ascension to that rarefied position."

Head of Kafer Advertising ... was that really possible?

"And," Larue continued, "you have years ... possibly decades ... ahead of you—at the top. Of your game. Of your profession. Choose."

And Larue stood, nodded in a priestly fashion, and saw himself out, leaving the deadly pills behind.

The next afternoon, with still no word from Jack, Joy—nerves jangled, exhausted after a sleepless night—drove to the motor lodge at Sunset and LaBrea. No one seemed to be following her.

Jack's white compact wasn't in any of the stalls.

Joy drove around the block several times, trying to see if the motel was under surveillance. It didn't seem to be. Letting herself in his room with the spare key, she breathed in air that smelled of his aftershave, which was sitting on the edge of the bathroom sink, next to a travel kit containing his shaver and toothpaste and pill bottle.

She waited, sitting on the edge of the made-up bed, waiting for Jack to show up to give her an update of the evidence he was mounting. She'd had no way to warn him that X-Gen was so thoroughly onto him.

How she needed to hear his voice. Needed to talk to him. How could she be expected to know what to think if she couldn't hear his side of it?

But two o'clock came and went without him showing, and after an endless hour, she darted into the bathroom where— among other things—she threw up. Then she wrote him a note on a little pad by the phone, saying she'd been there, and telling him how much she loved him.

Then she slipped out, driving home, numb, a zombie behind the wheel of a Jag.

The following morning—with no word from Jack either yesterday or on this, the day they were to go to the FBI and the media, the day they would begin a new life together—Joy was eating a breakfast of fresh fruit on her tiny back patio under an overcast, hazy sky, reading the paper.

The front page had an interesting story. A neo-Nazi militia in Montana had blown themselves to kingdom come, their very illegal and well-stocked secret ammunition dump somehow detonating, destroying itself and most of their membership.

Fired their asses was right.

It was on an inside page, local news, where Jack's name jumped out at her, straightening Joy in her chair. So fast, so soon … she'd thought tomorrow maybe, but …

She clutched the newspaper, hands shaking as she read the sad news of the successful private investigator, in charge of the local office of a prominent Denver firm, found dead in a motel room, struck down in the prime of life, the victim of an apparent heart attack.

The newspaper floated to the cement patio floor as Joy folded her arms on the table, and put her head down on them, like a child at a school desk. She didn't cry; she just stared—her stomach ached, though. Maybe she'd eaten the fruit too fast. That stapled stomach did give her fits….

She stumbled into the living room and looked at the gold couch where they'd made love. She could imagine Jack was sitting there, grinning at her, the big goof, the tousled dark hair, big dark eyes—or was that an accusing expression?

"I had to do it," she told him.

Jack had already been doomed by his own actions—he was a liability, as Larue had said. His defiance against X-Gen's rules had sealed his fate—she didn't have anything to do with that. With or without her actions, even if she hadn't switched Jack's pills with the ones Larue had left her, Jack was a dead man—right?

Then she collapsed onto the couch and buried her head in her hands and wept. And when she could cry no more, she stood and staggered to her bedroom, where she flung herself onto the rumpled covers, making pitiful, whimpering sounds.

She attended Susan's funeral that afternoon and sat in the back of the tiny, well-attended chapel and wept. Mr. Kafer comforted her, afterward, commenting on the nice things the board-member minister had said about a young woman he hadn't known; Joy agreed that it had been very nice, but of course she'd heard none of it.

That night, tossing and turning in bed, sleep beyond her grasp, she tried to figure out at what point she had decided she couldn't go with Jack into a new life, and she wasn't quite sure. She knew the thought had been forming before Larue appeared on her doorstep.

Perhaps it had been Jack's mention of Boulder. She liked the Colorado town well enough—but the last time she was there, as Joyce Lackey, conspicuously consuming along Pearl Street Mall, her arms laden with packages, she had spotted a homeless woman, sitting on a bench in the cold. The woman had asked for a dollar. Joyce had given her a quarter, and, disturbed, hurried on by.

If she had gone to Boulder with Jack, would she have been that wrinkled, raggedy, toothless woman with dead eyes in just a few years?

Or maybe she'd decided a new life wasn't for her when Jack spoke of settling for a lower-level job, a job beneath her qualifications and accomplishments and intellect. What a waste that would have been. Hadn't history taught her that a person is remembered for the work he or she does … for what he/she accomplishes in life?

The only lovers remembered by posterity were the tragedies—Lancelot and Guinevere, Romeo and Juliet, Bonnie and Clyde—and she had never liked stories with unhappy endings. Anyway, you weren't memorialized for loving someone, but for the work you did—your contribution.

That's what was really important, wasn't it?

Joy returned to the ad agency the following Monday, throwing herself into her work, staying late every day that week, making up for the time she had lost. She had her usual vitality and did typically first-rate work and would start sleeping again, soon— and makeup covered the dark circles just fine; Visine took the red out, too.

Nearly a month had gone by since Jack's death, when, on a warm Saturday morning, Joy kept her next appointment with Dr. Green.

After his usual checkup, he pulled the chrome stool over to Joy, who was seated quietly on the examination table.

"You did the right thing," he told her.

She responded with one curt nod.

"If you're having any difficulty falling asleep at night," he said, eyes unreadable in the bisque-baby face, "I can give you something."

"I'm fine," she said, not wanting anything negative in her file. "Really I am. I don't need a thing." She thought her voice sounded funny, funny strange, that is—distant, and like someone else's.

"All right, then," the doctor said. He dug into the pocket of his white smock and handed Joy her monthly supply of pills. "Here are your capsules."

Usually the nurse gave them to her.

Joy took the silver-capped bottle and put it in her purse.

At home, in the living room of her bungalow, with the afternoon sun streaming in, she fussed with the fern on the pedestal.

Something was wrong with the plant. Its green leaves were turning a yellowish brown. Was she watering it too much, or not enough? Was it getting all the sun it needed, or maybe too much? She wasn't sure what to do.

Giving up, Joy sauntered into the bathroom. Time for her pill. Drawing some water from the sink, standing at the mirror, she uncapped the silver lid of the new bottle Dr. Green had given her and shook one of the clear capsules into the palm of her hand.

She stared at the glimmering capsule.

What if it contained something other than her rejuvenating medicine? What if it contained the stuff that had given Jack his heart attack?

She shook her head. No, no, she'd shown them she could be trusted.

But could *they* be trusted?

The pill was an inch from her mouth, and she saw her reflection in the mirror—saw her young face, staring into the old eyes— and she wondered whether or not to take it. Wondered whether life was in the capsule or something else.

With a little shrug, she popped the pill in her mouth and took a swallow of water.

One way or the other, her future was inside that clear-coated capsule.

ABOUT THE AUTHORS

MAX ALLAN COLLINS is the author of the Shamus-winning Nathan Heller historicals (*Target Lancer*) and the graphic novel *Road to Perdition*, basis for the Academy Award-winning film. His innovative '70s series, Quarry, has been revived by Hard Case Crime (*Quarry's Ex*) and he has completed six posthumous Mickey Spillane novels (*Lady, Go Die!*). Collins wrote and directed the Lifetime movie *Mommy* and the documentary *Mike Hammer's Mickey Spillane* on Criterion's edition of *Kiss Me Deadly*.

BARBARA COLLINS is the co-author (with her husband Max Allan Collins) of the award-winning Trash 'n' Treasures comic cozy mystery series, beginning with *Antiques Roadkill* and continuing through the current *Antiques Disposal*. The fourth entry, *Antiques Flee Market*, won the Romantic Times award for Best Humorous Mystery of 2008. Barbara and Max have also written two stand-alone thrillers (*Bombshell* and *Regeneration*), now back in print. Barbara has published several dozen short stories to much acclaim.

Made in the USA
Charleston, SC
23 November 2012